FATE'S FAULT

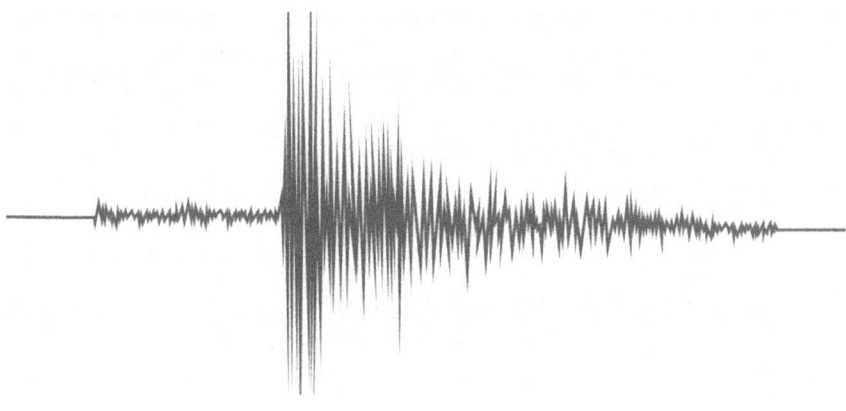

A ROMANTIC THRILLER BY
H. P. OLIVER
WITH
TIARE PEÑA

HPO Productions
8698 Elk Grove Boulevard, Suite 1-271
Elk Grove, California 95624

Cover art and book design by Steve Eitzen

Printed in the United States of America

MYSTERIES IN HISTORY

ISBN 978-0-9994150-4-7

DEDICATION

This novel is respectfully dedicated to those who, a century ago, began making California all it could be with self-indulgent, avaricious behavior. Sadly, we lost that spirit and now look at us.

AUTHOR WEBSITE

You are cordially invited to visit the author's website at http://www.hpoliver.com for many free features related to this and other H. P. Oliver books. These include a unique visualization section providing illustrated quotes from FATE'S FAULT that will increase your reading enjoyment by allowing you to "see" parts of the story (use link below).

www.HPOliver.com/BOOKS/FATESFAULT/VISUALIZATIONS/INDEX.html

ACKNOWLEDGMENTS

The authors gratefully acknowledges the following research sources used in the writing of this novel: California State Library; California Department of Transportation; California Institute of Technology, Seismological Laboratory; Las Vegas Convention and Visitors Authority; Reno-Sparks Convention and Visitors Authority; Eureka Police Department; and Valley Hospital Medical Center, Las Vegas, Nevada. Also, special thanks to Gary Weisenberger for keeping us honest.

ONE

It was one of those rare times in life when everything was going according to plan and years of hard work were finally paying off. That's Fate's favorite time to sneak up and kick you right square in the keester.

I'm a freelance photographer and I just landed a fat contract with a major Los Angeles agency. The list of locations on my itinerary would take me on a month-long journey down the California coast, beginning in Eureka and ending in San Diego. If everything went according to plan, the end of that journey would see my bank account fatter by enough to live on for at least six months.

The agency's client was an up and coming fashion sunglass manufacturer named E-Clipz. The company is located in Torrey Pines down near San Diego and they were after a cool and classy west coast image. To build that image they planned a series of high-gloss magazine layouts using an upscale female spokesmodel with whom they hoped their market would identify. Their number one criteria for the model was, in their words, "We do not want another goofy looking California blonde."

I arrived just in time to pick up the non-goofy model and the account executive accompanying her at the Humboldt County Airport in McKinleyville, about fifteen miles north of Eureka. I walked into the tiny terminal building and stood around until a United Express commuter plane landed and taxied up to the gate. Well, there isn't a gate in the big airport sense of the term. A couple of guys rolled a boarding ramp on wheels out to the little Bombardier CRJ200.

When the pilot followed ten or so passengers down the ramp and I had not yet seen the account exec or the model, I began to get the feeling old man Fate was taking direct aim at my posterior again. I poked a name in my cell phone directory and waited while the number rang.

"Good morning, Winchell and Dreyfus Advertising, how may I direct your call?"

I asked for the account exec I expected to be on the plane from LA. "Carlos Alonso, please."

A long period of ominous silence followed, after which the receptionist asked, "May I say who is calling, please?"

"Yeah, you may tell him Kevin Turner is calling. I'm the photographer Alonso was supposed to meet in Eureka a few minutes go."

"Oh . . . Yes sir. Please hold."

Something was definitely out of whack, and when a woman whose voice I recognized as that of Olivia Winchell, a senior partner in the agency, came on the line I knew for sure Fate had scored a direct hit. "Hello, Kevin. This is Olivia. I fear I have some bad news."

"What's up?"

"The model we were sending you for the E-Clipz shoot has disappeared. She and Carlos Alonso, our account exec, seem to be wanted by the FBI, and according to those guys, Rita and Carlos are across the border and well into Mexico by now."

I'd like to say I couldn't believe my ears, but I could. Fate came up with a real lollapalooza this time. "You're right, Olivia. That definitely falls into the bad news category."

"Tell me about it. The federal boys got me out of bed at o' dark-thirty this morning, banging on my door and demanding I come down to the office and open up. By the time they were through here, Alonso's office looked like it was hit by a tornado. While they were destroying the place, they found time to tell me Alonso and Rita are wanted for illegal importation of controlled substances and a bunch of other charges they rattled off. Needless to say, your coastal photo junket is off, and we'll probably lose the E-Clipz account over this."

I said nothing for several seconds while a did I little quick scheming. Then I said, "Olivia, if you'll trust my judgement, I might be able to save that account."

Ms Winchell did not sound hopeful. "How?"

"I know a model with the sort of high-class image the client wants. She is also downright gorgeous, and savvy. What's more, this woman works out of San Francisco, so with a little luck, I could get her up here tonight, shoot some images tomorrow, and e-mail them to you in the afternoon. If you don't like her, you're only out the cost of a roundtrip airplane ticket and a day's pay for her. If you like her, we're back in business. What do you think?"

It was Olivia's turn to be silent, but she eventually gave me the answer I wanted to hear. "All right, Kevin. You've seen the layout sketches, so you know what we need. Give it a try. I'm making no promises, but your idea could work."

"Okay. Same deal as Rita had, a grand a day?"

More silence came down the line. "Yes . . . or less depending on what we think she's worth."

Sounding braver than I felt, I said firmly, "Forget it, Olivia. The girl I have in mind has a hell of a lot more experience than Rita and she looks the part. I'm not going to drag her up here without promising her professional terms if you decide to use her."

"Geez, Kevin, what are you, this girl's agent?"

"I wish I was. She's that good. What's it going to be?"

"Okay, Kevin, a grand per day plus expenses for a one day test shoot. But make it clear that's all I'm authorizing until we see the goods. Same terms if we decide to use her."

I breathed a sigh of relief. "Fair enough. I'll see how fast I can get her up here and we'll shoot some stuff for you to look at. Unless you hear otherwise, watch for it in your email tomorrow afternoon."

I scrolled through my cell phone contacts until I came to "Bishop, Kieley." She pronounces her first name like "Keeley" in case you aren't familiar with the spelling.

Since I was in her phone's contact list, she knew who was calling and sounded genuinely happy to hear from me. "Kev! What a nice surprise. How are you?"

"Hi, Kieley. I'm all right, but I've got a client in a jam. Are you booked, or do you have a few weeks open?"

"Kev, I could kiss you. You just said the words I've been hoping someone would whisper in my ear. Work has been scarce lately. What's the deal?"

I described the situation and Kieley said, "Kev, now you get a kiss for sure. How soon do I need to be up there? Do I need to bring my own wardrobe?"

"Yes on your wardrobe. Just the classy casual outdoor stuff in your closet will do. As for when you need to be up here, according to the schedule in my hand, there's a United Express flight leaving SFO at five-twenty this afternoon. Can you make it?"

"Sure, I have plenty of time." Then in a quieter tone, Kieley asked, "Do I have to buy my own ticket?"

That told me her credit cards were close to maxed and her bank account was running on empty. "No, Kieley. I'll go to the United Express counter here in Eureka and pay for your ticket. All you have to do is pick it up when you check in at SFO. I'll text you the info. See you in a while."

"Kevin?"

"Yeah, Kieley?"

"Thank you, friend. You just saved me from flipping burgers at Mickey D's."

At the United Express counter I bought a one-way ticket from SFO to ACF on flight 5555 to be picked up at San Francisco International. The flight would depart at 5:20 p.m. and arrive here at 6:44. The price was $296. As I texted the flight info to Kieley, I wondered how many people actually thought it was worth three hundred bucks to be here instead of where they were. My guess was not many.

After picking up a packaged sandwich and a small bag of chips at the airport snack bar, I set out for the McKinleyville Holiday Inn Express I passed on my way to the airport. I drove a fair part of the night to meet a plane I didn't need to meet and I was dog tired.

I checked in and got an additional room for Kieley. After eating my sandwich and leaving a wake-up call for five p.m., I sacked out. As I drifted off to sleep, my thoughts drifted off to the woman who would soon be on her way to meet me.

Kieley and I met at UC Berkeley. We were very close back then—practically engaged, but I graduated in 2015 and traveled south to look for work in LA while she finished two more semesters. During those semesters, Kieley was "discovered" by a top Bay Area agency, and on the day she graduated, she went to work full time making good money. She made enough to pay off her college loans and start building a small nest egg. All of that seemed to necessitate our romance being put on permanent hold.

Still, we kept in touch and worked together when opportunities presented themselves. I love photographing Kieley. The camera loves her, too. Plus, I never have to tell her what I need from her more than once. She's a natural.

Then, about a year ago, the advertising business suddenly flipped topsy-turvy. That's when our industry discovered the "Information Highway" and realized social media reached way more people than print and other electronic media and was much less expensive. At the same time, untrained models whose boyfriends owned digital cameras came pouring out of the Internet woodwork.

High tech automatic digital cameras made "pros" out of guys who didn't know an f-stop from a bus stop. Of course, in a quality print ad you could see the difference, but at internet resolutions of a few hundred DPI, many of the differences disappeared. There were still a few glossy print publications and a handful of agencies in the market for quality work, but they were a vanishing breed.

After a restless nap, I pulled up in front of the Humboldt County Airport again a few minutes before six. This time United Express was on time and I watched Kieley Bishop walk down the roll-up ramp. Seeing her always had the same effect on me. A small pang of sadness passed through me along with the lyrics to *THIS NEARLY WAS MINE* from Rogers and Hammerstein's nineteen-fifties musical, *SOUTH PACIFIC*.

Kieley walked into the terminal, saw me, and ran into my arms. We hugged and I was about to ask how her flight was, when she blurted out, "Kevin, I've missed you so much! We had such wonderful times together. I really, really miss that."

Kieley's sudden outpouring of nostalgia threw me. Trying to catch up, I said, "Yes we did have wonderful times together. Have you been especially remembering those days?"

She nodded. "Yes, I've had a lot of time to think lately, and you always seem to be in those thoughts. When you called today, my heart jumped a foot."

I didn't feel comfortable with her reminiscing because it was so unlike Kieley. She was no softy, and while she could be as romantic as the next girl, romance was no longer a component of our relationship. Of course, things change, but I needed a little time to think before I did something I would regret.

I simply said, "It felt pretty good to hear your voice again, too."

We walked to the baggage claim and she pointed to her bag. I grabbed the black Eagle Creek Gear Warrior bag and we walked out into the cool evening air of the northern California coast. Kieley looked at the vehicles lined up in the parking area just outside the terminal, and said, "Let me guess."

"Okay. Which one?"

She pointed at a blue Jeep Wrangler. "That one there."

"Bingo. What gave it away?"

"It's the only blue one and you've always loved blue."

"I'm too predictable."

I heard the smile and something else in her voice when she replied, "That's one of the reasons I . . . I've always liked you so much. No surprises."

I mumbled something about sounding boring as we climbed into my blue Jeep and drove out to old Highway 101, which we followed in a southerly direction. Old 101, or more correctly, Business 101 is a two-lane highway that was built back when folks didn't mind slowing down to go through a town on its main street. Now there's a multi-lane freeway that bypasses the whole shebang.

Old Highway 101 took us to the Redwood Coast Brewery, which I was told by a helpful woman at the United Express ticket counter offered a good dinner bill o' fare. Actually, it is what folks in the big city call a brew pub. She-she had reached the boondocks.

Kieley, always figure conscious, ordered a Cypress Salad, which was full of healthy stuff I would not eat if I was starving. I, in turn, ordered something called Long Island tacos, which was actually a pair of beer battered fish tacos nobody in Long Island would ever consider ordering. Still, it all tasted pretty good . . . or we were both very hungry.

Most of our dinner conversation centered on me and the jobs I was getting. Kieley, on the other hand, didn't have much to say about her own career. She indicated on the telephone things were slow, but I had the feeling there was more to her lack of enthusiasm and I said so.

Kieley frowned at me. "You've always been able to tell when I was keeping something to myself. If you must know, I ran into some trouble.

"Oh? What happened?"

Kieley sighed and looked down at her salad. "I was raped and I made the mistake of reporting it to the cops."

She said it quickly as if the words were painful. I could understand that because it was certainly painful to hear them. The only information she added was her assailant was an account executive at one of the big agencies she often worked for.

I sat there looking at the pain in her eyes and deciding what to say. Most of what I was feeling was anger at whoever hurt someone I cared about. Eventually I came up with something I hoped told her I cared without aggravating the situation. "I guess I don't need to say I'm sorry that happened. You already know that. Why was reporting it a mistake?"

Flames flared in her bright blue eyes. "Because the San Francisco cops are nothing but a bunch of good old boys protecting their own interests and not giving a damn about the law or justice. The only thing that resembled justice in any way was the guy's agency sacked him and the word is out. I hear no other agency will touch him with a ten-foot pole now."

"Well, that's a little something."

Kieley shrugged. "I suppose. The only reason that happened, though, is several of the most influential agencies in town, including the one he worked for, are owned by gays and lesbians who especially hate anyone who does what he did. Unfortunately, I now seem to have a stigma attached to me. I can't even get work from the agencies who supported me back then. It seems I am no better than the ass who . . . did that to me."

Softly, I said, "Kieley, why didn't you tell me about this when it happened?"

After staring into my eyes for a long moment, she said, "I wanted to. In fact the first thing I wanted to do after it happened was call you."

"So, why didn't you?"

"I think I was ashamed and embarrassed. I guess that sounds strange, but I'd gone to a lot of effort proving to myself I could get along without you. Calling you would have meant admitting to myself I failed and I needed you."

It was obvious she was upset, but there were no tears. The only thing in her eyes was anger. The system had screwed her around and she was stuck with it. Now, however, her greeting at the airport made a lot more sense. What I thought might be a desire to rekindle our long dead romance was more of a cry for help from a friend.

An idea suddenly occurred to me. "Kieley, how tied to San Francisco are you? I mean there are a lot of agencies in southern California who don't know what happened to you, and probably wouldn't care if they did know about it."

"But the competition is much heavier down there, isn't it? In San Francisco I am one of a more elite group, or at least, I was."

"Yes, there might be more competition, but you have an ace in the hole."

Kieley looked puzzled. "I do? What's my ace in the hole?"

I shook my head, feigning frustration. "Me, you ditz. I'm riding high right now, especially if we can pull this assignment off. Then, you'll be the 'E-Clipz Girl' and I'll be the guy who made you a star."

She smiled softly. "Yes, you're right. I'm not thinking too clearly right now. If you think there's enough work to pay the bills in LA, I'm willing to give it a try. Heck, maybe we could even save . . . ."

I studied her face. I thought I knew what she was going to say and I wondered why she didn't finish the thought. "You okay,

Kieley?"

Nodding, she said, "Yes. Like I said, I'm not thinking real clearly right now."

"I'm not surprised. We've both had very long days. If you're through grazing your greens there, let's be on our way. There is a nice comfy bed waiting for you at the Holiday Inn Express by the airport."

Stepping off the Holiday Inn's elevator, I led Kieley down the hallway to room 219. I opened the door for her and carried her bag in. Then I handed her the key and said, "I'm in 220 right across the hall if you need me. They serve sort of a breakfast here starting at six-thirty. That's also a good time for us to get started. If we're going to pull this off, we've got a lot of ground to cover. Okay?"

Kieley was watching me intently, and for one of the few times since I've known her, she actually looked like she was going to cry. I guess I was being kind of tough on her, but damn it, I was being just as tough on myself. If I didn't get out of that room, I was definitely going to do something stupid.

She sat on the edge of her bed and in a quiet voice said, "Yes, Kevin, I'll be there and thank you."

I crossed the hall, closed the door to 220 behind me, and locked it. Anyone watching me would think I was taking precautions to keep the Bogyman out instead of a small adorable woman who didn't weigh a hundred pounds soaking wet.

I got my shirt and shoes off and was heading to the bathroom for tooth brushing kinds of activities when I barely heard a timid knocking on my door. I knew who it was, and if such things are possible, I might have willed her across the hall to my door.

Peeking through the little lens in the door, I saw Kieley out there. Her arms were folded across her chest as if she was cold. I opened the door and Kieley looked up at me. "You . . . you forgot to tell me what I . . . I should . . . wear in . . . ."

Then, as they say in the bodice-busters, the dam broke. Tears flooded her eyes and Kieley leaned forward and fell into my arms. "Oh God, Kevin! Please . . . please don't send me away. Please!"

Wrapping her quivering body in my arms, I said, "I would never send you away, Kieley. Never. Come in and let's talk. Sit on the couch there while I grab some tissues."

She sat while I pulled the chrome cover off the tissue dispenser in the bathroom so I could bring the whole box out. When I came back into the bedroom she was leaning forward and looking up at me as if she was afraid I wouldn't come back to her.

I offered her the tissue box and she pulled a couple of tissues out of it to dry her eyes and blow her nose. When I sat down next to her, though, she abandoned the eye drying and turned back into my arms. I could feel her warm tears on my bare chest.

"I'm sorry, Kevin. I feel like such a fool. I've messed up my life and now I'm messing up your life."

I took her face gently between my hands and turned it so she could see me. "Tell me, did you ask that guy to rape you? Did you wiggle your sexy little ass at him to make him crazy with desire for you?"

She jerked back. "No!"

"Then, I'm not clear on how you messed up your life by being a rape victim."

"Yes, but . . . ."

"Kieley, do you know what my very first reaction was when you told me what happened?"

She looked up into my eyes shaking her head and I said, "I'll tell you. It was rage. I wanted to find the man who hurt my woman and kill the son of a bitch."

Kieley just asked softly, "Your woman?"

"Yes, I know that's a rather one-sided view of our relationship now, but that's still who you are way back in the closet of my mind."

She managed a tiny smile. "Kev?"

"What?"

"When I'm honest with myself, that is exactly how I see me, too. I am your woman. I have been all these years. Moreover, you're my man. We lost those visions of each other when other things seemed more important. Now, I want more than anything to bring them back. Can we?"

I leaned back on the couch. "Kieley, I'm going to be honest with you. I've always hoped we could bring those good days back. Nothing would make me happier, but . . . ."

Her blue eyes showed fear and there was a quiver in her voice. "But . . . but what?"

"Honey, my old antagonist Fate has treated you horribly and you're upset. I know you mean every word you say, but we changed our minds once before. How do we know that won't happen again, hurting each other even worse this time?"

"I won't! I promise I . . . ."

"What would you say to a compromise?"

There were tears on her cheeks again, but she was listening. "How would it be if we agree to reconcile until this job is done with the understanding that we will be completely honest with each other about our feelings as we go. If after that, when things are looking better, we still feel as we do now, the ring is on me."

She smiled a little at the last part, but then her eyes got big again. "Does . . . does that mean we can sleep together and . . . and be together the way we were before? I've missed that closeness so much."

I grinned. "Just as horny as you always were, huh?"

"No! This has nothing to do with sex." After a very brief pause, she gave me a small smile and added, "Well not much to do with it."

"Kieley, if sleeping together would make you happy, it would please me, too."

Her arms were around me so fast I hardly knew what was happening, but her lips were another matter. There was no doubt what her lips were doing. They were kissing me with a passion that brought memories flooding back. I wasn't sure I made the right decision, but I didn't care. Even bringing back just one night of our love was a treasure.

TWO

After a night of passion that didn't include much sleep, we somehow managed to get out of bed, pack, and stagger down to the hotel's breakfast bar. The thought of a greasy strip of bacon and an omelet you could use to patch a tire did nothing for my appetite, so I settled for coffee and a cinnamon roll, both of which HIE does quite well. Kieley made herself a bowl of instant oatmeal from a paper packet and stirred in a little strawberry jam from a plastic packet.

By seven o'clock, we were headed south on US Highway 101, also known in these parts as The Redwood Highway. Just before entering Eureka, I turned west on Highway 255, which took us out to the Samoan Peninsula, home of the world-famous Samoa Cookhouse and my favorite breakfast on the entire planet. Unfortunately, we already had sort of a breakfast and didn't have time to dawdle. I promised Kieley we'd come back and visit the cookhouse.

When I described the menu—eggs, potatoes, ham, toast, and oatmeal—served all-you-can-eat family style—she said, "I shouldn't need to remind you, Mister Turner, both of our paychecks depend on me staying slim."

"Oh, hell, Kieley, by that time you'll probably be pregnant, so it won't matter."

Feigning indignity, she said, "Is that so? And just how do you expect I might end up in that condition?"

"The usual way, by sleeping in the same bed as your husband."

She leaned over the console and kissed me on the cheek. "And if I was pregnant and fat, would you still love me?"

"Assuming I was said husband, more than ever, Ms Kieley."

"I sure hope so! It would certainly be a new experience for

me."

"Being pregnant or eating?"

"Both, wise guy."

We stopped for what is commonly called a "grab shot" with Arcata Bay and the town of Eureka in the background. It wasn't particularly inspired scenery, but Kieley saved the shot with poses and facial expressions that made me smile as I looked through the viewfinder and tripped the shutter.

Next, we retraced our steps up the Samoan Peninsula and cut back over to Highway 101. Upon entering Eureka in the southbound direction, the highway splits onto two parallel city streets, one for northbound traffic and one for southbound travelers.

I turned right on M Street and pulled to the curb two long blocks later in front of the amazing Carson house, a huge Victorian mansion I've heard called the grandest Victorian in the country. It was built in the 1880s by William Carson, one of California's first lumber barons. Today, the mansion is a private club and signs make it clear trespassing will not be tolerated.

I have been allowed on the grounds for photographs before, but this time all we needed was the sidewalk and the mansion's elaborate wrought iron fence, so permission wasn't required, but sunlight was. The sun was still hiding behind the fog and it took some doing to get an exposure with the depth of field for what I had in mind.

The fence runs along right next to the sidewalk, and through the viewfinder of my Nikon D-5, it appeared to go on forever. Stopped-down as far as the Nikon's 27 millimeter zoom lens would go for the best depth of field I could get, I asked Kieley to walk slowly toward me smiling and swinging her arms as though she didn't have a care in the world. Of course, she donned a pair of white-framed E-Clipz sunglasses for the occasion.

She did the walk for me twice and I came away with at least three or four useable shots that included the mansion off to the right side of the frame. At the slow shutter speed I was using, I got some artsy blur from her arms swinging. Then the camera bag and tripod went back in the Jeep and we were back on US 101 heading south.

South of Eureka, we left Highway 101 on a county road that headed off to the southwest toward the town of Ferndale. We were nearly forty miles south of Eureka when we got to our next planned location of the day.

I pulled to the shoulder of the road in an area known as the

Lost Coast. South of Eureka the coast is flatter than a pancake and covered with grasses and low shrubs. This is not where you get dramatic shots of waves crashing against towering cliffs. This is the Pacific ocean's more docile side.

From the spot I picked we had a little elevation and looked down on the point where a meandering creek drains into the pacific. We spent almost an hour fooling with angles, poses, and giving the 21 megapixel D-5 a workout.

One of the beauties of a professional digital camera is you can evaluate your results instantly and without the time and fuss of a changing bag and setting up an E-6 processing line in a motel bathroom. A lot less stink, too. Anyway, we looked at what we shot and judged it well done for what we had to work with.

Kieley was especially gorgeous in the cloud filtered sunlight. Her skin seemed to glow with a radiance I had not seen before, even though I have probably exposed several thousand frames of her over the years. I mentioned this to her.

Giving me a kiss on the cheek, she said, "Maybe it isn't the filtered sunlight. It just might be the man I've loved for so long I can barely remember where we met."

Trying to sound as if I was quoting chapter and verse, I said, "We met during a Golden Bears football rally at the base of the Campanile. Oski, the mascot, was cutting capers and the cheerleaders were trying to generate enthusiasm for the 'big game' with Stanford. You were there with your girlfriend . . . ah . . . Sandy . . . she never cared much for me."

Grinning widely, Kieley said, "You do remember! That's amazing."

"I don't think you can call remembering one of the most exciting moments of my entire life 'amazing'."

"No, Darling, it's all of you that amazes me."

I got another kiss on the cheek and one on the lips that threatened to delay our travels. However, we persevered, and after another hour and some change of driving we were back to Highway 101 and entering the Avenue of the Giants.

While nowhere near a beach, this region of giant redwood trees is a landmark known far and wide, so, we stopped for another hour of photographing Kieley cavorting among the Sequoia Semperviren trees. As always, she was a real trooper, scampering among the trees like a squirrel. We came away with two series that stood out from the rest.

By then the lunch hour had arrived and it was about time to end the day's shooting so I could send some images to Olivia

Winchell. Even though we had five good to great series, I really wished we had one more. Then an idea hit me that would kill two birds with one stone.

Twenty minutes down 101 brought us to the historic Benbow Inn near Garberville. It is a luxury hotel, restaurant, and spa that began attracting celebrities in the mid-1920s. The Benbow has the appearance of a Tudor castle nestled in the redwoods, which made a decent setting for another photo series. The inn would also give us a place to stay that kept us on track location-wise if Oliva said, "Go."

I sent our bags up with the bell boy, and since we didn't have permission for a commercial shoot, Kieley and I tried to look like tourists while filling a few dozen frames with images of her in a classy leather jacket and, of course, E-Clipz sunglasses. She looked for all the world like a sexy Ms Gotrocks enjoying the swanky inn.

Around one o' clock we went into the lounge for lunch. It was the only restaurant at the inn open for lunch and the menu was limited. Kieley found a kale salad and she was set. For me, fried rock shrimp with snap peas and garden herbs, all in a Wasabi emulsion sounded like the best choice. Actually, despite the Asian fusion thing the dish was trying for, the shrimp was quite tasty.

Up in our suite, I sat at the small desk and set about transferring our images from the Nikon's Compact Flash card to my laptop. Kieley stood in front of the gas fireplace and watched what I was doing.

Once I had the contents of the memory card on my laptop, I used a simple photo manipulation program to convert the frames from their original NEF raw format to low-res JPGs so the files would be a manageable size for email attachments. I made no other enhancements to the images. For one thing, they didn't need much enhancement. For another thing, I wanted to be telling the absolute truth when I described the images to Olivia Winchell as "raw."

Saying photos are raw always buys a photographer a little leeway in the mind of those who will judge his or her images. Given the lack of natural ocean drama in the section of coast we worked, a little leeway wouldn't hurt.

Next, I wrote a cover note to Olivia describing the attached images and telling her we needed a decision before the end of the day. Reading over my shoulder, Kieley nervously asked if I was pushing Olivia too much.

"I don't think so. This is one of those rare situations where I'm in the driver's seat. First, we shot some good stuff this morning;

plus, she will lose a fat account if she can't deliver the layouts on time, and the only way she can do that now is with our work. Her approval of these images is mostly a formality and reassurance for her that you fit as the E-Clipz model."

Kieley nodded. Still, I could tell she was anxious about keeping the job now that we started it. "Kev, what if this woman says no?"

I smiled at her. "Then we catch a tramp steamer for Tahiti and live on pineapples and bananas."

Frowning, she said, "Be serious, Kevin. I'm really nervous about this."

"Kieley, let me ask you something."

"What?"

"Do you still want to be my woman?"

She smiled a small soft smile. "Yes, for now and for always."

"Then I will take care of you now and for always. In fact, we will take care of each other. We're both talented and smart. We're gonna come out on top no matter what."

"It's just that sometimes I don't feel very talented or smart."

"Remember the reason your situation turned bad in San Francisco. It wasn't your fault. Old man Fate gave you both barrels, but you're still the same smart talented woman who became the hottest model in that city. It is not resting on your laurels to remember your accomplishments and use them to climb back to the top of an emotional ladder."

Kieley leaned over and kissed my cheek. "I'll try, Darling. I really will."

Finally, I bypassed the hotel's complimentary Wi-Fi Internet connection and hooked up with a 5G satellite account for which I pay a hefty monthly fee. The six series of four or five images each and my cover letter took off for LA via the super highway in the sky. I finished my photographic chores by uploading all of the photos to a secure storage cloud for safekeeping.

As I made sure my cell phone's volume was turned up, I said, "There we go, Darlin'. Now all we have to do is sit around and wait."

Kieley gave me a risqué smile. "If sitting around is all you can think of to do while we wait, I must be losing my touch."

My cell phone's incoming text alert caught us at a rather awkward moment, so it took a few moments to finish what we were doing and untangle ourselves. Actually, I was in no hurry to do either, but Kieley was frantic to know what Olivia Winchell said about the sample images we sent her.

I opened the phone and pulled up the text. It was from Olivia, all right. Her message was also short and to the point. "Good work. You've saved us! Proceed with shoot. I authorize the following terms for model: $1K/day plus daily expenses and travel. Keep me informed of your progress. ~O"

I wanted to see the message before reading it to Kieley and the suspense was driving her crazy. Still in her birthday suit, she was jumping around trying to grab the phone. Finally, I said, "Okay, okay! Here, read it for yourself."

She looked at the screen for a few seconds, did a fist pump, and yelled, "Yessss!"

I took the phone back from Kieley and sent Olivia a brief text acknowledging her message. It simply said, "Received your text. Terms acceptable."

Kieley jumped into my arms and said, "Oh, Kev! You did it. You did it!"

"No, Darlin', WE did it. Olivia would have told us to forget it if she didn't like you and your work." Looking at her message again, I added, "Say, I just realized something. You're making two-hundred-fifty bucks a day more than I am."

With her big blue eyes shining brightly, Kieley said, "I'll split the difference with you so we're equal."

"Nope. I want my $250 per day in trade."

Feeling her naked body against mine was getting my attention and she was noticing. "But, Darling, what could I possibly give you every day that's worth that much?"

I kissed her hard, after which she said, "Oh. At two-fifty a day, that makes me a pretty high-priced piece of . . . ."

I interrupted her with another kiss, after which I picked Kieley up kicking and squealing and deposited her on the bed.

THREE

After searching the entire one mile length of Garberville's main drag, Redwood Drive, we determined the town to be the only settlement in the northern hemisphere without a single fast food joint. They had not so much as a Taco Bell. That left the Chevron station convenience market as the only place we were going to find coffee and something quick for breakfast at seven o' clock Wednesday morning.

I bought a cup of stale coffee for myself, an equally stale cup of decaf for Kieley, a package of brown sugar cinnamon Pop-Tarts, and an apple somebody might have been using for batting practice. I couldn't interest her in a highly caloric Pop-Tart, so she got the apple and I promised better chow for lunch.

From Garberville south to the town of Leggett, Highway 101 winds around like its builders couldn't decide where they wanted to go. After Leggett, the highway straightens some, but we didn't get to go that way. We turned west onto State Highway One and wound around for another 45 miles until we got to the tiny settlement of Hardy, which consists of exactly five buildings, two of which are deserted. From Hardy, Highway One skirts beaches and cliffs that are much more dramatic than those we saw up to that point.

I pulled off the road at an overlook where we thought the cliffs and the surf smashing into the rocks a few hundred feet below us looked promising. We discussed the best ways to take photographic advantage of nature's drama.

Our overlook was adjacent to a highway bridge and Kieley pointed to the bridge railing, suggesting she sit on it facing south so the scene would have the surf and the cliffs at the other end of the bridge as background. I walked to the railing and looked down.

I looked a long, long way down.

I've never been fond of heights and this height went on for hundreds of feet. I felt my stomach give a lurch. "Kieley, did you see what's on the other side of that railing?"

"Yes, but if you line up the shot before I sit, I'll only be there for a short time. I think it will be okay."

I shook my head. "I don't like it."

"I know you don't like heights, Kev, but they don't bother me. I'll be fine."

I let her talk me into it because the set up was exactly the sort scenic drama E-Clipz wanted. We might have found something similar and safer down the road, but I was trying to make the best use of our time. We would use what we had.

I set up the shot while Kieley put on a pair of ugly black E-Clipz sunglasses that made her look bug-eyed. When I had everything in the viewfinder the way I wanted it I was in the roadway about twelve feet from her to get the angle I needed. Fortunately, there was no traffic to worry about.

I said, "Okay, let's get this over with."

Kieley started trying on expressions and I started pushing the shutter release. That is precisely when the world in my viewfinder went nuts. Everything began jumping up and down, including the bridge we were on. Of course, being a native Californian, I know an earthquake when I feel one and they don't scare me, but what I was seeing in the viewfinder sure did.

Kieley was clinging to the railing for dear life while the bridge whipped up and down like a mechanical bull in a cowboy bar. Her expression was somewhere between panic and determination, but it was clear her grip on the railing, and life, was slipping. I dropped eight-thousand-dollars' worth of Nikon camera and lens on the road and staggered forward to grab Kieley.

She saw me coming and reached for me. I grabbed her arm and pulled. Her slim body offered little resistance and we flew backwards, ending up sprawled in the roadway. Yelling to be heard over the freight train rumble of the quake, I said, "Come on, we have to get off this bridge."

We crawled like crazy and I grabbed my Nikon as we passed it. Then, we were on relatively solid ground again and a few seconds later the shaking abruptly stopped. I got to my feet and helped Kieley up.

Her voice was a little shaky when she said, "That was damned close! If it had taken another two seconds for you to grab me, I don't think I would have been there to grab."

"Yeah. Next time I . . . ."

Another one hit. It was much shorter in duration, but seemed just as strong.

When we had our footing again, I said, "Come on, climb into the Jeep. Let's get out of here before the world comes down around us."

She looked around. "Those rocks up there haven't moved. I think we're . . . ."

"It's not rocks I'm worried about. It's water. That quake was at least a mag-six and the epicenter was close. We're gonna see a Tsunami heading our way any minute."

Kieley said, "Oh God, I didn't think of that."

While we were strapping into the Jeep, another shaker gave us a jolt and sent an avalanche of rocks down on the roadway south of us. I didn't like driving back over the bridge, but that was the only direction open to us and the shortest route to high ground.

We made it across the bridge, and after dodging a few rocks on the road, we passed Hardy. There was nobody in sight, but one of the abandoned buildings was now a pile of splintered kindling.

Then we were in tall timber. I spotted several downed trees alongside the road, but so far, none were blocking our way. While I was paying attention to the road ahead, Kieley turned on the Jeep's radio, hunting for a station. I wasn't surprised when she found the dial empty of anything but static. It was likely the local stations were put out of commission by the quake and we were in a lousy reception area to pick up stations in Eureka or San Francisco.

Finally, we came to a switchback on the edge of the ridge that offered us a view of the coast below. I pulled as far off the road as I could get to see if my guess about a tsunami was right.

Also, as soon as we parked, radio reception improved. There were still no local stations on the dial, but good old KCBS in San Francisco was coming in crystal clear:

"According to initial reports from Caltech Seismological Laboratory in Pasadena, the major earthquake that hit the west coast at eleven-forty-seven pacific standard time registered a record seven-point-four magnitude and was felt as far as Los Angeles to the south and Seattle to the north.

"The National Oceanic and Atmospheric Administration is warning that a tsunami of record proportions will hit the northern California epicenter of the quake within the next 30 minutes. California residents are urged to evacuate coastal areas

and move to higher ground inland.

"Stay tuned to News Radio Seventy-Four for the latest information on the earthquake and tsunami as it comes in."

A commercial for Chevy trucks came on and I lowered the volume. With a note of awe in her voice, Kieley said, "Seven-point-four! I've never heard of an earthquake that strong before."

"Neither have I. They said it was a record. I'd say Old Man Fate just took his best shot at us and we beat him out by inches."

Kieley took my hand. "Thanks to you. I was literally inches from going over that railing. I'm still shaking!"

I smiled and made a weak attempt at humor. "I couldn't let that happen. Who else would have my children?"

She smiled back at me. "The way things are going, we'd better get started on that while we're still alive. What do we do now?"

"I'm not sure. As much as I'd like to stick around here where we might see the tsunami, I feel we should keep going to see if we can get back to what passes for civilization at Leggett and head south on Highway 101 from there."

Kieley squeezed my hand. "Kevin, I'm a city girl. I vote for civilization, too. That way we'll have more information to help us figure out if we can save this shoot."

"All right. That makes the best sense, and we may encounter road conditions on the way that could slow us down."

I estimated we were almost to Rockport, which didn't really qualify as civilization. That meant there were still about 18 miles of winding mountain road through tall timber between us and Leggett. Mentally crossing my fingers, I put the Jeep in gear and continued up and over the ridge.

The best thing we had going for us was our fuel situation. I filled the tank at the Chevron Station in Garberville, so we had no immediate worries on that score. We could make it to Leggett. After that finding fuel could be tricky depending on how much damage the quake caused.

We made it just past a wide spot in the road called Hale's Grove before Fate took another shot at us. I negotiated a curve and we came face to face with a downed tree across our path. I stopped and we got out to size up the situation.

Outside the Jeep everything was dead quiet, except for a faint sound of rushing water in a creek somewhere not far away. When we spoke there was a slight echo to our voices as the sound bounced off the trees and mountainside. The words that passed through my mind were "forest primeval."

The tree came down nearly parallel to the roadway and

smackdab in the middle of it. What was left of the roots were at our end of the fallen tree and close enough to the embankment on the high side of the road to prevent us from sneaking the Jeep by over there. A sheer drop-off left us no room to clear the tree on the other side of the road.

In a dejected tone, Kieley said, "It looks like we're stuck."

"Maybe not. Maybe we can scoot that tree far enough to the right that we can get by between it and the bank."

"How can we move it? That tree must weigh tons."

"I'm sure you're right. That tree is much too heavy for us to move by hand, but our trusty Jeep might be able to do it."

Her expression brightened. "You mean like we could push it out of the way?"

"I don't think we have the maneuvering room to do much pushing, but maybe we can apply the laws of physics in a different way and rotate it out of our way."

"Okay, what do you want me to do?"

Gesturing toward the Jeep, I said, "Look in the back. There's a black plastic bin with a bunch of stuff in it. One of the items in there should be a fifty-foot coil of canvas tow strap. It's yellow and has a loop at each end."

While I looked for a workable fulcrum on the fall-off side of the road, Kieley found the tow strap. Holding the large yellow coil up, she said, "Is this it?"

"That's it. Let's see if it's long enough to do what we need it to do."

I started at the base of our fallen tree, looping one end of the tow strap around a sturdy-looking root. Next I uncoiled the strap across the road in the direction of the tree at the roadside I'd picked as our fulcrum. I passed the strap around our fulcrum and walked it back toward the Jeep until I ran out of strap about a dozen feet from the from the edge of the road.

"Kieley, would you please move the Jeep over here so the front bumper is just above the end of this strap?"

"Okay."

"Try to angle the Jeep in so the it's aimed at our fulcrum tree over there."

"You mean the one with the strap around it?"

"That's the one. I'll stay here near the end of the strap so I can signal you when we're close enough to it."

It took her two attempts because she was trying so hard to do it exactly as I asked, but she got the Jeep lined up just right. I shouted, "Stop there. Set the brake and take it out of gear."

She did as I asked, and then trotted over to see what I was up to. I said, "Good job."

Kieley said a quiet, "Thank you," and watched me drop the built-in loop of the tow strap over the closest of two tow hooks bolted into the Jeep's front bumper. I hoped to hell Chrysler did a solid job of mounting those hooks and they weren't just for show.

Finally, I turned to Kieley and said, "I think that will work. Let's give it a try."

"Where do you want me, in the Jeep?"

I gave her question a moment of thought, and then said, "No, I think at least thirty feet behind it and on the driver's side so I can see you in the side-view mirror. If that strap snaps or something else lets go under the strain we're about to put on it, the strap will act like a giant rubber band. We don't want to be in its way."

"Aren't you going to be in the Jeep?"

"Yes."

"What happens if the strap snaps and hits the windshield?"

"I'm a fast ducker."

"Kev, don't forget; for us to have those kids you keep talking about, we both have to survive this."

The fact that she still had her sense of humor was a positive sign. "I don't really think we'll have a problem. That's a four-ply strap rated at seventy-thousand pounds. I just don't see any reason to put you in a risky position when there's no need for you to be there."

Nodding, she began walking toward where I told her to stand. Over her shoulder she said, "Good luck, Darling."

Shifting the Jeep into reverse, I slowly took up the slack until there was tension on the strap. Then I gradually stepped harder on the gas pedal and rode the clutch. That earned me a lot of snapping and creaking noises, but the strap held.

More gas . . . more snapping and creaking. More gas . . . more snapping and creaking, but the fallen tree moved a few inches. That was a relief because the way my fulcrum tree was bending. I didn't think it would take much more stress.

Once more I pressed lightly on the gas. The fallen tree moved again, this time nearly a foot. More gas and the gap between the fallen tree and bank opened further. I kept at it until I had a clearance of what looked to be at least eight feet between the tree and the uphill embankment.

I was about to let the tension off of the tow strap when an idea struck me. I set the brake and put the Jeep in neutral. Then I reached behind the seat and grabbed my Nikon. Praying the thing still worked after being dropped during the quake and hoping the tow strap would stay put for a few seconds, I walked around to the passenger side of the Jeep and leaned across the hood.

Putting the taught bright yellow tow strap at the bottom center of the frame, I zoomed out to show the road and the tree blocking our progress. Making slight adjustments to the zoom ring, I shot half a dozen frames.

Back in the Jeep, I put my foot on the brake and shifted into first. Taking my foot off the brake pedal, I eased the clutch out and drove the Jeep a few feet up the hill to take tension off the strap. My fear was the fallen tree might roll back where it had been, but nothing moved. We'd foiled Fate for the second time in an hour.

I put the Jeep in neutral and set the brake. Opening the door, I was met with a Kieley kiss, my favorite kind.

"You did it! You're a genius!"

Hugging her, I said, "No, WE did it. Come on, let's free the tow strap and roll it up in case we need it again."

"By the way, Mister, I saw you risking life and limb to make a photo of the strap and the tree. I hope the image will be worth the risk you took getting it."

Back in the Jeep, I eased us through the gap we created between the hillside and the tree and resumed our trip up Route One toward Leggett with my fingers crossed that Fate wouldn't throw us an even bigger impediment to our progress.

We were already descending the eastern slope into the Leggett Valley when we encountered our next challenge. It wasn't, however, nearly as difficult as the fallen tree.

This time Fate left a rockslide in our path. Hitting it in a passenger car or in any vehicle after dark would be a nasty surprise, but we handled it with relative ease. I simply slowed and shifted the transfer case into its four-wheel-drive mode. Then it was just a matter of picking our way over and through the rubble, carefully avoiding any rocks big enough to damage the Jeep.

Back on our way again, Kieley asked, "Do you have an idea when we'll get there? I need to . . . ."

With a grin I said, "Pee?"

"Yeah, that."

"Okay, but it's hard to know what conditions we'll find in Leggett. I see a pullout up there and we have a roll of TP in the back. How about I pull over and you can take care of the problem without waiting."

She sounded completely serious when she said, "You promise you won't peek?"

I laughed. "Kieley, I won't peek, but even if I did, what is there to see that I haven't seen many times before?"

She thought about that for a moment and came up with an answer. "That was pleasure, this is business."

Shaking my head in amazement, I pulled off the road and parked next to the trees. Hitting the rear hatch release button, I said, "TP is in that black plastic storage bin where you got the tow strap."

Opening her door, Kieley said, "Don't forget, you promised not to peek."

"I know. Don't worry."

A few minutes later, as we got back on the road, Kieley said, "You peeked, didn't you?"

I smiled and said, "Yup."

"I knew you would. I guess that tells me how much your solemn promise is worth."

"Yes, but what if a bear came charging out of the woods and grabbed you? I was protecting you!"

Kieley gave my arm a whack. "Next time I'll just pee on this fancy leather seat and we'll see how you like that."

I gave her a grin. "I'd still love you."

Shaking her head in something like aggravation, Kieley said, "Yes, I bet you would."

Then she snuggled as close as she could get with her shoulder belt and the console in the way and gave me a kiss on the cheek. About twenty minutes worth of twists and turns after that, we rolled into what was left of Leggett. Actually, there wasn't much there to begin with.

The wooden sidewalk awning in front of the Leggett Valley Mercantile had collapsed and flattened the hood of a small Ford pickup. The three tall glass windows and a matching glass door at the front of the Post Office were nothing but long shards dangling from their weather stripping. I pulled onto the shoulder of the road and shot a few frames of the damage to beautiful downtown Leggett.

Under the heading of good news, the Leggett Patriot gas station seemed to have survived the shaker mostly intact. I pulled up next to one of their two pumps wondering if they had power. A bright pink neon "open" glowed in one of the service bay windows telling me they did.

I got out and a fellow in grubby jeans and a denim jacket came running over. "You'll have to pay cash, Mister. The credit card machine works on the telephone and our lines is out."

Since I always travel with a few hundred in small bills, I said, "No problem. You want the cash up front?"

He looked up at me. "Naw, you look like an honest sort of fellow. Go ahead and pump your gas."

While I pumped he said, "Where'd you folks come from, up north?"

"No, sir. We just came over Highway One from Hardy."

That surprised him. "You did? I was figurin' One was closed over the ridge. A shaker that strong is sure to bring down some rocks and timber."

"It did, but we managed to clear our way through. I wouldn't try it in anything that doesn't have decent ground clearance, though. There's a rock slide on this side of the ridge that would be tough going in a low-riding passenger vehicle."

"Thanks for tellin' me 'bout that, Mister. Now I can let folks know who wants to go that way. Was you there for that big wave, or whatever it was?"

Returning the pump nozzle to its holder, I said, "No, sir. We beat it up the hill right after the shaker. The last place I wanted to be was on that coast road with a tsunami coming. Do you know if it ever showed up?"

He shook his head. "I surely don't. We was gettin' that religious FM station from over to Garberville for a while, but they quit not long after the shake. There ain't nothin' else on the dial now."

The tank took seven gallons and I handed him a twenty and a five, saying, "don't worry about the change. Tell me, though, is there a motel around here where we could spend the night?"

He shook his head again. "The nearest place with motor lodges is Laytonville, 'bout twenty miles down 101. Heck, they even got them a Injun casino there!"

"How about something to eat?"

The fellow smiled a semi-toothless smile. "That we can help you with." Pointing up the road, he said, "That place right up there on the right is Janie's Diner. They don't have nothin' hot cuz their propane tank is on the blink, but Janie can make you a sandwich or somethin' else cold."

I offered my hand. "Thank you for your help. I hope you folks can get things fixed up and running again soon."

He shook the hand I offered. "We surely will. Most of us was borned and growed up in these parts. We ain't gonna let no little old earthquake run us off!"

Getting back into the Jeep, I said, "Looks like lunch is about to be served."

"Yes, I heard. At Janie's Diner no less."

It was chilly inside Janie's, but she did have food for us. Kieley ordered Janie's take on a Cobb Salad, which had a little of most everything in their refrigerator on it. I got a turkey and cheddar sandwich with a little bag of chips. It wasn't fancy, but we were hungry.

While we ate lunch, I fired up the Nikon to look at the images we had from the coast. I discovered we had more shots of Kieley on the bridge railing than I remembered making. The last one showed Kieley leaned way back over the bridge railing and hanging on for dear life. I showed her the frame.

She took a look, and then quickly turned away. "I don't even want to think about that, let alone see it!"

Before leaving, we ordered two more sandwiches to go and two bananas Janie said she used in their fruit salad when she made it. Thus equipped with emergency rations, we climbed into the Jeep and drove back to the Highway 101 junction at the north end of town.

According to a mileage sign that showed up soon after we got on the highway, Laytonville was 21 miles ahead. The same sign also informed us San Francisco was 175 miles in the same direction. I glanced at Kieley, wondering if she noticed it.

She not only read the sign, she also read my mind. "Yes, I saw it, and no, it does not make me homesick. In fact, except for picking up my things from my apartment and checking on my roommate, Kris, I'm not sure I really care if I ever see San Francisco again."

"I know some bad things happened to you there, but you can't blame the whole town for that."

"Yes, I can!"

I laughed at her vehemence. "Okay, I guess you **can** blame the whole town."

"Besides, I have another reason for not caring about San Francisco anymore."

"Oh? What reason?"

"I plan to begin a new life with the man I love and he's in Los Angeles."

"You sure you should do that? I heard the guy nearly pushed you off a bridge."

"That's not the way it happened! My man damn near got himself killed saving my skinny butt."

"Skinny butt? I thought it was a sexy butt."

"It's my butt, I'll call it what I want."

Suddenly she was leaning over the console again kissing my cheek. "Gosh, I love you, Kev. I guess I always have and I know I always will. If I didn't realize that for sure before, I sure as hell know it after today."

"I love you, too, and I still say it's a sexy butt."

Compared to the other bergs we visited recently, Laytonville was a veritable metropolis. They even had a Chinese restaurant, a gym, and a Chevron Station.

They also had four motels. The one that struck our fancy was a place called the Long Valley Inn, which advertised color TV, air conditioning, and wireless Internet. However, I had to laugh when Kieley told me to wait a minute while she ran the joint through Yelp on her cell phone. The connection was slow, but what she got were a whole lot of one-star reviews that said, "Do not stay here."

Acting on the advice of the Internet just as if we could afford to be choosy, I drove diagonally across the street and parked at an economy chain motel which had significantly better Yelp reviews. The office door opened when I tried it and a fellow behind the registration counter welcomed me. I asked if they were open and he said, "Sort of."

His explanation went like this, "We have no power, no heat, and no hot water. What we do have is cold running water, candles, and lots of warm blankets. Under the circumstances, I'll let you have a room for ten bucks cash . . . our credit card machine isn't working."

As I opened my wallet and pulled out a ten, I said, "Yeah, there's a lot of that going around."

Before taking our bags in, we checked the radio for KCBS. It was there, but only barely. What we could hear of the news was the tsunami had been much larger than anticipated and a lot of the Great Highway along the ocean beaches on the west side of San Francisco was literally washed away and the Golden Gate Bridge was closed because engineers were concerned it might have suffered structural damage.

Kieley said, "God, Kevin! What's happening? Is this global warming or something?"

"Darned if I know. Maybe we just had a whopper of a quake. We haven't heard what fault line it's on, but I don't think it was the San Andreas fault. It can't cause tsunamis."

I backed the Jeep up and parked it where nothing like the sidewalk awning was going to fall on it if there were more shakers. As we carried our bags in, I felt Kieley walking close beside me.

Once inside our room, we set our bags down and I led Kieley over to the bed. "Let's sit and have a conversation."

She cuddled close to me and I said, "Talk to me. What's going through your head?"

"Honestly?"

"Honestly."

"I'm scared, Kevin. Really, really scared."

"Can you narrow that down a little. I mean can you say what's scaring you?"

She waved both of her arms in the air like the answer should be obvious and said, "Everything!"

When I didn't respond right away, Kieley said, "No, that's not right. The thing that scares me most is we don't know what's going on. For all I know, this could be the end of the world." After a momentary pause, a little sob crept into her voice as she said, "I'm not ready for my world to end. Not now. Not after we've found each other again."

My arm was around her waist and I gave her a squeeze. "Okay, Kieley, I think I get it now. We're both suffering from the same thing: severe uncertainty. It doesn't help our situation any, but I suspect a lot of other people are experiencing the same fears.

"I don't have any answers for us, except one. We're together and we love each other. Do you think we could make that our rock—the thing that keeps us from getting panicky and makes us less scared?"

She looked up with a small smile. "I think it just became our rock because of what you said. My mind was going in all directions at once, but when you said that . . . everything sort of popped into focus. I could see you and I could see myself clearly in my mind, and I could see us going on to make our dreams, even dreams we haven't talked about yet, come true."

I said, "That pretty well describes how I feel. It's sort of like that old Sonny and Cher song, *I Got You, Babe.*

Kieley pulled my face down to hers and kissed me. "Yes, exactly like that, and I just realized something else."

"What?"

"You never asked me a question like that before. I mean you never came right out and asked me what was scaring me before. It's like we never wanted to admit to being afraid, but you just made it all right. We can be scared and we can help each other through the scary times. You just helped me, but I don't know how to help you. Please tell me."

After a moment of thought, I said, "The most important thing is stay close. When I look at you, the world always seems brighter . . . and let me know you have faith in me. I try to let you know I believe in you and I need to know it works both ways. Sometimes you can do both of those things at the same time by just holding my hand. Does that make sense?"

Her eyes had a sheen to them when she looked into mine. "Yes. It makes perfect sense, and I will remember to do those things for us. I'll begin right now by reminding you that you literally saved my life today, and maybe you just did it again. Most women never get to see how far their men will go for them, but I got to see that in you today.

"It was scary as hell, but in a small way, I'm glad that earthquake came along when it did, because now I know without a doubt I am loved by a man who is willing to risk his life for me. As long as I live, I will always remember that."

I leaned down and kissed her lips. They felt warm and alive, but not with passion. They were alive with love.

Half an hour later we were both stripped down to our underwear and under several blankets piled on top of us. It was only late afternoon, but we were both exhausted and by mutual consent we decided sleep was what we needed most. We drifted off in the warmth of each other's arms.

FOUR

When I woke up, the room was dark and it took me several seconds to figure out what awakened me. I eventually figured out it was a combination of things. One was the rattle of our room's heater fan. That meant the power was back on.

It took me even longer to realize the other thing that woke me was not a dream. I thought I was reliving the earthquake we experienced earlier, but when another tremor shook the bed it was clear we were having another round of shakers.

These were not as strong as the last tremors, but they were enough to wake Kieley, too. She grabbed my arm and sat up. "What? Are we having another earthquake?"

"Yeah, but these are baby shakers. The good news is we have electricity again. The room heater is working now."

"What time is it?"

I looked at the glowing hands of my watch. "Two-fifteen. You think you could sleep more or do you want to get up?"

"I think I'd like to get up for a while, but that means getting dressed."

"Well, I can offer a reward for that effort."

Leaning over to kiss me, Kieley said, "Mmm. What's the reward?"

I chuckled. "Not what you're thinking. We don't need to get dressed for that."

She put on a pouty expression. "Phooey. Then what?"

"This room has a coffeemaker, and now that we have power, we can make hot water which is one of the two primary ingredients for hot cocoa."

"What about the other ingredient? Where do we get that?"

"We already got it at the McKinleyville Holiday Inn Express

breakfast bar. So, putting two and two together, we have everything we need to make hot cocoa. Doesn't that sound good?"

"It does, but how many calories does it . . . Oh, to hell with it. Yes I want some, as long as you'll still love me if my skinny butt isn't quite as skinny."

"Darling, I'd love you even if you weighed as much as a hundred and twenty pounds."

She smiled broadly. "Oh goodie! I can put on sixteen pounds. Make that cocoa!"

I plugged in the coffee maker gizmo and loaded it with tap water. While I was doing those things, Kieley put her clothes on. Watching her get dressed is almost as much fun as watching her get undressed.

As I mixed the hot cocoa, Kieley tried the flat screen TV. After some fussing with the remote, we were suddenly watching a cable news network. What they were saying got our attention in a hurry.

"The second major earthquake to hit Califiornia in as many days struck less than thirty minutes ago. Centered near the small community of Goshen, about thirty-six miles south of Fresno, this quake registered a seven-point-three magnitude, only slightly less powerful than yesterday's trembler centered on California's northern coast not far from the town of Eureka.

"With most lines of communication already down because of Friday's quake, reports of damage and injury from the affected areas are still spotty. It is suspected, however, that San Francisco suffered major damage over and above that caused by the tsunami following yesterday's earthquake. A second tsunami will likely follow this most recent quake, but the NOAA has not issued a statement or warnings yet.

"We are currently working on satellite links we hope will put us in direct communication with our reporters in California. In the meantime, ..."

Kieley pressed the mute button on the remote and the blonde woman reporter's mouth kept moving, but no words came out. Kieley grabbed my hand when the news report began and she was still hanging onto it.

"Whatcha thinking, Kieley?"

Looking discouraged, she said, "I'm thinking our shoot is over. We won't be able to get anywhere near the beaches down the coast, especially if another tsunami comes along."

"Agreed, but there are other things in our lives we have to think about. We need to make some big decisions about those things and prioritize some plans to accomplish them. I think survival trumps bug-eyed sunglasses at this point."

"That makes sense, but what kinds of things do we need to decide about? I don't mean to sound dumb, but I'm not seeing things very clearly now."

"We need to look at are the big things first and work down to the details. Big Thing Number One: How far-reaching are these disasters and how many more are ahead of us? We can't know that without help and time, but we need to keep our eyes open for the information."

"Yes, I see."

"Big Thing Number Two: We are together right now, but is that how we want to continue?"

Kieley looked a little panicky. "That's what I want. Isn't it what you want?"

"Yes, it's what I want, too, but in this instance saying it to each other becomes a commitment . . . like we are committed to surviving this crisis together. See what I mean?"

She nodded. "Yes, I see now. What else?"

"Well, if we're going to survive this, we need to gather our resources. That probably means getting into your apartment in San Francisco and recovering whatever you need from there, and then getting down to my home in Los Angeles to see how it's holding up and to recover some resources there if we have to move on."

Taking a swallow of her hot cocoa, Kieley said, "All right. By the way, this cocoa really hits the spot. Thank you."

"You're welcome. Any other high-priority issues come to mind?"

"Sort of. Thinking about getting my things out of San Francisco has got me wondering how Kristina is doing. She's my roommate and the closest thing to a sister I've ever had. We have always looked after each other. Besides that, a decent apartment in The City runs three to five grand a month. The way things have been, I couldn't afford that on my own.""

"Checking in with Kristina and finding out how she is certainly a reasonable priority."

"I've tried calling her a couple of times, but the cell towers must be out of whack. All I get is a busy circuits recording. I don't seem to be able to send text messages, either."

"Is Kristina alone there—no family or anything?"

"She has a brother in Los Angeles somewhere, but she's been seriously dating a guy in The City. Hopefully, he's with her."

"How much do you need to get from your apartment? I mean

would it fit in the Jeep?"

I don't need much. Mostly, just some clothes and a few pictures and mementos. My little treasures are more important to me than the clothes. Some of them are things you gave me."

"Then maybe we can kill two birds with one stone. How would it be if we made getting your stuff from San Francisco our first priority? That makes sense geographically, and you can check on Kristina while we're there."

I could feel her physically relax. "Could we do that?"

"Sure. First, let's get out of here and see if we can get something to eat in this town. We passed a couple of markets and restaurants coming in. With the power on again, maybe one or two of them will be open. It could be a while before we get another chance."

"We still have the sandwiches and bananas we bought yesterday."

"We do, but I'd like to hang on to those just a little longer to make sure we can get something here."

Kieley frowned. "How long will it take us to get to The City?"

"That depends. Based on the sign we saw yesterday, we have about a-hundred-and-fifty miles to go and that would typically take about three hours. Given the road conditions we encountered yesterday, though, I don't think we can count on averaging anything near the speed limit. It could take a lot longer depending on what we run into along the way."

She looked thoughtful. "That's sort of what I figured. It's more of that not knowing. What about gas?"

"We've got a little less than three hundred miles' worth, so we can get into and away from San Francisco, but I would not pass up any opportunities to top the tank off if we find a working station down the road. What do you think? Are we ready to hit the road?"

Kieley looked into my eyes. "I guess I don't need to tell you I'm getting scared again."

"I am, too. For me, doing something . . . working toward a goal helps me stay positive. Will that work for you, too?"

"Yes, I think so."

"And if I suggest anything you don't think is the right thing for us to do, I want you to speak up. I'm playing this strictly by ear and I'm certainly no survival expert. Promise you'll do that?"

Slipping into her jacket, Kieley said, "I promise. Let's hit the road."

The Jeep started on the first crank. While I let it warm up a little, I said, "Kieley, do you have your cell phone charger with you?"

"Yes, it's in my bag."

"It would probably be a good idea to plug our phones in so we aren't out of battery power when we need them most."

With our phones plugged into the Jeep's power system and charging, we set out to find some food before we left town." I pointed us north on the Redwood Highway, which also served as Laytonville's main street, and headed back toward the center of town.

Nothing we passed, including the Chevron Station, showed any lights until we got to the Long Valley Grocery Store. They not only had lights on, there were several cars in the parking lot.

We went in and found a sort of party going on. About twenty folks were sitting around in the store's deli sandwich shop drinking coffee and discussing earthquakes. Chalk one up for small towns where neighbors are their own support group.

Kieley went straight to the produce department and picked out some fruit and veggies. While she did that, I found a block of medium cheddar cheese, an entire box of brown sugar cinnamon Pop-Tarts, a box of Quaker instant oatmeal packets, and a box of Saltine crackers.

She caught up with me in the cracker aisle, where she looked kind of sheepish as she eyed the shelves. I said, "Okay, Kieley, what is it you want me to get, but you're embarrassed to ask for?"

Kieley came over and whispered in my ear, "Cheez-Its, please."

I couldn't help smiling. "I must say that is a very strange request coming from you."

"I know, Darling, but I loved Cheez-Its as a little girl and I haven't had any since . . . well, I don't remember when, but it's all right. I shouldn't eat them anyway."

Adding the biggest box of Cheez-Its I could find to the cart, I said, "The hell you shouldn't, and I'm going to have as much fun watching you enjoy those crackers as you'll have eating them."

When she didn't reply, I turned to look at her. Kieley was actually blushing. I hugged her. "Don't let me ruin your fun. I know how important your figure is to you, and you do a great job of keeping it. I promise I won't kid you if you put on a pound or two. You need to have a little more energy reserve now than you have in 'normal' times."

She hugged me and we were off to the deli where we ordered sandwiches for breakfast. That's right, *we* ordered sandwiches. Kieley wanted a roast turkey on whole wheat bread, hold the mayo. She was really living it up. Mine was a ham and swiss on rye. After all, ham is a popular breakfast food.

We found an unoccupied table in the corner of the store's deli shop and ate our breakfast. As we did that, I looked around and was reminded of something I always find fascinating about being out in public with Kieley. It wasn't just that she attracted the eyes of everyone in the room, it was the ways different people looked at her.

Often women who were with their husbands did a kind of double take, first noticing her, and then looking to see if their husbands noticed her. Unaccompanied women noticed her and sort of smiled to themselves. I thought that might be a sign of admiration.

Young men, on the other hand, tended to gawk, making no effort to hide the fact they were staring at a beautiful female. If they were with a woman, their gawking often got them a smack on the arm or an elbow in the ribs. Mature men were more surreptitious about looking at Kieley, especially if they were with their wives.

The one thing everybody did after staring at Kieley was glance at me. I think most of them figured if I was with a woman that beautiful, I must be somebody rich, famous, and/or important. It was all kind of fun to watch.

About three-forty-five we pulled back out onto Highway 101 in the southbound direction. Kieley played with the radio, which gained us nothing but static and gibberish.

South of Laytonville, the highway carries one lane of traffic in each direction and runs mostly straight through a long narrow valley. With no other traffic on the road, it felt like the most desolate spot on earth.

The roadway surface was asphalt, and while some deep cracks had opened up here and there, the highway seemed to have survived the quakes without damage serious enough to block our progress. That being the case, I pushed the 55 mile per hour speed limit a little, making good time while we could.

As we neared the southern end of the valley, it narrowed and we were back in the timber with an increasing number of curves in the route. I slowed down to the 45-50 range and paid better attention to what was in our headlights. We were still at least two hours away from sunrise.

We passed what I thought might be an RV park and some tourist cabins along the way, but they were dark, leading me to think the power had not made it much beyond Laytonville. Then all of a sudden we were back in civilization.

The town of Willits is, or was, considerably larger than the other communities we passed since leaving Eureka. It was also in shambles. With no street lights and some pretty large pieces of debris littering the road, I slowed to a crawl.

Watching the carnage roll past our windows, Kieley said, "This is awful. Such a pretty little town, but it looks like somebody fought a war here."

"One of the reasons it's so bad is most of the buildings are older unreinforced wood frame structures. In a light quake they give and flex pretty well, but in something the size of what hit yesterday, they are literally shaken to pieces."

We passed the Willits Veteran's Memorial Building with every one of its many windows broken, but that wasn't the worst of it. The greatest damage was in the old downtown area. What once was a four-story brick hotel at Commercial Street was reduced to about a floor and a half with most of its bricks scattered over the sidewalk and across the roadway.

I turned left on Commercial Street to go around the debris, and what we saw as the Jeep's headlight showed us the way was an old theater with a collapsed marquee and a partially collapsed roof. Despite what it said on a coming attractions poster, a Disney animated feature would not be coming to the Noyo Theater anytime soon.

I planned to turn right at the next block, but debris from a stone building and an old Purity Market building on opposites sides of the intersection blocked our way. The next street we came to was Main, but it was a dead end. I finally turned south again on Madden Lane, a residential street lined with older wood frame houses that were now mostly kindling.

Weaving back and forth across the road to avoid debris, we made it to the next intersection, which was Mendocino Street. It look as if it might take us back to the highway, so I turned right. Back at the main drag, I turned left to continue south.

Once again, our progress was slow with a lot of weaving back and forth to get around debris. At one point I actually had to drive on the sidewalk. Nobody minded, though. There wasn't a soul in sight.

That part was especially bothersome to me. We were in a town of about five thousand people, and at that hour at least a few of them should be starting their day, but as far as we could tell there were no people left in Willits.

Kieley picked up on the same line of thought. "This is so eerie!

I feel like we're in a science fiction movie where we are the last two people on earth. This is way scarier than driving out in the country."

"I was thinking more or less the same thing. I'm not sure I would be surprised to see a crowd of zombies coming up the street."

"Kevin! Don't say that! I'm already spooked out of my wits." She looked at the door on her side of the car. "Are the doors locked?"

"Yes, Kieley, they're locked. They lock automatically when I put the vehicle in gear."

"I hope so."

A few minutes later I got a surprise when we passed a highway sign telling us that we were on State Route 20. "What the hell?"

With a touch of panic in her voice, Kieley said, "What? What's the matter?"

"Somewhere along the way we got off of Highway 101. We're on something called State Route 20."

"Yes. I thought you did that on purpose to look for a gas station. The road split way back before we got into town."

I smacked the steering wheel with the palm of my hand. "I should be using the damned GPS, but oh, no, I know the route. God only knows how far out of our way we've gone."

Putting her hand on my right leg, Kieley said, "Relax, Darling. We're okay. We just passed a highway sign that said, "Highway 101 South Right Lane."

Slowing to look for the turn off, I said, "Thanks, Kieley. I'm sorry. I guess I'm not as sharp as I thought I was."

"You're doing fine, Kev. Really you are. I think 101 just skirted the town. I should have asked you about it when I saw the highway split, but in a minute we'll be back on track. "

Kieley was absolutely right. I took the onramp to our right and we went right back onto the highway, and better yet, while we were wandering around Willits, 101 turned into an honest-to-god freeway.

A little simple arithmetic told me something else that wasn't particularly good news. Even though it seemed like we'd been driving for hours, we were still more than a hundred miles from San Francisco. We only covered about forty-five miles since leaving the motel in Leggett.

"Kieley, do you know how to work a GPS?"

"I think so. My cell phone has one I use sometimes."

"Well this Jeep has one, too. I'm gonna pull over to the

shoulder and get it running so we can make use of it."

I got the dashboard GPS display turned on and pulled back on to the highway. Kieley finished the process by entering her apartment address into the destination blank. The electronics instantly confirmed my simple arithmetic. We were 104 miles from her address in San Francisco by the shortest route.

I sighed and said, "Thanks, Kieley. At least we're making pretty good time now that we're on a real freeway."

The sun was starting to show in the east and we were seeing an occasional car on the road as we got closer to the heavily populated Bay Area. We rolled past Ukiah and Cloverdale, and by a little after five we had knocked the remaining distance down to seventy-two miles. Then Fate took another shot at us.

A ways north of Healdsburg, we encountered a California Highway Patrol Dodge parked diagonally across the lanes ahead with its light bar flashing. A temporary orange highway sign on a sawhorse stood between us and the cruiser. It said, "Road Closed Ahead." Another sign that said "Detour" pointed us toward an off ramp.

Following more detour signs, we ended up on a county road that more or less paralleled the highway. Half a mile later we saw why the freeway was closed. The two concrete highway bridges over another county road at a flyspeck on the map called Lytton were collapsed.

We had to stay on the parallel road until we were allowed to rejoin the freeway in Healdsburg. What little we saw of Healdsburg looked very much like Willits, except the sun was nearly up and we got a better look at the destruction.

As we drew closer to San Francisco, the towns along Highway 101 appeared with greater frequency. After Healdsburg came Windsor and the largest town we encountered so far, Santa Rosa. Then we zipped through Rohnert Park, Cotati, Petaluma, and Novato so quickly it was hard to tell where one ended and the next began.

The last major town we came to before the Golden Gate Bridge was another big one, San Rafael. We had to leave Highway 101 again because of more road closures ahead. I half expected the closures. Much of 101 through San Rafael is elevated, which means there were more overpasses to collapse. Apparently many of them had.

We were shunted off of 101 on North San Pedro Road across from the fancy Frank Lloyd Wright-designed Marin civic center. That was fine with me because I could already see there were functioning gasoline stations in in San Rafael.

It was also nearly time for Kieley to call her roommate in San Francisco. San Rafael was a good place from which to do that because, if the Golden Gate Bridge was closed as had been reported hours ago on the cable news channel, San Rafael was as far as we could go before deciding on a different route into San Francisco. Our first stop, though, was an open Chevron Station Kieley spotted from the off-ramp.

With the Wrangler's 22 gallon tank filled and our bladders emptied, we pulled into a small shopping center parking lot next to the station. All the shops were closed and ours was the only vehicle in the lot.

Kieley unplugged her cell phone charging cable and tapped in a number. When the number began ringing, Kieley tapped the speaker phone icon.

I looked at my watch. "It's only seven, I hope Kristina is an early riser."

"Normally she'd be up by now, but not much is normal any . . . ."

A female voice coming from the cell phone said, "Kieley! I'm sure glad to hear from you! I was afraid you might be hurt or something."

Kieley said, "I'm fine, Kris, but cell reception where we've been was limited or nonexistent."

"Then you're okay?"

"Yes. There were a few scary moments, but Kevin got us through them. I've got the speaker phone turned on so he can listen, too."

Kristina said enthusiastically, "Hi, Kevin! Nice to meet you, and thanks for taking care of my best friend."

I said, "Kieley and I did it together. We're a pretty good team."

"When are you coming home, Kieley, or are you?"

"Well, that depends. I can explain it better when I see you, but . . . ." Kieley looked up and smiled at me. "But Kev and I are picking up where we left off a few years ago. We're back together and this time it's for keeps."

Kristina sounded truly excited. "That's wonderful, Kieley. I'm so happy for you guys!"

"Thanks, Girlfriend. Now, I have a question for you. Our ultimate destination is Kev's home in Hollywood, but I want to pick up some important stuff from our apartment. The question is, can we get there from where we are? We're in San Rafael."

"Yes, you can get here, but not by way of the Golden Gate. It's closed."

"We heard something about that on one of the few newscasts we caught. Can we cut over to Oakland and come into The City by the San Francisco/Oakland Bay Bridge?"

"Yes. It'll be slow going, but last I heard the Bay Bridge is open. Everything here has been sort of minute to minute. When are you coming?"

"As soon as we finish talking."

"That's good because things are kind of touchy here at the Edgewater. Everybody got eviction notices this morning."

"What?"

"Eviction notices. The buildings suffered some structural damage, and they want to do repairs, but they say they can't do it with tenants in their apartments. They've given us until next Friday to move out. And just to make it harder, we can't use any of the elevators. Thank God we're only on the second floor."

"Well, I only want to take my clothes and personal stuff . . . pictures, and like that. I collapsed and kept all the boxes I used to move in, so it shouldn't be too bad."

Kristina said, "That will work out well. My brother is coming up this morning to help me pack my stuff. I'm moving in with him until things are better here. We'll have a moving party."

Kieley laughed. "Kris, it doesn't matter what's going on, you figure out a way to make it a party."

I said, "What's wrong with that? Sounds like a good philosophy."

"Oh, she's just a party pooper, Kevin."

"Well, unless you ladies have anything else you need to discuss right now, we'll get on the road."

"Okay, see you guys in a little while."

Kieley said, "Okay, Kris. See you soon," and disconnected the call.

I said, "Anything else we need to do before we leave San Rafael?"

"I don't think so. Do you know how to get to the Bay Bridge from here?"

"I'm pretty sure I can get us there, unless we run into a bunch of blocked roads."

We got back on 101 and followed the signs for Interstate-580. Eventually, we passed the front door of San Quentin State Prison and drove onto the Richmond-San Rafael Bridge. The Jeep's GPS was going nuts trying to keep us on track to our destination. It was clear the satellite it was talking to didn't know anything about any earthquakes.

Across the bay, 580 continues down the San Francisco Bay's east shore past Berkeley and to the Oakland end of the Bay Bridge. As we passed a University of California off-ramp sign, I heard Kieley sigh.

"You okay, Kieley?"

"I'm fine. Just seeing the University Avenue off-ramp reminds me of better times. I miss them, especially the times when we were together at Cal and hardly had a care in the world."

I laughed. "Yeah, no cares, just midterms, finals, term papers, tuition, grade point averages . . . ."

"All right, smarty. I remember those things, too, but the world wasn't falling apart around us then."

"True, but it took the world falling apart to put us back together."

"Maybe it reminded us what's important in life."

Kristina was right about traffic on the Bay Bridge. The bridge has two decks. Originally the top deck carried all of the auto traffic and the bottom deck carried trucks and electric trollies. Beginning in 1963, the lower deck carried cars, trucks, and busses in the eastbound direction, and the top deck carried all traffic in the westbound direction. The freeway leading to and from the bridge eventually became part of the Interstate Highway System, the beginning of I-80 to be specific.

The westbound traffic was bumper to bumper moving at five miles an hour and frequently coming to a standstill. We had plenty of time to study our view of San Francisco before we got there.

From our viewing distance, The City looked surprisingly intact. That changed when we got off the bridge onto city streets. We did that at Ninth Street and Kieley took over the navigation chores, and getting to her apartment was definitely a chore.

The problem was San Francisco's elevated freeways were all rebuilt and strengthened to higher seismic standards after the 1989 Loma Prieta quake, and so were the modern high-rise office buildings, but the older buildings lining the surface streets below were not. As a result, getting off the freeway was like driving into a metropolitan version of Willits.

Just as in Willits, surface thoroughfares were clogged with debris—sometimes with entire buildings. Kieley just kept steering us around this block and that block until we finally arrived at 355 Berry Street in the Mission Bay District, about three blocks south and west of the Giant's baseball stadium, Oracle Park.

Kieley's apartment complex had an underground parking

garage for tenants, but a gate blocked the way in with a large hand-lettered "closed" sign attached to it. That explained why Berry Street was lined with parked cars. That left me expecting to carry Kieley's moving boxes several blocks. Then a van left the parking space directly in front of the building's entrance. I grabbed the spot and cut the Jeep's engine.

Kieley leaned over and rested her head against my arm. "That was awful. For a while I wasn't sure we could actually get here."

I kissed her forehead. "You did a great job of navigating through the maze. Shall we go in, or would you like to sit here a little longer?"

"No, let's get this done and get out of this town before the rest of it comes down on our heads. Besides, I'm anxious to see Kris."

Making sure the Jeep's doors were locked and the alarm was activated, we entered 355 Berry Street, but even getting in the front door was a challenge.

The doors were the automatic kind that slide sideways to open, and their doorframes were warped during one of the quakes, jamming the doors halfway open. I made sure they could be pushed the rest of the way open so we could get Kieley's boxes out.

FIVE

Thursday, August 18, 2022
Edgewater apartments, San Francisco, California

Inside 355 Berry Street's lobby, large "OUT OF ORDER" signs decorated the elevator doors. I followed Kieley to a stairway behind a door next to the elevators. Leaving the stairwell through similar door Kieley unlocked on the second floor, we walked down a hallway to apartment 215.

The door was ajar, so Kieley walked in with me trailing along behind her. She shouted, "Hey, anybody home?"

A female voice answered from a hallway. "Hi, Kieley. You made it!"

The girl who ran into the living room and hugged Kieley was one of the most beautiful women I have ever seen. Kieley introduced us. "Kris, meet Kev. Kev, this is Kris."

I shook a warm hand with a firm grip and looked into two clear dark eyes in a perfect face finished off with a Mona Lisa smile. Her hair was a dark shade of brown and her slim body was clothed in a black sleeveless T and jeans.

Kristina said, "It's so cool to meet you, Kev. Maybe I shouldn't say this, but when Kieley told me she was going on location with you, I had a feeling you two might get back together."

I smiled. "Good to meet you, too, Kris. Forgive my curiosity, but what gave you that feeling?"

She gave me a conspiratorial smile. "That's private between me and Kieley, but I think you'll get the **picture** before you leave."

The way she emphasized the word "picture" made me think I ought to keep my eyes open for something in a frame. Kieley just said, "Geez, Kris."

Taking another look at Kristina, I asked, "Tell me, by any chance are you in the same business as Kieley?"

Brightly, she answered, "I am. What gave me away?"

Feigning annoyance, Kieley gave me an elbow to the ribs. "Step on the brakes there, Mister. You've already got all the woman you can handle. Besides, Kris is spoken for."

Kristina said, "I hope I am. I've only talked with Bailey a couple of times by telephone since the first quake. The city has gone nuts and they have him doing two shifts a day."

Kieley explained. "Bailey, Kris's guy, is a San Francisco homicide cop, which is another good reason you should stop staring at her and help me get the boxes packed."

"I am NOT staring at Kristina!"

Kieley looked at Kris. "How do you vote, Girlfriend, staring or not staring?"

Kristina looked at me and winked. "I'm not going to get in the middle of this, but remember what Kev does for a living. If he was looking at me, it was with a photographer's eye."

Kieley grumbled, "Oh, brother," and then we all trooped off to what I discovered was Kieley's bedroom. Six empty cardboard boxes of various sizes were assembled on the bed.

"Thanks for getting my boxes out, Kris."

"You're welcome. I didn't have anything else to do until Tony gets here, so I decided to be helpful." She looked at a small gold and black wristwatch. "I thought he'd be here by now. He was going to leave at three or four this morning."

Kieley said, "Kev, Tony is Kris's brother and I hope he gets here soon. It's a mess out there on the streets."

Looking at the boxes, I said, "What's the most efficient way to do this so we get the right stuff into the boxes and leave the stuff you don't want?"

Kieley looked around the room thoughtfully. " Kev, please start with packing my clothes from the closet—just jeans, casual tops, and maybe a hoodie or two. Don't get fancy packing them—just cram stuff into the large boxes until they're full. Okay?"

I nodded and dragged one of the boxes to the closet. While I did that, Kristina said, "What do you want me to do, Kieley?"

"Would you please take smaller boxes and empty my underwear, stockings, and the other stuff from the chest of drawers? While you do that, I'll start packing treasures and mementos."

Kieley left the room to visit the bathroom and Kristina said my name softly. I looked in her direction and she pointed to a gold-framed color eight-by-ten on the nightstand. I recognized it as a posed photo I made of Kieley and me when we were at Cal. I'd posed us looking at each other face-to-face, using the camera's self-timer to include myself in the image. It was a romantic mood shot and I always liked it. Apparently, Kieley did, too . . . enough to make it the last thing she sees before going to sleep every night.

I looked back at Kristina and she smiled warmly. I nodded my thanks to her for showing it to me before Kieley packed the photo away. I hoped Kieley would bring it out again for our bedroom, if and when we ever had one.

Kristina and I finished our packing assignments in about 45 minutes. Kieley took a little longer, checking through every drawer in the room. Then she looked in the direction of the closet.

"Oh, hell, my shoes! Kev, is there room in one of the clothes boxes for them?"

I looked at about eight pairs of shoes from red spike heels to white running shoes. "Yes, I think so." I looked at the top shelf, and added, "There's also some bedding up on the shelf in here . . . ."

Kieley was running out of patience. "Oh, I can't leave my great-grandma's quilts behind. And the pillows . . . we might need those."

When we were done, there were six boxes stacked inside the front door to the apartment. The good news was none of them was particularly heavy. For our first trip down to the Jeep, we each carted a large box out the door.

When we had them stacked next to the Jeep, I opened the rear doors and hatch so I could move stuff around to make room. While I did that, Kieley and Kris went back upstairs for the remaining smaller boxes.

Feeling like I was trying to solve a Chinese block puzzle. I tried three or four combinations for positioning the boxes so they would all fit. Ultimately, with a little bending and squishing, I got all six boxes in with our travel bags, camera gear, and the stuff I usually carry in the Jeep. In the process, I shared the two bananas we bought the day before with Kieley and Kris. I discarded the two sandwiches we bought with the bananas in . . . Leggett. Life was moving so quickly, I had to stop and think where the hell we bought the stuff.

Then the three of us were standing on the sidewalk. Kieley and Kristina hugged with tears in their eyes. Kieley said, "I'm gonna miss you, Girlfriend."

Kristina said, "I'll miss you, too . . . a lot. You're the bestest roommate I ever had."

I said, "Kris, where does your brother live?"

With an expression that made her look as if she had tasted

something bad, she said, "He lives down in your part of the world, in West Hollywood."

Trying to cheer the girls up, I said, "Hell, we're practically neighbors!" I dug one of my personal cards out of my wallet and offered it to her. "This is my home address along with the landline and my cell. When you get down there, you and Kieley can get together anytime you want."

"That's wonderful! Thank you, Kev."

Kieley said, "And please let me know when you're safely out of San Francisco . . . even just a text message so I know you're okay."

Kris glanced at her watch again, and said, "I will, I promise."

Kristina stood on the sidewalk waving as we drove away. Kieley was turned in her seat with the window open to wave back. Just before we turned the corner, I looked in my rearview mirror. Kris was still there on the sidewalk, looking very sad and lonely.

Kieley navigated us back onto Interstate-80, also known as the Central Freeway. Once we were on it and headed south toward its junction with our old friend, Highway 101, Kieley asked, "Why am I suddenly so sad? I feel like I'll never see Kris again."

I looked at her. "What if Kristina's brother can't get up here?"

She jerked her head around to look at me. "You think he might not?"

"I don't want to create problems where they don't exist, but it pays to be realistic in times like these. These quakes have caused a lot of highway and infrastructure damage, and with cell coverage so iffy, he might not be able to call Kris. Does she have a car?"

Kieley shook her head. "No. She sold hers like I did. We needed the money to live on. After that we used Uber or public transportation. I doubt if either is available now. Is there anything we can do?"

"I think we should at least offer her an option. How 'bout calling her and asking if she would like us to come back and wait for her brother with her or take her south with us?"

Kieley picked her cell phone up from the console. "I'll do it."

There was a long wait for the connection to complete. Kieley, said, "Hi, Kris. Kev and I were wondering if you heard from Tony yet?"

After another pause, Kieley said, "Well, Kev is concerned Tony might not have cell coverage coming up from LA, or the road might be closed. Would you like us to come back? Kev said we could wait for your brother with you or take you south with us, your choice."

The pause was shorter this time. "Yes, Kris, Kev would do that for you just like I would. I wish I'd thought of it, but calling you was Kev's idea."

Another short pause. "All right, Girlfriend, you pack a bag of essentials and stuff you don't want to lose and wait for us out front. We'll be back as soon as we can get there."

As I took the Ninth Street ramp off of I-80 and got us back on the freeway in the opposite direction, Kieley said, "She sounds as scared as I've been for the past few days. Kris said she would like to leave town with us."

"Good. I feel better now."

In a tender tone, Kieley said, "Thank you, Kevin. Not everyone would put a person they hardly know ahead of themselves like that."

"Kris is important to you and that makes her important to me, and I promise I won't stare at her."

"You do know I was kidding about that, don't you?"

"I do."

We played the maze game again, this time with a whole new set of surface streets because we were coming from the opposite direction. Eventually, though, we pulled up in front of the Edgewater Apartments at 355 Berry Street again.

Of course, the empty parking spot we used in front of the building entrance before was filled, but we didn't need it this time. Kristina was waiting for us and came running with a backpack and a small carry-on. I double parked, jumped out, and opened the driver side rear door. I wedged her heavily loaded bags in behind Kieley's seat, and then made a little room behind my seat for Kris. It's a good thing she has a skinny butt like Kieley.

I closed the door behind her, and as I climbed back into the driver seat, I made a decision. Kris was saying, "I can't thank you enough for coming back for me. I left Tony a couple of voice messages and a text message. Hopefully he'll get them before he gets all the way up here."

Kieley said, "You don't have to thank us, Kris. I think Kev just likes the idea have driving around with two hot babes . . . ."

I interrupted her. "Excuse me, hot babe, but I'm making a slight change in our plan."

"Oh?"

"Yeah, can you get us back onto the bridge?"

"You mean back the way we came? I think so. Why do you want to go that way?"

"I've been so fixated on Highway 101 all the way down here I wasn't thinking clearly. Interstate-5 is a much faster route to LA from here and is less likely to have serious quake damage than 101 because it's newer. I could be wrong, but I think it's a better choice."

"Okay, Darling. Go straight ahead and see if you can turn left on Fourth Street."

Luck was on our side. The route back to the bridge was direct with the main surface streets open. Almost as good, the bridge's eastbound lanes were a lot less crowded.

At the end of the bridge, we transitioned to I-580, which continues east toward the Oakland hills, and then turns south until it gets to Castro Valley, where it turns inland. The Jeep's dash clock was showing ten-fifty-one when 580 turned east toward Stockton.

I noticed Kieley turned around and look at Kristina a couple of times. I, in turn, looked at Kieley and she gave me a worried expression, and then mouthed the words, "Talk to her."

I wasn't sure how I got appointed as leader of the pep squad, but I did as asked. "How are you doing back there, Ms Bryant?"

She sniffed and said, "Just fine, Kev." The sob in her voice said she was anything but fine.

"Kris, I guess I should have explained the rules on this bus."

Softly she asked, "What are the rules?"

"They're very simple. We tell each other the truth no matter what. For example, if you're sad, you don't have to say why you're sad if you don't want to, but you do have to be honest about how you feel. Okay?"

A quiet "Yes" came from the back seat.

"Now, let's try it again. Kris, how are you doing?"

I saw Kieley look back at Kristina and nod. Kris cleared her throat and blew her nose.

After all that preparation, all she said was, "I'm scared."

It was déjà vu all over again. I remembered having the same conversation with Kieley quite recently. I said, "There seems to be a lot of that going around these days. Do you want to tell us what's scaring you?"

With a little more life in her voice, Kristina said, "Everything . . . the earthquakes . . . I'm worried about my brother . . . I miss Bailey . . . and if it weren't for you and Kieley, I'd feel like I don't have a friend in the world."

"Well, Kris, there's one piece of good news in all that. You do have at least two friends in the world who care about you."

"I know. Thank you both for caring when I really need friends. I think I'm just a coward at heart."

"There's something else you should know. A couple of days ago Kieley and I were feeling about as low as you are now, and for the same reasons. Am I right, Kieley?"

"Yes. I swear I was about to come completely unglued, but Kevin let me in on a secret."

Curiosity got to Kristina. "What secret, Kieley?"

"He told me he was just as scared as me and made me believe it. That confused me. I mean, here was the guy who risked his life to save me from falling hundreds of feet off a bridge in the first quake, and he is telling me he's scared. Now, I know for certain anybody who can do what he did, can't be a coward. That means he can be scared without being a coward, and so can you."

"Wow, did Kevin really do that?"

"He did and we have photos to prove it. The other thing he told me that night is what was scaring us was . . . what did you call it? Severe . . . severe uncertainty. Is that right?"

"Those are my exact words. Severe uncertainty is the result of trying to live in a world that's so messed up you can no longer count on the things you used to be sure of."

Kieley picked up the pep talk again. "But when we talked about it, we realized we do have someone we can count on. We can count on each other, and Kris, the same goes for you. You can count on us, too. We're like the Three Musketeers, one for all and all for one!"

Kristina said, "I understand what you're saying. I remember how I felt when you guys drove away earlier. I feel pretty good now compared to that."

I simply asked, "Why?"

She didn't have to think about that. "Because I know I have friends. You cared enough to turn around and come back to take me with you."

Kieley said, "And would you do the same for us?"

Without hesitation Kris answered with an emphatic, "Yes."

Kieley smiled over her shoulder. "There you go."

Outside our windows, the world was in better order than Kieley and I had seen it in a while. The parts of Dublin and Livermore we could see from the freeway looked relatively undamaged, certainly not as bad at the communities we saw north of San Francisco.

We stopped for lunch at an Applebee's in Dublin. Applebee's is never my first choice among chain eateries, but it was handy and it seemed like a big deal to actually sit at a table and order from a menu.

Kieley and Kristina both ordered Thai shrimp salads, which according to the menu went for four-hundred-and-ten calories each. I ordered a brunch burger with a fried egg and hash browns on it. The burger also came with fries. I don't know how many calories it had because I deliberately didn't look. My activity level for the past few days was more than enough to burn off a fried egg and a few hash browns. I'll worry about my butt getting big if and when we ever get back to a normal world.

From Dublin we rejoined I-580 east for about twenty miles through rolling hills and over the Altamont Pass. A few miles further, 580 turned south to head for a junction with I-5. Actually seeing a sign that said Los Angeles raised my spirits considerably.

The less desirable part of our progress was we were driving through some of the most desolate country in California. Aside from some large agribusiness operations, there was nothing out on the west side of California's central valley but jackrabbits and a few tiny farm towns.

Kieley made note of this fact. "You were sure right about civilization being scarce out here. I don't see anything besides the freeway that bears any resemblance to civilization." Then she picked up her cell phone and woke up the display. After looking at it for a few seconds, she said, "You were also right about cell phone coverage. I've got zero bars and a no service available notice."

Adding to the feeling of desolation was the fact there were very few cars on the road. We saw a few eighteen-wheelers heading southbound, but even they were in short supply. Around three p.m. we stopped at a Shell Station in Kettleman City to top off our gas tank and stretch our legs. San Francisco was four hours behind us and Los Angeles was something like three hours ahead of us, or it used to be.

We were making the best progress we'd made since leaving the coast south of Eureka after the first quake on Thursday. Now the immediate goal was to get home to my house in the Hollywood Hills and regroup.

With a few low calorie energy bars from the Shell Station's convenience market aboard, we got back on the highway. We were rolling along at something close to 70 when things suddenly got very strange.

With no assistance from me, the Wrangler swerved sharply to the left. I caught a glimpse of Kieley grabbing for the panic bar above the glove compartment and Kristina squealed from the backseat, but they were on their own. I had my hands full trying to regain control of the Jeep.

Then, just as abruptly, the Jeep reversed course and took off for the right shoulder. By this time I had my foot off the gas and onto the brake pedal. When I got a second to look up the road, I clearly saw what was happening. Interstate-5 looked like a long gray ribbon somebody was flapping from one end to make waves.

Kieley was white as a ghost when I got the Jeep stopped and she let go of the panic bar to grab my arm. Meanwhile, the quake just kept shaking us. Kristina let out a panicky yell from the backseat, "What the hell is happening?" The shaking kept right on going.

I found myself yelling to be heard over the loudest quake rumble I've ever encountered. "It's another quake, but we're okay, Kris. We just have to ride it out. Brace yourself so your head doesn't hit the window or the door frame."

I can't give you a precise duration for the quake, but a habit picked up in photographic darkrooms over the years kicked in and I mentally counted to "sixty hippopotamus" five and a half times before the shaking finally stopped. Three-hundred-and-thirty hippos convert to about five-and-a-half minutes. Typically earthquakes lasted about thirty seconds. I was pretty sure Mother Nature had just set herself a new record.

Kristina interrupted my mental arithmetic. "Is it over?"

"It seems to be, but there are bound to be aftershocks."

I'd no sooner said "aftershock," when one bounced the Jeep on its springs. "Like that one."

Kieley said, "I didn't think it was ever going to end!"

"According to my mental stopwatch, the quake lasted about five-and-a-half minutes. That has to be a record. I'm surprised we don't have the Pacific Ocean lapping at the roadside here. Kieley, would you please see if we can pick up KCBS in San Francisco or KNX in LA? KCBS is around seventy-four on the dial. KNX is at ten-seventy."

While Kieley looked for a radio station, Kristina said, "Are we okay here? Nothing's going to fall on us or anything?"

I opened the moon roof shade and looked up. "There's nothing out there to fall on us. I'm more concerned about these cracks opening up in the ground and in the pavement. They could make for some rough going if the cracks are wide enough and deep enough."

Kristina said, "The road's all broken up behind us, too."

"I think we can handle these cracks if they don't get much worse. Can you see any cars behind us?"

After a few seconds Kris said, "I think there's a big truck back there, but it's on its side, like it tipped over."

I turned around to take a look at the truck. It was at least a half mile behind us, and there was nothing we could do to help him anyway. I could see nothing on what remained of the road ahead of us.

Suddenly KCBS cut through the static. Jeff Bell was reporting.

. . . tuned to News Radio Seventy-Four. So far, we have been unable to contact Caltech Seismological Laboratory in Pasadena for specific details, but indications are the quake was centered near the Salton Sea at the southern end of the Fortuna earthquake fault.

The Fortuna is a subduction fault about one-thousand-five-hundred miles in length, running from Mexico along California's coastal mountains and through the Cascade range in Oregon and Washington. It ends in the Overseer Mountains north of Victoria, British Columbia. Most Westerners have never heard of the Fortuna Fault because it has been inactive for more than a century.

The National Oceanic and Atmospheric Administration is using the Emergency Alert System to transmit warnings for everyone within ten miles of the California, Oregon, and Washington coasts to move inland immediately. They are expecting a tsunami of record proportions to strike momentarily. It could reach 100 feet or . . . .

KCBS disappeared abruptly and Kris sounded a little panicky as she asked, "Another tsunami! It can't get us here, can it?"

"No, Kris. We're safe from tsunamis here. There are two mountain ranges between us and the ocean."

After relieving Kris's worries about stray tsunamis, I added up the sketchy facts we had. We were faced with a quake centered five-hundred miles away that lasted five-and-a-half minutes, tore up a four-lane freeway like it was tissue paper, and could kick up a hundred foot tidal wave. On top of that, the quake was on a fault line that hadn't so much as twitched in a hundred years.

Feeling like we were trapped in a Harvey Corman horror flick about the earthquake that ate California, I said, "Kieley, keep trying for a station about every fifteen minutes, any station. If the NOAA is using the Emergency Alert System, the broadcasts should automatically be retransmitted by every local radio station still on the air. If you locate one on the dial, we should be able to find out more about what's going on."

"Okay, but what are we going to do now? Can we keep going to LA?"

"It looks like we can, but what I really want to do is hole up somewhere until we can get information about how things are to the south. I don't want to drive us out of the frying pan and into the fire, so to speak."

Kris said, "No, we don't want to do that! I'm scared enough as it is."

"Ladies, the facts are we just experienced what could be the most powerful earthquake in history and that puts everybody else in the same boat we're in, including emergency services. In other words, Mother Nature is in the driver's seat and we're on our own for now; maybe for quite a while."

Kristina's mind was on more immediate matters. "But what about the road. It's all busted up. We can't drive on it, can we?"

"We probably could, but it would be a rough ride. This, however, is an off-road vehicle and we've got a nice flat off-road shoulder to drive on for now."

Kieley was studying the GPS display on the Jeep's dash. "It looks like the closest places we could go are Kettleman City, where we just came from, and a place called Buttonwillow, which is about fifty miles down the road. It looks like Buttonwillow has motels and restaurants."

"Yeah, I'm familiar with Buttonwillow. It offers us the most options. That okay with you ladies?"

Kieley nodded, I heard a shaky yes from the backseat, and an aftershock gave us a shake of agreement. I shifted into low and we moved out along the shoulder.

I figured our progress would be slow, and it was. There were places where the banks of the highway cut were too narrow for a shoulder to drive on. That put us on the cracked asphalt and slowed us down even more.

After about 30 miles of skirting the highway, we finally got a break at State Route 46. I can't say why, but the earthquake gods decided to spare some of the highway south of that point. We were back on solid freeway paving and making good time again. All told, the fifty-four miles to Buttonwillow took us about two-and-a-half hours. We pulled off the freeway just as the last rays of the sun were slipping behind the hills to the west.

Lights were already blinking on at some sort of large industrial complex off to the southwest. I was wondering what was out there in the middle of nowhere when I realized I photographed that complex a while back. It was the Elk Hills Oil Field, a federal oil reserve. It held more than a hundred-million barrels of crude and had some two-thousand wells to pump it out of the ground if the oil was needed in a national emergency. I momentarily wondered how all that stored oil was affected by the shaking. Since that wasn't our problem, though, I stopped thinking about Elk Hills and pulled into a Rodeway Inn parking lot.

There were four other motels along a frontage road that paralleled Interstate-5, but the Rodeway looked like the newest. There were also numerous fast food burger joints, a Subway sandwich shop, and even a Starbucks. Buttonwillow had it all. Well, all but electricity. There wasn't a light in sight except those in the distance at the oil field.

I tried the Rodeway's office door and it opened. From that point my conversation with the fellow behind a registration counter lit by a candle was a replay of one I'd had at the Laytonville Budget Inn last Friday, except this time I needed two rooms and the guy thought his rooms without power, heat, or hot water were worth fifteen dollars a night instead of ten.

Since his credit card machine wasn't working, either, I handed him three tens in exchange for the keys to two adjoining ground floor rooms with a connecting door. I moved the Jeep close to our rooms without being right next to the building.

I took a look at the Jeep's gas gauge before shutting the engine off. It was pointing just below the three-quarter mark. Our off-road route from Kettleman City sucked up a lot more gas than cruising down the highway at a steady speed. Under normal circumstances three-quarters of a tank was plenty to get us over the grapevine to LA, but normal circumstances were ancient history.

Getting our gear out of the Wrangler, I suggested we have a conference to discuss our situation after we were settled in. Kristina carried her backpack into Room 101, while Kieley and I carted our stuff into 102.

We had two queen-sized beds and they were looking awfully inviting. I was tempted to stretch out on one of them for a few minutes. Realizing I would probably be asleep within seconds of laying down, I opened our half of the connecting doors with Kristina's room. I thought she might feel safer with the doors open.

After stashing our bags, Kieley came over to me for a hug. We embraced and we were kissing when Kris poked her head into our room through the connecting door. When she saw what was going on, she said, "Oops! Sorry."

Kieley said, "It's okay, Kris, we still have our clothes on."

I could tell Kris was embarrassed, but she laughed at Kieley's comment, and then we made ourselves comfortable and commenced to discussing how we ought to proceed. The first item on the agenda was dinner.

"The fellow in the office told me Subway was going to stay open with a limited menu for as long as their supplies lasted. He said it was the only place he knew about where we might get something to eat."

Kris frowned. "Maybe I'll pass. I don't think I want all the starch in one of their sandwiches."

Kieley said, "You don't have to have a sandwich, Kris. Subway has salads now. You can make one up with lots of flavor, very few calories, and no starch. What about you, Kev?"

"A foot-long rotisserie chicken with everything on nine-grain wheat, a bag of Doritos, and cookies for everybody."

Kieley stood. "C'mon, Kris, let's go get dinner and let Kev rest up from all the driving he did today. We started out before four this morning."

Kris said, "Good idea."

Then I stood up and said, "A thoughtful idea, but not a good one."

Kristina looked hurt and Kieley said, "Why not, Darling?"

"The way things are, our world can turn upside down in a split second. We need to stick together so we don't have to go searching for each other if something else happens. Tell you what, I'll drive you over to Subway and wait in the car while you guys get the groceries, how would that be?"

By six-thirty, we were back in Room 102 eating dinner. Something about having the world fall apart around you must boost appetites. When we were done, there wasn't a scrap of lettuce or a cookie crumb left in sight.

"All right, ladies, I'm going out to the Jeep and see if I can pick up anything on the radio. I'll be just outside the door."

Kieley said, "Can we come, too?"

"Sure, if you want to."

Thus, we all piled into the Jeep again and I started its engine. I hated to waste the gas, but all the gas in the world wouldn't do us any good if we ran the battery dead.

I started my search at the high end of the dial and hit pay dirt right off the bat in the form of a Fox news station at fifteen-sixty:

. . . is the National Oceanic and Atmospheric Administration broadcasting on the Emergency Alert System. Here are the latest seismic events along the country's west coast. Aftershocks from the record nine-point-seven magnitude earthquake centered near

*Palm Springs, California that struck at three-eleven p.m. Pacific
Daylight Savings time today continue to be felt from Eureka to
San Diego.*

*The resulting tsunami arrived at the California coast at five-
forty-nine this afternoon with wave heights of one-hundred-
twenty to a hundred-and-fifty-feet. The worst tsunami damage
reported thus far occurred in San Francisco. The death toll in
that city alone may be as high as one thousand.*

I heard Kristina gasp at the news of San Francisco's fatalities.
I turned the radio off. We'd all heard enough tragic news for one
day. Back in Room 102 I could tell the news about San Francisco
clearly shook Kristina to the core. "All those people dead! It's
horrible! And if you guys hadn't come back for me I would have
been one of them!"

I said, "Maybe, but we did come back for you, so you're alive
and safe."

Kieley added, "Yes. We're all okay. Thank God for that."

I said, "Yes, and now the trick is staying that way. It doesn't
sound like LA is a very good place to be right now, but there are
personal items at my place I'm pretty sure we're going to need
before this is over, besides that, I'd like to know if I still have a
home."

Kieley asked, "Can we find out before we try going there?"

"Unfortunately my neighbors aren't very neighborly, so there's
no one I can call. The only sure way to find out is go there, and
getting there requires going over a mountain range and crossing
the San Fernando Valley. There are a couple of ways to accomplish
those things, but I need to think about which one would be safest.
Right now, what I need most is some sleep."

Kieley seconded the motion and from the corner of my eye, I
saw a sad expression passed over Kristina's face. She said, "I guess
I'd better get back in my own room."

I glanced at Kieley. She was looking at me with a questioning
expression. I knew what she was thinking and I had no real
objection. I just wanted some sleep. I nodded an answer to her
silent question.

As Kristina got out of her chair, Kieley said, "Kris, would you
feel better sleeping in here tonight? We have two beds."

"I don't want to invade your privacy. You guys deserve some
time alone without me hanging around, especially after everything
else you've done for me today."

Kieley was standing next to me and she rested her head
against my shoulder. "Kris, look at Kev. He's asleep on his feet,

and so am I. I'm pretty sure there won't be anything going on in our bed besides sleeping."

I yawned and Kris looked at me. "Are you sure this is okay with you, Kevin?"

"I've got no problem with it." I picked up my ditty bag and walked into the bathroom, thus ending the discussion.

I returned to the bedroom at exactly the moment Kristina came back from her room. All I had on were my briefs and she was in a long sleep shirt like Kieley's, but I could not have cared less. I noticed however, she almost fell over the corner of the couch trying not to look at me. I climbed into bed and thought, "To hell with propriety."

Kieley was the last into bed, so she switched off the light and cuddled in next to me. She said, "Goodnight, Kris. Sleep well."

A quiet voice from the other side of the room said, "You, too."

Kieley whispered in my ear. "I think Kris is embarrassed she saw you in your shorts. She is definitely not a woman of the world."

"And you are?"

"No, but sleeping in the same room as a half-naked man doesn't upset me."

"Seems to me that would depend on who the man was."

"Oh, never mind. I love you, Darling. Sleep well."

Kieley rolled onto her side and draped her leg over mine the way she often did. That put her thigh right where, despite my exhaustion, it caused an involuntary reaction. Of course she noticed and whispered, "Oh, oh."

"You did that on purpose. Knock it off and go to sleep."

Kieley giggled softly. "I was just checking."

"Okay, woman of the world, you've checked, now go to sleep."

SIX

Friday, August 19, 2022
Rodeway Inn, Buttonwillow, California

At first, I thought the jostling that woke me was Kieley getting out of bed, but she was still sound asleep. I guessed it was another damned aftershock, and a strong one at that. Then something hit the floor with a crash and I bailed out of bed.

Trying to keep my balance against violent shaking, I shouted, "Kieley, grab some clothes and get out of here! Kristina, wake up!"

I grabbed my pants and shirt from a chair by the bed and headed for the door right behind Kieley, who was carrying her jeans and a jacket. Then I noticed Kristina stumbling in the darkness. She seemed confused. I put my arm around her waist and latched on to a blanket from her bed.

Outside, the shaking seemed even more violent. I let go of Kristina and leaned against the Jeep to put my pants and jacket on. While I was doing that, Kristina managed to get the blanket wrapped around her, but Kieley fell getting into her jeans. She used the Wrangler's fender to pull herself up before I could get to her. All the while, the quake rumbled like a dozen locomotives going by at the same time.

My keys were in my pants pocket. I fished them out and pressed a button on the Jeep's electronic key fob to unlock all four doors. I yelled, "Come on, into the Jeep."

Kristina was having trouble getting her blanket through the Jeep's door. I hopped out, and hanging onto the vehicle for support against the ceaseless motion of the ground, I stuffed the offending blanket parts inside and closed the door.

Back in the Jeep, I slipped the key into the ignition switch and was just about to start the engine when the shaking stopped. The world suddenly got very quiet. It was like somebody pressed a mute button.

Kieley said, "It's over."

It wasn't a question. She was simply stating fact. I glanced at my watch: 3:57 a.m.

A flash of light in the rearview mirror caught my eye. I looked again and saw fire. It was a long way off, but it was a big damned fire. Opening my door, I stepped out and looked behind us. I couldn't say for sure, but it looked as if the Elk Hills oil field was ablaze.

Kieley asked, "What is it, Kevin?"

"Nothing that affects us directly; at least, I don't think it does. The big oil field off to the southwest seems to be burning."

I heard a faint boom and a spot of fire flashed higher and brighter for a moment. Kristina asked, "Can we go back in yet?"

I turned and looked at the motel. The Rodeway Inn seemed to have withstood yet another shaking without any noticeable damage.

Answering Kristina's question, I said, "Let's go in, get dressed, and gather up our gear. We can figure out what comes next after we've done that much."

Back in Room 102, Kris unceremoniously dropped her blanket and ran over to hug me. She looked at Kieley who was standing close enough for us to see her amused smile even in the dark.

"Kieley, I'm sorry. I'm not trying to steal your man, as if I even could, but I owe him something because he just saved my life . . . for the second time."

With that, she turned and kissed me full on the lips. I looked at Kieley. Her amused smile turned to a wide grin. "That's okay, Kris. Just return the unused portion when you're done with him."

That gave us all a laugh and Kristina trotted off into her room for her gear. Kieley came over and gave me the same treatment Kris had just given me.

When the kiss ended, she grinned again. "Don't worry, I'm not going to ask which of us is the better kisser. I'm more concerned that my best girlfriend just gave me a very sexy kiss by proxy."

I lowered my voice so Kris wouldn't hear me. "You win the kissing contest hands down, but that might have as much to do with how I feel about you as it does with kissing skill. As for kissing your Girlfriend by proxy, I won't tell."

"You'd better not!"

Then Kieley finished buttoning her blouse and said, "What do we do now, Darling? I mean, with the quakes still going on, does it make sense to go to LA, even if we can get there?"

"I think it does. If my house is still standing and hasn't been destroyed, there are things hidden there—papers, cash, and such—that will be hard to replace, and we will need no matter where we end up going.

"As for getting there, I have an idea, but first, let's get our gear out to the Jeep and try the radio once more before we make a final decision about how we might get into LA."

Kristina joined us and with our gear stowed in the Wrangler, Kieley took a stab at tuning in an emergency alert station, and for a moment she had one. We heard:

. . . Alert System. A third major . . . minutes ago . . . east of Los Angeles . . . extensive damage . . . Highway Patrol is reportedly closing all major highways, including Interstate Five over the Grapevine . . . .

"All right, Kieley, let's shut it off and save some gas. We can go back inside for a while to stay warm."

Inside, Kieley said, "Is Interstate-5 over that Grapevine place important?"

"Yes, The Grapevine they referred to is the shortest route through the mountains between here and Los Angeles. The main alternate route would take us over to the coast to pick up Highway 101, which we could follow into Los Angeles. Besides being much longer, I don't think that route is worth trying because of tsunami damage along the coast, plus there's probably another one about to hit from the quake we just felt."

Kieley frowned. "We may not be able to even get to LA, then."

"I think we might. There are a couple of other mountain pass routes, and I know one that isn't far from here. It's the long way around, but the route may be open because it's just a two-lane road with no overpasses or elevated sections to collapse. What do you guys think? Should we give it a try?"

"I trust your judgement, Darling. If you think it's important to try for LA, I'm game."

I looked at Kristina. She sighed and unenthusiastically said, "Me, too."

"All right. I'm not especially keen on trying the route I'm thinking of in the dark, so I suggest we hang here for a couple of hours until sunrise."

We spent the next two hours dozing, talking, and generally killing time. When it was light enough to clearly see the Jeep outside our window, I said, "I think we can go now, if you two are ready."

While the Jeep warmed up, I asked Kieley to enter Taft,

California into the GPS. She did, and the first driving instruction the computer gave us was to head west on State Route 58, which ran right alongside the Rodeway Inn's parking lot.

As we drove away, I looked at the gas gauge. I would much rather have started this trip with the needle on "F" rather than on the three-quarters mark, but that situation wasn't going to improve unless or until we got someplace where they had gasoline and electrical power to pump it.

State Route 58 is a two-lane road running more or less due west across a lot of flat land from where we joined it at I-5. A railroad track paralleled our route. I guessed the track might go to the Elk Hills oil field, which was easy to spot off to our left because of the large black cloud of smoke hanging over it. Evidently the fire was still burning.

Our first turn was only a few miles west of Interstate-5. We turned south on Wasco Road. The terrain remained flat, but the scenery became more agricultural.

Soon the GPS instructed us to make another turn. This one was back to the west on another arrow-straight two-lane road. We were still in farm country and even passed close to a farm house—a pretty snazzy one at that.

Then our straight road suddenly made a 90-degree turn to the left and changed its name. We were then on Buttonwillow Drive. Half a mile or so after that, we crossed a large canal and the road changed its name again, this time to Elk Hills Road.

Now the scenery outside our windows changed significantly. We were climbing slightly and the terrain took on an inhospitable and desolate look. A vulture perched on one of the utility poles alongside the road would have been a perfect addition.

Elk Hills Road ended at State Route 119, also called the Taft Highway. Our trusty GPS said turn right. Taft Highway wandered around some, but generally tracked south. Then, quite suddenly the desolation was replaced by civilization, and a lot of it. According to a sign, we had arrived in Taft, which according to the same sign was a town of about ten thousand folks. What Taft is doing out there in the middle of nowhere, I have no idea, but I was glad to see it.

Amid heavy quake damage, something caught my eye and made me even happier to be in Taft. What I saw was a porchlight attached to a sagging house close to the road. Despite the house's condition, the porchlight was on. That meant Taft had power. If Taft also had a functioning gas station, my spirits would positively soar.

A "Business District" sign detoured us to the right. Entering the commercial area of Taft, it was obvious the town suffered heavy damage. Seeing small towns with such devastation was a familiar experience for Kieley and me, but here, the local citizens were out early clearing debris. They had a determined look about them. I stopped long enough to shoot some images of the activity.

The best news was a Chevron Station on our right. It appeared essentially undamaged and was already open for business at seven in the morning. I pulled in and filled up the tank while Kieley and Kristina went into the station's food mart to stock up on provisions, including fresh coffee.

Kieley made a point of showing me a box of Brown Sugar Cinnamon Pop-Tarts among the supplies they purchased. Pop-Tarts were now kind of a joke between us, but even so, it reminded me how nice it is to have someone close who really cares, even about the little things.

On our way out of town we passed the West Kern Oil Museum across from the local Dollar Store. Under different circumstances I would have stopped at the museum. Local museums are a passion of mine. I suspected, however, they were closed for repairs, and now was no time for lollygagging.

Back on the road with gas in the tank and hot coffee in hand, it was time to give the GPS a new destination. I asked Kieley to enter Ojai, California, pronounced "O-high." She did so, and after looking at the new route display, Kieley announced we were beginning the toughest part of the trip thus far, describing it as eighty miles of bad road.

If the scenery we were passing on State Route 33 south of Taft was any indication, there wasn't going to be much to look at along those eighty miles either. About the only scenery amounted to a few oil pumpjacks here and there. Then we ran out of oil wells and were left with just mile after mile of desolation.

Out of the blue, Kristina said, "May I ask a question?"

I said, "Sure. Ask away."

"I've been kind of wondering what we will do if we find out there's nothing left of Los Angeles. I mean what if it's all knocked down and . . . and there's no place there for us?"

I gave her the best answer I could think of, which was no answer. "That's certainly a good question, and to be honest, I haven't given it much thought. What would you suggest we do under the circumstances you described?"

Kristina was quiet for several seconds. I was paying attention to the road, but I took a quick look in the rearview mirror. I could see her back there and she appeared to be absorbed in weighty thoughts. Kieley had a worry frown on her face.

Finally, Kris said in a quiet voice, "The only thing I know is there are bad people in Los Angeles, especially men who hurt women. They do evil things even when there are policemen around. Now, there may be no police around and they will do even worse things."

I pondered Kris's observation about Los Angeles while moving along the very edge of the road to get around a boulder that rolled down from somewhere and ended up in the middle of our path. Once we were around it, Kieley said, "Kris, is it okay with you if I tell Kevin about your sister so he'll understand why you don't like Los Angeles?"

Quietly, Kristina said, "Yes, I guess so."

"Kev, Kris's older sister had a good job with an electronics company that transferred her from Silicon Valley to LA. One day after work she drove home to her apartment—it was in a good neighborhood, but some bad guys were hanging around in the underground parking garage. They were reported to the cops earlier, but the cops never showed up. Those bad guys raped and murdered Kris's sister, and then went joyriding in her car."

I glanced up into the rearview mirror again. Kristina looked like she was about to cry. "Kris, I'm sorry, but now I see what you mean about bad people."

She said, "That's one reason I depend on Bailey so much. This is a violent world and he makes me feel safe . . . like nobody can hurt me. I bet Kieley feels that way about you, too."

Nodding, Kieley said, "Yes, very much so. It's a very good feeling to have someone bigger and stronger looking out for you."

I asked, "Kris, have you heard anything at all from Bailey?"

"No, and I'm terribly worried about him. I've sent several texts and emails telling him where I am and what we're doing, but there haven't been any replies. I don't even know for sure he got what I sent him."

I told myself finding this fellow, Bailey, needed to be a priority. At the moment, however, I had to focus on getting us to our destination. Up ahead I could see we were heading into the mountains. Things could get hairy up there.

Actually the going wasn't any worse in the mountainous area than it was in the flatlands. The trees weren't the kind we encountered way up north that tended to fall down and block the roadway. These trees were shorter and better anchored.

The main dangers we faced crossing the mountains were

rocks on the road and buckled pavement. With Kieley helping me spot hazards, however, we got through them without damage to us or the Jeep. Finally, we topped a low ridge and saw what was left of Ojai below us.

Ojai was mostly an artsy residential suburb northwest of LA. The majority of homes we passed, however, were little more than piles of rubble. We saw very few signs of life along our route. As before, I stopped for a moment in a couple of places to make photos of the destruction. From a photographer's point of view, it was dramatic stuff.

The GPS and a lot of careful driving to avoid debris got us to a modern commercial district at the junction of State Route 33 and State Route 150. I pulled into a mini-mall parking lot just off of the highway, being careful to avoid the Spanish tile and other adornments scattered by the mall shops as they fell.

It felt good to get out of the Jeep and stretch my legs. Kieley was also happy to unbend and stretch. Kristina didn't look happy about much of anything.

Personally, I wasn't too happy about our progress. We'd been driving for nearly six hours since leaving Buttonwillow and we only covered about a hundred miles, some of it in the wrong direction. The good news was we bypassed I-5 over the Grapevine.

What concerned me most was the needle on our gas gauge. I was keeping an eye on it, and when we pulled into the parking lot, the gauge was indicating just over half a tank. That meant we burned up about ten gallons since we left Taft.

The up and down terrain we came through, along with running in four-wheel-drive to circumvent obstacles burned up a lot of gas. We weren't in trouble yet, but the way things were going, it wouldn't take long to get there.

Looking around at her surroundings, Kieley asked, "Are we near where you live?"

"Not yet. We're a lot closer, but we're still a ways west and a little north of Hollywood."

Kristina was frowning as she asked, "How far do we still have to go?"

"From here we need to work our way east through the Simi Valley, and then across the San Fernando valley to where Highway 101 will take us south over the mountains into Hollywood. That's a distance of about another 80 miles."

"How long do you think it will take?"

"Under normal conditions we'd be there in about ninety minutes. Today . . . ." I shrugged. ". . . I have no idea."

Kieley changed the subject. "I'm hungry. I'm sure glad we got some food when we stopped for gas. Kev, you want a Pop-Tart?"

I nodded and Kieley asked Kris if she wanted a nutrition bar. The response was a shake of the head and, "No thanks. I'm not hungry."

I was watching Kristina. She seemed nervous and jumpy. That made me think we needed to get back on the road. A few minutes later we were in the Jeep and I was telling the GPS to find "home," which was my address in the Hollywood Hills.

"Before we go, let's see if we have any cell signal."

I looked at my phone and was surprised to see two bars of signal. Kieley had the same. I turned to ask Kristina how much signal she had and saw tears in her eyes.

"What's wrong, Kris?"

"My cell phone is dead and I forgot to bring my charger. Now I'll never know what's happened to Bailey."

I looked at Kieley and she said, "Here, Kris, let me see your phone."

Kieley looked at the phone and smiled. "It's okay, Kris. Your phone is the same kind as mine, and we have a way to charge it in the Jeep. I'll plug it in. Your phone will turn on right away, and stay on while it charges."

"Oh, thank you, Kieley. I don't know what's the matter with me. I'm a mess."

I said, "Sit back and take a deep breath. Remember we're all in this together. Your problems are our problems. Between us we'll make it through."

While Kieley got Kris's phone charging, I looked at the two route options to my address the GPS offered us. One took us west to Ventura, where we could pick up US 101 and follow it back east to Hollywood. The other was a longer, but safer, inland route that took us southeast on State Route 150.

The mini mall lot we were parked in was right on 150, so all I had to do was pull out of the lot and turn left. In a short distance, State Route 150 became a winding mountain road with lots of cracked pavement to take us over a couple of ridges in our path.

Watching the countryside go by, Kieley said, "This is so rural. I didn't realize there was so much open country in LA."

"I'm afraid you had it right. This isn't considered Los Angeles. We are in the northernmost mountain range that runs east from the coast to Interstate-5."

"Oh."

Ultimately, 150 delivered us to the town of Santa Paula, where there once were a lot of older wood frame houses. They were mostly rubble now and I was reminded of the towns up north we saw after the first quake. Once again, we were forced to do a lot of twisting and turning to avoid the debris.

Fortunately, the GPS was able to follow our meanderings and the stops I made for photos. Sort of like a good hunting dog, it kept pointing us toward our next turn. That turn was east onto State Route 126, which took us east to the town of Fillmore.

Destruction from an earthquake can be like what is left behind a tornado. Sometimes the damage in one place is total, and just up the road the destruction is relatively minor by comparison. That was the case with Santa Paula and Fillmore.

The earthquake gods took pity on Fillmore, where the destruction was significantly lighter than what we saw in Santa Paula. I even noticed lights on in a couple of businesses, which started me looking for a gas station. I found one at C Street.

A pickup truck was parked next a gas pump and a fellow was filling its tank. I pulled in and got out to do the same.

A fellow in a white Shell work shirt came running over, and I'd hardly gotten the Jeep's gas cap off when he said, "I'm sorry, sir, but we are only selling gas to local residents. Are you from the area?"

"I am if you count Hollywood as part of the area."

He nodded. "That's close enough, but I'll need to see your ID."

I handed him my driver's license. He looked at the license and handed it back to me. "I'm sorry to be so picky, but we figure our first obligation is to local customers."

"I understand. Do you need cash or is your credit card system working?"

"Credit card will be fine, but we have limit of fifteen gallons."

"No problem. It won't take that much to fill the tank."

I inserted my Visa card into the pump's card reader and tapped 90068 into the keypad when the display asked for my zip code. While I set about filling the Jeep's tank, Kieley and Kris headed for the station's restrooms.

The pump clicked off at 13 gallons and spit out my receipt. I climbed back into the Jeep and drove over to park next to the restrooms. I'd just gotten out to take advantage of the facilities when I heard a telephone ringtone somewhere in the Jeep.

I looked in the console and it was Kris's phone. I answered the call.

"Hello, this is Kristina's phone."

A man's voice said, "This is Detective Sergeant Bailey of the

San Francisco Police Department. Who are you?"

"My name is Kevin Turner. I'm a friend of Kristina's roommate, Kieley, and you have no idea how happy I am to hear from you. Kris has been very worried about you."

"I thought she might be. I received her texts, but when I finally got a chance to call back, I tried over and over without getting through. This is the first time I've gotten an answer. Can I talk to Kris?"

"She'll be here in a minute. We stopped for gas in the town of Fillmore. Kris and Kieley are in the restroom."

At that moment, Kris came out of the restroom. She saw me talking on her phone and broke into a run. Into the phone, I said, "Hang on, she just came out."

Handing the phone to Kris, I winked and said, "It's for you; some guy named Bailey."

She wiped tears from her eyes and said, "Hello? Bailey?"

I turned and headed for the men's room, meeting Kieley on the way. She saw Kris on the phone and said, "What's going on?"

Smiling, I gestured toward Kris and answered Kieley's question with one word. "Bailey."

When I came back from the restroom, Kieley was talking to Bailey on Kris's phone. Well, she had been talking to Bailey. Now she was saying, "Hello? Bailey? Hello?"

She looked at the screen and pressed something on it. "I'm sorry, Kris. We lost the signal."

Grinning from ear to ear, Kris said, "That's okay, Kieley. I got to talk with him and I know he's okay."

Kieley added, "And he's on his way to be with you." To me, she said, "He was in San Jose and I was telling him the route we took to get here. When the cell phone signal is better, I'll text him the information in case he didn't hear it."

I said, "He's going to be on the road a while just getting to Buttonwillow. With a little luck we might be through with our business by then and we can meet him somewhere up north."

Kris hugged Kieley. "Thank you so much for figuring out how to make my phone work again." She looked at me and said, "Thank you, too, Kev. I'd give you another kiss, but I'm afraid Kieley might slug me if I did it again."

Kieley said, "I'll do it for you, Kris." And she did.

When we hit the road again about one o'clock I was feeling pretty good. We had a full tank of gas and Kris's Bailey was no longer among the missing. Things were looking up. I hoped Old Man Fate was busy somewhere else.

Our next turn was up the road a few blocks at A Street, which was also State Route 23. The GPS said to take it south and within a few blocks we were out of town and looking ahead at another small mountain range to climb.

On the other side of the mountains we found ourselves in the town of Moorpark, just west of Simi Valley. We continued south on State Route 23, and after crossing one more peninsula of low mountains, we arrived in Thousand Oaks. There, 23 turned into the Moorpark Freeway and a temporary orange sign next to a green one that said "Begin Freeway" told us State Route 23 was closed.

That put us back to picking our way through numerous housing tracts that were more debris than housing. Along the way, I added to my photo record of quake damage, including an entire section of collapsed elevated freeway.

We were heading for Highway 101, which runs, or ran, east to west on its way to Hollywood and Los Angeles from the coast. I had no reason to expect 101 to be any more passable than State Route 23, but now we were in my backyard and I knew my way around.

Just before we got to 101, I turned left onto Thousand Oaks Boulevard. It parallels what remained of 101 and would get us through if we were careful and paid attention to the hazards. We were passing through one of Los Angeles's largest bedroom communities—now row after row of houses, thousands of them, all flattened into tidy piles of kindling.

Kieley pretty well summed up the situation when she said, "I can't get used to the idea that all this is real. I keep thinking it's a scene in a science fiction movie."

I said, "Yeah, it's hard to get my head around the fact that every one of those piles of rubble was once a family's home."

Kris asked a question none of us wanted to contemplate. "Where are all the people?"

The only fortunate part of our situation was we were making good time. I knew, however, that was about to end. Thousand Oaks Boulevard only went as far as Agoura Hills.

I turned south on a major cross street and we picked our way past a crumbled Highway 101 overpass and turned left on Agoura Road. It parallels 101, but I couldn't remember where the road ends.

It turned out Agoura Road got us as far as Calabasas, where another low mountain range blocked our path. There was, however a cut through the range just wide enough for the freeway and one surface street. That street was Mureau Road and we used it to get over the mountain pass.

That's more or less how our progress went as we worked our way east past West Hills, Tarzana, Encino, Sherman Oaks, Van Nuys, and several more LA bedrooms. There was very little to set them apart before the quakes, and there was even less now. One pile of rubble looks pretty much like another.

Finally, around four o' clock, we got to the point where Highway 101 turned south to go through the Cahuenga pass. Once again, there was an alternative route. Cahuenga Boulevard parallels the freeway through the pass. We were now almost literally in my backyard, and I said so.

Kieley said, "Thank goodness! Getting here has been like a nightmare."

At four-fifteen I turned into my driveway, and we all bailed out of the Jeep. I breathed a small sigh of relief because, at least from the street, everything looked okay.

My luck held when we walked through the front door. Besides a few items shaken off the walls and shelves, everything looked pretty much as it had when I set out for Eureka nearly a week ago.

Looking around the living room, Kieley said, "Very nice Darling. You can be in charge of decorating our new home . . . when we get one."

"Ha! My idea of decorating is hanging stuff on the walls until I either run out of walls or stuff to hang."

Grabbing a flashlight from the kitchen, I made a quick check of the utilities. I had no power, but the water and gas were still on. While Kieley and Kristina made use of the bathroom, I went out through the garage and grabbed a small monkey wrench. I used it to turn off the gas in case there was already a leak somewhere in the house or another shaker caused one.

That chore completed I rounded up the girls and we headed for my bedroom for some packing. Lifting the largest duffle-style bag I owned from the closet, I opened it on the bed, and said, "Shorts and socks are in the top two drawers of the dresser. Please load them all. I'll lay out the shirts, slacks, shoes, and jackets worth taking from the closet."

After the packing job we did for Kieley in the San Francisco apartment, we had the drill down pretty well. With the duffle loaded, I went into the second bedroom, which served as my office, and picked up the briefcase beside my desk. I opened it and dumped its contents onto my desk. Most of it no longer applied to the world in which we now lived.

Then I knelt on the bedroom closet floor and turned the dial of my floor safe. I removed a variety of documents, including personal items like my birth certificate and paperwork pertaining to my various bank and retirement accounts. I also removed a Rolex watch that was a birthday present from an uncle I admired. After the Rolex came two banded stacks of one hundred twenties each, which I dropped into the briefcase.

Finally, I reached deep into the safe and removed the last two items. I placed the Glock 19 pistol and a box of nine-millimeter ammunition into the briefcase and closed it. Then I relocked the floor safe.

As I stood up, Kieley said, "I sure hope we don't need those last things you put in there."

"Me, too. They're just a precaution."

I glanced at Kristina. She said nothing, but nodded solemnly.

"Now the question is, what do we do next? What do you think, Kieley? Kris?"

Kris spoke first. "Could we go back to where we stayed last night and meet Bailey there? I know it's a long way to go, but is there any reason to stay down here?"

I said, "No, I can't think of any particular reason to stay here, and yes, I think we could make it back to Buttonwillow. In fact, I have another route for us to try. It's not a shorter distance, but it might be a little faster and safer. Kieley, what are your thoughts?"

"I've been thinking a little further into the future, like where are we going to live when we stop wandering around like a band of Gypsies? Judging by what we've seen so far, I don't think any of the big cities in California are going to be habitable in the near future." She glanced at Kris and added, "Still, I think meeting up with Bailey should be our first priority."

I said, "I go along with that. There are a couple of things we need to think about before we set off on another road trip. First, we ought to find a way to fill up the tank again before we hit the road. Second, the way things are out there, I don't want to try the trip in the dark, so we need to find a place to spend the night."

Kieley said, "Could we stay here? We have real bathrooms where we could clean up and everything."

I thought about her suggestion for a moment. "Yes, I guess we could, but there is a risk involved. This house is perched on the side of a hill. Everything looks solid right now, but a big enough quake could shake the house right off its foundation and we might wake up at the bottom of the hill."

Kris said, "Could we stay in a motel again tonight?"

"We could, if we found one that's open. We could also waste a lot of gasoline wandering around looking for one that's open."

Kieley said, "I vote we stay here. We could sleep with our clothes on in the living room near the door so we could take off fast if the shaking starts again."

"Kris?"

"I agree with Kieley."

I wasn't sure we were making the right decision, but I didn't have a better solution, so slipping back into my jacket, I said, "All right, we stay here. I'll be right back."

Kieley quickly asked, "Where are you going?"

"Out to turn the gas back on so we can have hot showers."

When I returned to the living room, Kieley and Kris were composing a text message for Bailey on Kris's cell phone. With only two bars of signal, it was iffy, so they also sent the text via Kieley's phone as a backup.

SEVEN

Saturday, August 20, 2022
Kevin's Home, Hollywood, California

    I slept uneasily, expecting the world to start shaking again at any minute. It did not, so around six Saturday morning I was back outside with my trusty monkey wrench turning the gas on again so we could heat water on the stove for some stale instant coffee I found in the back of a cupboard. I have one of the K-cup gizmos, but without power, it's worthless.

    The coffee, along with some of the provisions left over from Taft served as breakfast. Then, with our gear, including my duffle bag and attaché case crammed into the Jeep, I buttoned up the house and duct-taped a message covered with clear acetate to the front door. It identified me as the owner of the property, said the property was not abandoned, and gave my cell phone number and e-mail for contacts.

    As I got into the Jeep, Kris was saying, ". . . glad Bailey got our messages. I'll never speak badly of Verizon again."

    I asked, "Is Bailey meeting us in Buttonwillow?"

    Kris answered my question enthusiastically. "Yes! He's checked into the Rodeway Inn where we were and will look for us sometime this afternoon."

    "Good. I hope we don't keep him waiting any longer than that."

    While I got us down out of the Cahuenga Pass and into Burbank, Kieley busied herself programming my new, more complicated route to Buttonwillow into the Jeep's GPS. It's a good thing the GPS wasn't the sensitive sort because Kieley called it a few bad names.

    When Kieley had everything programmed, she said, "The total distance is 182.6 miles to the Rodeway Inn there at State Route 58 and I-5. You were right. The route we took to get here is a little shorter, but only by about seven miles."

I said, "I figured this way would be a little longer, but I'm fairly certain it will be shorter in total time on the road. Do you feel up to crunching some gas mileage numbers?"

"Sure. What are the numbers?"

"Well, let's see. According to the trip odometer, we drove about fifty-five miles from the Shell Station in Fillmore to my place. Figuring we've only been getting around fifteen miles to the gallon with the kind of driving we've been doing, how many gallons did we use?"

"Three-point-six."

"Okay, let's call it four. The Jeep has a twenty-two gallon tank, so that leaves us around eighteen gallons. Right?"

I think Kieley was actually getting a kick out of our number crunching exercise. She quickly replied, "Right."

"Okay then, using the same average gas mileage figure, how far can we go on what we have left in the tank?"

The answer came back almost as quickly as the calculator in my phone could have figured it. "We can go about 270 miles on the remaining 18 gallons. If we're right, we can make it to Buttonwillow with 87.4 miles to spare."

"Hey, you're pretty good at this stuff."

Kieley grinned at me. "Yeah, it's nice to know I'm good at something besides wiggling my butt at a camera."

"Actually, I can think of a couple of things at which you excel besides looking good through a camera lens."

Sounding shocked, Kieley said, "Kevin! You shouldn't talk like that in front of Kris. She'll get the wrong idea about us."

Kris laughed. "Hah! I've got news for you, Kieley, I never figured you kept that photo of you and Kev on your nightstand for its esthetic value."

Feigning despair, Kieley said, "Oh, my. Now I feel like a fallen woman."

I said, "That's okay as long as you're fallin' for me."

Out of the corner of my eye I saw Kieley look at me. "Mister, I fell for you a long time ago and I've been falling for you ever since. You're stuck with me and that's all there is to it."

From the backseat: "You go, Girlfriend!"

The first leg of our journey took us northeast across Burbank on Olive Avenue to San Fernando Road. A week ago the buildings we passed were fast food joints, small retail stores, and auto repair shops. Now, like so many other places we'd seen, the former businesses were just colorful rubble.

While I hated to lose time, I felt I needed to keep up my photo record of the quakes' damage, so I stopped a few times for more images. The way the debris was distributed along the edges of the street and on the sidewalk, I had the feeling somebody tried to clear the street so it was passable. If that was the case, we seemed to be the only ones taking advantage of their efforts.

We saw very few signs of life until we drew close to Interstate-5. Being closed to auto traffic, the freeway was now a thoroughfare for hundreds of folks carrying their belongings on their backs, or pushing them along in supermarket carts. The scene reminded me of FIDDLER ON THE ROOF when the peasants are trudging away from their village with all their worldly goods piled on wooden carts. The melancholy procession made a powerful photo study.

San Fernando Road parallels Interstate-5 for a long distance and ends at Foothill Boulevard clear up in Pacoima. From Foothill Boulevard, we took the Sierra Highway north through the mountains east of Santa Clarita. Sierra parallels State Route 14, which is a full-fledged freeway and was closed with its onramps blocked. The Sierra Highway took us over the San Gabriel Mountains to Palmdale in the high desert.

It was becoming apparent the high desert was the place to be during the earthquakes we experienced. The destruction was nothing like what we saw in the San Fernando Valley north of LA. Of course, it's also true there aren't nearly as many buildings to destroy up in Palmdale and Lancaster. We actually saw only one destroyed building, and for all I knew it might have looked like that before the quakes.

I was also happy to see indications Palmdale had power. We cut over to a street that had every restaurant and retail chain store known to man on it to look for a gas station. When we came upon a USA station in a strip mall, I pulled in and filled the tank while Kieley and Kristina made use of the restrooms. I did the same after pumping our gas.

When we were all back at the Jeep, I said, "Did you guys notice the Albertson's Market over there on the other side of this center?"

Kristina grinned. "Of course! A woman is always aware of any nearby shopping possibilities."

I chuckled and Kieley said, "Do you think we should stock up on provisions while we're here?"

"Aside from the fact it's lunch time and I'm hungry, you may recall there weren't many choices for food in Buttonwillow. Things may be better there now, but remember, even though it seems like days since we were there, it was only yesterday morning."

Kieley looked surprised for a second or two. "You're right! It really does feel like days ago. Okay, Kristina, let's shift into shopping mode."

Cheerfully, Kris said, "Done!"

"Then get in, I'll drive you . . . ."

Kieley said, "I'd like to walk if that's okay with you. I need to stretch my muscles. I feel like I've been sitting for weeks."

Kris said, "Me, too."

"Okay, I'll follow you over there in the Jeep so you don't have to carry the groceries back. Here, Kieley, let me give you some cash."

"No, save the cash for when we really need it. I'll use a debit or credit card."

I stopped her again. "Here's my Visa debit card. The pin is 4132."

Kieley looked up at me a little sheepishly. "Thank you. I forgot I haven't got enough in my bank account to buy a box of raisins."

"Unless you've changed your mind about the stuff we've been talking about, you might as well get used to sometimes being a Turner instead of a Bishop."

Her sheepish expression changed to a thoughtful look. Slowly, carefully pronouncing each syllable, Kieley said, "Ms Kieley Bishop Turner. Missus Keven Turner. Kieley Turner. You know what?"

"What?"

"I like 'em all! C'mon, Kris, let's go before he wises up and takes his debit card back."

Thirty minutes later, Kris and Kieley showed up where I parked the Jeep with two large paper grocery bags of stuff, including a couple of sandwiches from Albertson's deli. Munching a fairly decent turkey on whole wheat with swiss cheese, I steered us back onto the Sierra Highway again and headed north through Lancaster and on to Mojave.

It was about one o' clock when we turned west on State Route 58, which would take us to Bakersfield, and from there to Buttonwillow. Kieley reported we only had about 80 miles to go, but I suspected those miles were going to take longer to travel than the last 80.

West of Mojave, Highway 58 is a divided four-lane road through the sort of country you see in old cowboy movies. Kieley, who is an avid fan of Randolph Scott and Gene Autry movies was soaking it all in.

"This is really cool! I feel like I should yell, 'Let's head 'em off at the pass!'"

I gave her an unenthusiastic, "Head for the roundhouse, Nellie. He can't corner you there."

Kieley gave me a punch in the arm. "It would serve you right if them varmints who robbed the stage got plum away."

"How come there were plums on the stagecoach in the first place?"

She said, "I give up. Have you no romance in your soul?"

"No, I keep my romance elsewhere."

Kristina said, "I'm so definitely not going to ask where that might be."

And so it went all the way through the little berg of Tehachapi at the summit of the mountain pass we were crossing. From Tehachapi we started a long downhill run into Bakersfield. We hit the eastern edge of town about two-thirty, and it was clear Bakersfield took a pretty damaging hit in one or more of the quakes we had.

We were still on State Route 58, which turned into a six-lane divided highway through town, but it was open because 58 has cross traffic and isn't considered a freeway. We were taking advantage of that technicality when we came to what looked like an abandoned railway line where a concrete overpass was built to allow the highway to cross the tracks. The overpass was collapsed onto the tracks.

Fortunately, we were able to roll down the embankment to the tracks, and then climb the other side. I've got to hand it to Jeep engineers. Despite all the junk we crammed into the Wrangler, it took us where we wanted to go without complaint or hesitation.

A short distance later, we encountered the same problem with an overpass crossing a surface road. Figuring there were more collapses ahead, I found a parallel surface street called Brundage Lane a block north of Highway 58 and we picked our way through the debris of an industrial area.

Bakersfield is mostly flat as a billiard table, so even when the street was entirely blocked, we were able to get through by driving around the blockage using empty lots, of which there were many. Despite our progress, though, I fully expected Old Man Fate to throw something big in front of us any minute.

He finally got around to it a few miles later. I'd been watching a tall column of black smoke up ahead for some time and when we reached the smoke it turned out to be a burning Chevron gas station at the corner of Brundage and Business US Highway 99.

A group of firemen blocked the road and seemed to be there

for the sole purpose of watching the station burn down since they didn't seem to be doing anything to extinguish the fire. They told us we needed to detour a few blocks north to proceed any further west. That turned out to be easier said than done. What remained of a housing development and a canal blocked the way west until we went a mile or more north.

Thinking we were clear of the obstacles, I turned back to the south and ran smackdab into a roadway bridge collapsed into the damned canal, which ran at an angle to our path. Once again, I had to turn back north, and then west to find a north-south artery that would get us back to Highway 58.

Ultimately, Chester Street accomplished that feat, but it was slow going because a supermarket seemed to have exploded and there were canned beans, asparagus, melting ice cream, and raw hamburger splattered across all four of Chester Street's lanes. Don't ask me what makes a grocery store explode because I have no idea.

We finally got back to Brundage Lane and continued west parallel to Highway 58. At US Highway 99 we had to cross the highway using the now familiar technique of rolling down one embankment and climbing back up the other.

I must have looked worn out after two solid days of driving over, under, and around stuff because Kieley put her hand on my arm. "Darling, you look really tired. Would you like me to try driving for a while? I've been watching you and I think I could do it."

"I know you could do it, and I'm tempted, but we should be out of Bakersfield before too much longer, and then we won't have far to go. Thank you for thinking of it, though."

She leaned over and kissed me on the cheek. "I'm just trying to take good care of my guy."

West of US 99, Brundage lane became the Stockdale highway and I thought we were still on the right track, but Kieley noticed we were no longer on State Route 58. It was paralleling our course on the other side of a mud wallow called the Kern River.

I was trying to figure out how the hell we strayed off course when Kieley discovered the GPS was taking us out to Interstate-5 south of Buttonwillow and expected us to go north on the freeway to reach our destination, which would quite likely be impossible. I told the stupid GPS what I thought of its skills, and Kieley took over the navigation duties.

Watching the map display, she said, "Turn right on Heath Road. It's coming up very shortly. There it is."

I turned right onto a two-lane farm road and Kieley said, "Next we want to turn left on the Rosedale Highway. It will be the third major road we come to after crossing what looks like another canal."

Fortunately, the road bridge over the canal was intact, so we were able to cross it and get to Highway 58. That elusive highway took another jog to the north a few miles later, and after a few more miles, I saw the cluster of buildings at Buttonwillow coming up. Hallelujah!

It was about three-forty-five when we pulled into the Rodeway Inn parking lot, which had only two other vehicles in it. One was a black Silverado pickup and the other was an unmarked pale blue Taurus Police Interceptor sedan. The Ford was parked in front of Room 101.

Kristina yelled, "That's his car! That's Bailey's car!"

I was pulling into the parking slot next to the Taurus when the door to Room 101 opened and a fellow stepped out onto the walkway. He was at least six feet with dark curly hair and one of those smiles you don't see often, but when you do, you get the feeling it's sincere. He was wearing white running shoes, jeans, and a gray t-shirt displaying a slightly faded yellow and black circular logo that said, "San Francisco Police Activities League."

Kris damn near broke my eardrums yelling, "Bailey!" The Jeep had not stopped rolling when she jumped out and ran into the fellow's arms.

I looked at Kieley and asked, "Bailey?"

Kieley nodded. "Bailey."

"Mission accomplished."

"Thank you, Kev. You just made my best friend one very happy girl. C'mon, I'll introduce you to Detective Sergeant Bailey."

The first things I noticed upon entering Room 101 were the lights. They were on. The local utility company was on the ball.

Kristina was still in Bailey's arms when Kieley said, "Hi, Bailey. Glad to see you alive and well."

"Likewise, Kieley. Who's that you've got with you there?"

Kieley said, "Detective Sergeant Bailey, meet Kevin Turner. Kev, meet Bailey."

I shook the hand Bailey offered. "Nice to meet you, Bailey."

He said, "You, too, especially since I owe you big time for keeping Kristina safe during the past few days. I gather you've had some adventures."

Kris said, "You can say that again!"

I said, "Yes, but you don't owe me anything, Bailey. We're a team and we look out for each other. So, welcome to the team."

Bailey smiled. "Thanks, Kevin. I'm glad to be part of the team. Listen, I'm curious. You were in LA, right? How are things down there?"

"We didn't get into the downtown area, but we got a good look at the San Fernando valley—from out in Thousand Oaks on in to Burbank and Glendale. To be blunt, everything we saw was pretty much leveled. God only knows what the final death toll will be."

Bailey nodded and I saw the understanding in his eyes. He'd come from San Francisco, which after the shaking they took yesterday afternoon, had to be as bad if not worse than conditions in LA.

Changing the subject, Bailey said, "When I knew you guys were on your way, I grabbed onto the room next door, 102, although I needn't have worried about them running out of rooms. So far as I can tell we're it. The pickup out there belongs to the guy at the desk."

"Thanks for getting the room. I'll reimburse you for the cost."

Bailey shook his head. "No you won't. Paying for a hotel room is the least I can do for you and Kieley." He handed me the room key and in a slightly embarrassed tone, asked, "Ah, us one room okay? If not . . . ."

Kieley let him off the hook. "I'm not letting Kev get more than a foot away from me these days, so even a closet would be okay."

After carrying our bags into 102, I moved the Jeep back from the motel's wooden awning over the walkway. Bailey watched me do it, and realizing why I did it, he said, "You know, that's a hell of a good idea. I think I'll do the same."

Looking at his Taurus, I asked, "Is that the all-wheel drive model?"

"Yes, and if I'm getting your drift, it was somewhat helpful when I had to get off the road coming down here, but the ground clearance on this rig is practically nonexistent. They built this car to do 130-plus on pavement, not for off-roading."

"Then we'll just have to be careful where we go, assuming we're going in the same direction."

Bailey said, "I haven't given that much thought yet. How about we hold a powwow later and see what we can figure out?"

I said, "Works for me."

In our room, I gave Kieley a hug. She returned it with interest in the form of a sweet kiss. Then she flopped onto one of the beds and asked, "What do you think of Bailey?"

I sat on the edge of the bed. "He seems all right. I can see why

Kristina feels safe with him. He's got an energy about him that exudes authority . . . the kind that would make most people think twice about messing with him.

"I'm curious, though. Based on what you told me about your experience with San Francisco cops, I'm a little surprised you even talk to him."

Kieley put on a thoughtful expression. "At first I put up with him to keep peace in the family. After a while, though, I got to know him and decided he's an okay guy. He treats Kris like a royal princess."

"They seem like an unlikely couple. How on earth did a fashion model and a homicide detective get together?"

"Mostly by accident. Kristina's roommate at the time was murdered at work and Bailey was investigating the case. He interviewed Kris, and according to her, there was so much chemistry in the room she could hardly breathe. He felt it too and asked her to lunch. The rest is history."

I shook my head. "Kris has certainly had more than her share of tragedy. Her sister and her roommate both killed, and now her brother is missing."

Sitting up and leaning against me with her head on my shoulder, Kieley said, "Yes. That's why I'm so glad we found Bailey for her. She's standing up under all this better than she has any right to and Bailey is her rock, just like you're mine." She paused, cocked her head to one side, and completely out of the blue asked, "Am I really a better kisser than Kris?"

I couldn't help laughing. "I think so, but it wouldn't hurt to confirm my earlier findings with further testing."

Kieley grinned. "I hope you mean a kiss from me. Going next door to kiss Kris right now could get you in big trouble."

An hour or so later we knocked on the door to Room 101. It took a minute for someone to open the door. That someone was Kris. She had a silly grin on her face and her hair was in a state of wild disarray.

Kieley said, "If we're interrupting anything we can come back later."

Kris giggled. "Is it that obvious?"

Kieley shook her head. "Only because we were up to the same thing next door."

That made me feel a little self-conscious. Sometimes the openness between Kris and Kieley was downright embarrassing.

Kieley sensed my discomfort. "Better get used to it, Darling. Kris and I are just a couple of randy broads with no shame whatsoever."

Still grinning, Kris nodded her agreement and we were invited in by Bailey who was just coming out of the bathroom. Once we were all seated, Bailey said, "Well, what do we need to discuss first?"

I said, "How 'bout tallying up our resources so we know what we have to work with?"

Bailey nodded. "Makes sense."

Kris said, "Well, we have the food Kieley and I got at that supermarket this afternoon, at least enough to last through tomorrow."

I said, "That's a plus. On the other side of the ledger gasoline is a constant concern, and now we've got two vehicles to feed."

Bailey said, "I think we can fill up before we leave here. I saw a couple of stations that seemed to be open when I got here."

I said, "Good. Given the way things have been going with the quakes, it probably would make sense to fill up sooner rather than later and at every opportunity."

Bailey nodded. "Agreed. What else do we have?"

"I've got four thousand and some change in twenties and other small bills, so we should be okay for cash until we get someplace where things are a little more normal and plastic is still in use." I paused, and then asked, "I assume you're armed?"

Bailey studied me for a moment as if deciding something, and then nodded again. "Yes, I have my Glock 19 and a Remington 870 12-guage Tactical in the trunk, along with ammo for both. How 'bout you?"

"I brought a nine millimeter Glock and a full box of ammo from home."

Obviously frustrated, Kris jumped up and said, "Okay, we've got money and food and enough guns to start a fricking war, but where are we going?"

I looked at Bailey, he looked back at me, and then we both shrugged. Apparently he didn't have any more idea about where we ought to go than I did.

Kieley said, "Well, I'll give you my two-cents' worth on that subject. From what Kev and I have seen during the past week, it's going to be a very long time before any of the big cities in California are up and running again, if they ever are. That means unless we're willing to live someplace like Chicago, New York, or maybe Miami, Kristina and I are unemployed with few prospects. I've got a BA in Graphic Design, but I doubt there are many opportunities in that field either with all that's been going on."

Bailey looked at me and I said, "Actually, the situation goes even deeper than that. California was a major retail market, but that's over. It might be a long time before the economy here can support luxury products again—high-end cars, top shelf cosmetics, and such—so it will likely be a while before the makers of those products who are still in business are prepared to do any quality advertising.

"Right now, it's safe to say the west coast, from Mexico to Canada, is closed for repairs. That means Bailey is the most employable person in this room based on experience and education."

Detective Sergeant Bailey nodded. "Yes, there will always be crime to fight."

Kieley was sitting next to me on the couch. Putting her hand on my shoulder, she reminded me of what might be a valuable asset that wasn't on our list. "Kev, what about all those photos you took on the way down from Eureka? If you still have them, they might be worth quite a bit."

"You are absolutely right, and yes, I still have them. If I can get hold of a publisher before too much time passes, they're worth a fortune. They are some of the most dramatic images I've ever made."

Kieley asked the next logical question. "How do we go about selling them?"

"I need a day or two at my laptop cataloging the collection and watermarking sample images to submit. Since I've been acting as my own agent, a copy of WRITERS MARKET would also be helpful."

Bailey said, "And while you're doing that, we can explore other possibilities for income. So it sounds like we need to go someplace where we can set up shop and get busy. Where would be a good place?"

I said, "The only big California city we haven't seen personally is San Diego, but one of the quakes was centered in the Salton Sea area to the northeast, so it's a safe bet that San Diego isn't much better off than LA."

Kieley said, "How about Las Vegas? It might be the nearest large city still standing."

Bailey said, "You could be right, but can we get there?"

Nodding, I said, "I know we can get as far as Barstow. We came through there today and I got the distinct impression the quakes did a lot less damage up in the high desert than they did in the other places we've been."

Bailey said, "How 'bout it then? Anybody object to Las Vegas as our next destination?"

When nobody else said anything, I said, "Sounds like we have a destination, so the next step is getting our ducks in a row for the trip, probably starting with filling the gas tanks."

"Bailey said, "Agreed. Ladies, while we do that, why don't you go to the office and see if they can get us booked into rooms in Vegas tomorrow? There must be several Rodeway Inns in a town the size of Vegas."

Kieley looked at me with a frown. I knew what she was thinking. I said, "Bailey, you aren't aware of this, but ever since the world started going crazy, we've held to a rule that we don't separate because another quake could hit at any time. If that happens, we don't want to waste time having to look for each other."

Bailey nodded. "You're right I didn't know that, but I think it's a very sensible precaution. Ladies, would you care to join us for a night on the town buying some gasoline?"

When we returned with full gas tanks, Bailey and I shifted some of the stuff crammed into the Jeep over to his Ford so the load would be a little more evenly distributed. Kris's bags and the three largest of Kieley's cardboard boxes ended up in the Ford's large back seat along with a dozen bottles of water from the provisions Kieley and Kristina purchased in Palmdale.

Since Bailey and I were less than a dozen feet from the Rodeway Inn's office door, I gave Kieley a Visa card and my Choice Hotels reward club card so she and Kristina could see about Las Vegas reservations. When they returned, Kieley reported the results.

"Apparently a lot of folks from California are headed for Vegas and rooms are getting scarce, so it's a good thing we planned ahead. Choice Hotels—they own several chains, including Rodeway and Comfort Inns—has four motels in the Las Vegas area and three of them are already full.

"The good news is we have a guaranteed reservation for two rooms at the Comfort Inn and Suites near Nellis Air Force base. I'm not sure where that is, but the guy in the office assured me it's not far from the strip."

Bailey shook his head. "That's stretching it a little. Nellis is off of I-15 at the north end of town, so getting to the strip is a bit of a drive. Not far, but not as close as he made it sound."

I said, "I'm not sure that's a bad thing. If we're going to set up shop there, the farther we are from crowds, the less traffic and fuss there will be. Kieley, how long is the reservation for?"

"I booked two rooms for ten days. The rooms go for a hundred-and-twenty-five each per night—that's the reward club member price. The total for a ten day stay will be twenty-five-hundred plus eight-and-a-quarter percent sales tax and a room tax of twelve percent. That brings the total up to thirty-one-hundred and some change."

Bailey whistled. "Wow, Vegas really socks it to the tourists. Listen, Kevin, I'll have 'em switch the cost of one room over to my MasterCard."

Kieley said, "Unless you have one of their reward club cards, that will add about ten percent to the room cost. It would be cheaper for you to pick up some other expenses, like gas or food."

I said, "Do whatever works best for you, Bailey. I'm not worried about the money."

He gave me a look like he thought I was nuts. "You independently wealthy or something?"

"Or something."

After a dinner of Hormel Compleats microwave entrees in little plastic tubs, we all agreed to call it a night. We also agreed to hit the road no later than seven in the morning.

When Kieley and I climbed into bed, she rolled onto her stomach and propped herself up on her elbows. "Kev, can I stick my nose into your personal business?"

I had a pretty good idea what peaked her curiosity and I figured it was time to give her the straight story. "I don't see why not. I have no secrets, at least none where you're concerned."

She grinned. "Just tell me to mind my own business if I'm being too nosey."

"Ask your question."

"Before, when Bailey asked if you were independently wealthy or something, he was kidding, but when you answered him, you said, 'or something,' and it didn't sound to me like you were kidding."

"And you want to know if I've taken up bank robbery or some other nefarious career?"

She gave her head a perish the thought shake and said, "Oh no, I . . . ."

"It's okay, Kieley. I was planning to tell you about this and now is as good a time as any. I had this favorite uncle—my mom's brother—and he was into the stock market with an uncanny ability to sniff out stocks that were about to skyrocket. He played the game so well that, when he died, Uncle Jake was worth roughly forty million bucks, and he left a big chunk of it to me. After taxes, the inheritance came to a little more than twenty million."

Kieley was now kneeling on the bed and her eyes were roughly the size of the hubcaps on Bailey's Taurus. She was also stark naked. That condition made it a little more difficult for me to concentrate on what she was saying, which was, "You're kidding! When did all this happen?"

"A little over a year ago. My take on it was Uncle Jake had an artist's soul and admired my belief I could make a living on my own as a photographer. He made sure I could do that by providing me an after taxes monthly investment income of about twenty-five grand to fall back on if I hit hard times."

She shook her head. "I don't know what to say, except I'm sure glad I didn't know that a few days ago or you'd have thought I wanted us to get back together because of your money. Even so, I suddenly feel like a gold digger."

"Kieley, I can't believe you said that. We fell in love years ago when I barely had two nickels to rub together. Why would I suddenly think you were interested in a little money I happen to have?"

"I don't know. I just feel funny about it . . . and twenty million is way more than a little money!"

"As far as I'm concerned that money is all on paper. It is managed by an investment firm in New York City and I never see any of it except on the statements they send me. The only thing I've bought with it is some camera equipment and that Jeep outside, and those were business expenses."

Tilting her head to the side, Kieley looked me in the eye. "Why?"

"Why what?"

"Why aren't you spending that money? You could live on it and just do photography as a hobby."

"I could ask you the same question. If you hadn't needed the money, would you have taken up modeling as a hobby?"

"That's not the same thing."

"But it is the same thing. Needing to make a living is a strong motivation for working my butt off, and that's why I've had some success. I've worked hard to develop my skills and use them to the best advantage I could. Uncle Jake's money is just sort of an insurance policy if I fail, which so far, I have not."

Kieley was studying my face closely as she said, "So, what happens now?"

"What do you mean?"

"I mean how does twenty million dollars affect our plans for the future?" She shook her head. "No, I mean . . . I don't know what I mean, but all that money has to have some impact on our plans, doesn't it?"

"Yes, I suppose it does." Then gently taking her hands in mine, I said, "That money buys us freedom. That's all it's good for and that's what we'll use it for."

She shook her head. "I still don't understand why you waited so long to tell me about such good fortune."

"I think there were two reasons. First, I wanted to be sure of us."

"And are you sure of us?"

"Yes. We've been through hell together and we made it. That says a lot about our love."

"And the second reason?"

"I didn't want you to think I was trying to buy your love with twenty million bucks."

Kieley cocked her head to one side again and thought about that for several seconds, and then she threw herself at me, and wrapping her arms around me, she said, "Darling, you couldn't buy my love for twenty million, but if you didn't already have my love, you could buy it for those two nickels you barely had back when we were in school."

EIGHT

Seismologists use three specific terms to describe earthquakes. Those terms are *magnitude, intensity*, and *duration*.

Magnitude describes the energy of a quake on the Richter Magnitude Scale. Most people living in earthquake country are familiar with Richter numbers, which describe the strength of an earthquake at its source or epicenter. Richter magnitude measurements are based on the physical length of the fault on which the quake occurs.

Each whole number on the scale represents a strength of ten times the previous whole number. For example a quake measuring five on the Richter scale would be ten times stronger than a magnitude of four. Since there are no faults on earth long enough to generate a mag-ten shaker such a mega-quake is technically impossible.

Intensity, on the other hand, is a measurement of an earthquake's energy at a specific place, but not necessarily its epicenter. The intensity numbers of a quake vary depending on how far the observation point is from the quake's epicenter.

Numbers from the *Modified Mercalli Intensity Scale* are used to describe the intensity of a quake's impact on people and/or structures at a specific point of measurement. The scale ranges from MM-One (imperceptible: barely sensed only by a very few people) to MM-12 (completely devastating: all buildings are damaged and most buildings are destroyed).

Lastly, duration describes how long an earthquake lasts according to a seismograph. Typically, earthquakes last ten to thirty seconds, although I timed one of the three we recently experienced at around five-and-a-half minutes. That one set a world duration record and left us wondering what would come next.

We found out what would come next soon after filling our gas tanks at a Union 76 Station in Barstow near the junction of Highway 58 and Interstate-15. Major quake number five struck at 11:42 a.m. on Sunday, August 21, 2022.

Kieley and I were cautiously leading a caravan of two east on I-15 when Bailey's Ford swerved violently across my rearview mirror. My immediate thought was he blew a tire, but when our Jeep did the same thing in the opposite direction a second or two later, I knew our tires weren't to blame.

We got both vehicles to the shoulder, but the shaking was still going strong. According to news reports we heard later, the quake's duration was an incredible 00:07:34. Now seven-and-a-half minutes doesn't seem like a long time in the grand scheme of things, but when the world is shaking to pieces around you, it's long enough to make you think you're experiencing the end of creation.

The quake's intensity where we were wasn't too bad, but seismologists placed it between MM-10 (very destructive) along the Washington coast and MM-12 (total destruction) from San Francisco to San Jose. The epicenter turned out to be the Sibley Volcanic Regional Preserve in the Oakland Hills across the bay from San Francisco. Seismologists rated it 9.9 on the Richter scale. It was as bad as any earthquake could be.

When things calmed down, Kieley and I walked back to the Bailey's Ford about fifty feet behind us. Bailey got out and met us, but Kristina stayed in the car.

As he approached us, Bailey asked, "You guys okay?"

Kieley nodded and I said, "Yes. You and Kris?"

"I'm okay, but Kris is pretty shook up, no pun intended."

While Bailey and I held a short conference, Kieley walked over to the Ford, where she leaned in and talked with Kris through the open driver's door. Having been through a quake and some aftershocks with Kris, I could imagine how she was reacting.

I said, "Your car okay?"

"Yes. All that sliding around didn't do the tires a lot of good, but everything seems all right. What do you think we ought to do from here?"

"I think we ought to press on and get as far away from that damned Fortuna fault as we can."

"You think this one was on the Fortuna like the others?"

"I'm guessing, but I blame the Fortuna for most of the evil in the world, anyway. What I do know is it runs through Palm

Springs on its way north from Mexico. That puts the fault about eighty miles south of where we're standing. Under these circumstances, that's too damned close."

"Agreed."

"We'll need to keep our eyes open for rock slides wherever the road passes through mountainous areas. Also, there are bound to be some heavy aftershocks."

"Got it. Let's hit the road."

Interstate-15 east of Barstow is a divided four-lane freeway with very few overpasses or underpasses to collapse, which may be why it was still open. The road's surface, however, was showing the effects of the monster quake in the form of cracks and missing chunks of asphalt. That along with recurrent and substantial aftershocks kept me on my toes.

As we rolled along at about thirty-five miles an hour, I said, "I saw you talking to Kris back there. How's she doing?"

"She's about half an inch from total hysteria. I hoped being with Bailey would calm her down, but I guess all this shaking is just too much for her."

I nodded. "And how are you doing?"

"I'm okay. I really am. I'm not happy about the danger we're in, but I'm surprisingly calm about it all once the shaking stops."

"I'm glad to hear that. Why do you think that is?"

She didn't have to think about her answer. "Because we have a future. I mean you and I do. If you hadn't called me from Eureka, I think I'd be where Kris is now. But you . . . you rescued me from where I was then."

"Don't give me too much of the credit. You did most of that yourself. I may have been a catalyst to help the process along, but you're stronger than you think you are."

From the corner of my eye I could see Kieley looking at me. "Maybe. Kev, do you mind if I change the subject and ask you a question about that future we have together?"

"Oh, oh. Sounds like you're about to get serious on me."

"Well, a little serious." After a brief pause and a deep breath, Kieley said, "Kev, would you be upset with me if I didn't go back to modeling? I mean assuming I could even find work as a model now?"

"Hell, no. That wouldn't upset me at all. I take it you've had all the glamour you can stand?"

I sensed her breathing a sigh of relief. "Thank you, Darling."

"You don't need to thank me. Did you think I would object?"

Kieley leaned on the console and put her head on my

shoulder. "Well, we'd be living on your money for a while and . . . no, I didn't think you would object. In fact, you were a catalyst in this, too."

"Oh? How so?"

"What you said last night—the part about all that money buying us freedom. I feel very strongly I need to get away from modeling. At first it was what you said, glamorous, and the money was amazing, but now it's . . . it just makes me feel dirty. No, that's not right. Working with you makes me feel proud. It's the rest of it that makes me feel dirty . . . like a prostitute who thinks she's above it all because what she does is called by a different name instead of whoring."

"Wow. Those are some heavy feelings you've kept well hidden, even from me. I had no idea you felt that way."

Kieley laughed nervously. "I didn't mean to shock you, and I certainly don't want you to think I plan to sit around all day and get fat eating Godiva chocolates."

"I don't think that, but you haven't said what you WOULD like to do."

She was quiet for several seconds. "I want to say this right, but I'm not sure I know how to do that."

Smiling, I said, "Oh, give it a try."

I could hear a smile in her voice as she said, "Okay, Mister, I will."

"First, I want to be your wife. I don't mean just legally. I mean I want to be half of us. I want to have our kids and work with you to raise them right. That is a big, important job.

"Second, I want to make you happy. I never want you to wonder what the hell you got yourself into when you married me. I couldn't stand that, so I will never let it happen, but you've got to help me with that part by telling me how I'm doing. I've never been a wife before.

"Third, I want to do something worthwhile in the world. Maybe something with wild animals, like helping them stay free to live the way God intended them to live."

Kieley was quiet again for several seconds, but I sensed she had something else to say, so I waited. Finally, she said, "Gosh, that all sounded pretty highfalutin as my grandpa would have said. I know I'm being very idealistic, but it's how I feel and . . . well, that's what I want to do."

"I can't think of a thing wrong with what you want. All I insist on is you be happy with your life. If doing what you just said would make you happy, then I'm all for it."

Around three o' clock we pulled off the highway at a place called Valley Wells Rest Area. In addition to very little else, there is a Shell Station there and it was open for business. Kieley calculated we used about six gallons since we filled the tank in Buttonwillow, for us that was nearly a third of a tank, so we pulled up to a pump island and Bailey followed us. He and I filled the tanks while Kieley and Kris made use of the station's restroom. Then we were back on the road. Oh, and Kieley's estimate of the gas we consumed could not have been more accurate.

Less than ten miles after we left the rest area, we climbed over a mountain pass and almost as if somebody waved a magic wand, the road cracks disappeared and the aftershocks stopped—at least they stopped as far we could tell in the vehicles. Since we were now on an intact freeway that seemed as safe as freeways used to be, I gradually picked up speed, watching the rearview mirror to see if Bailey was getting the message. He was.

Kieley recalculated our arrival time in Las Vegas at fifty-five miles per hour. She figured we would cover the remaining 209 miles in less than four hours, assuming everything kept going smoothly. That would give us an ETA in Vegas of about seven-thirty.

When she finished her calculations, Kieley said, "Kev, are you sure what we talked about before—I mean me quitting modeling— is really okay with you?"

"Didn't I say it was?"

"Yes, but . . . ."

"But what?"

"Well . . . I guess even though I think I know you pretty well, I sometimes have trouble believing you're real. I mean, it's not that I think you're trying to deceive me or anything like that . . . you're just very different from so many guys I know." Kieley paused for a moment, and then quickly added, "I'm sorry. I'm not trying to compare you to anyone else. I just don't know how to say what I mean."

"Okay, let me give you another one of my theories about people that might help you sort out your thoughts."

"All right."

"No matter how pure their intentions, everyone expects something in return from their relationships with other people. Even people like clergymen get something out of helping the members of their flock. If they didn't, they wouldn't be doing what they're doing. That make sense to you?"

"I never really thought about it before, but yes, it makes

sense."

"All right, now think about those other guys you know for a moment. What do they want out of their relationships with you?"

Kieley was quiet for several seconds, and then she said, "In most cases they wanted money because they were agency execs and using me as a model was a way to please their clients, which in turn made money for them. You mean like that?"

"Exactly like that."

"Then, some of them just wanted to get into my pants. I always thought that was kind of funny. I mean, some of the guys I knew thought I was cute and sexy, but I also know I was a disappointment to them. I didn't live up to their fantasy expectations. The good part is, after that got around, they weren't so anxious to get into my pants. I'm sorry if I shocked you by saying all that, but we have an honesty deal in effect, don't we?"

Smiling, I said, "We do. The part I'm not sure about is how they could have been disappointed when you always exceed my expectations."

She looked over me. "Oh, come on Kev, is that really such a mystery? No, wait. Don't answer that. Instead, tell me what you get out of loving me and making me happy? What's your hidden motivation where I'm concerned?"

"Well, let's see. First, your love fills an empty place . . . a need in my life no one else has ever even come close to filling. Your love makes me feel good and needed and cared for. Oh, and you're a fantastic sex partner."

"You're dancing all around it, Mister. Now say it. I want to hear you say it out loud. Go ahead, say it."

Not quite sure what she was looking for, I tried something more direct. "Okay, My motivation for loving you is to receive your love in return."

"And?"

When I figured it out, I laughed. "Okay, okay. And you are such a fantastic sex partner because you love me."

"You're getting warm, but that's still not all of it. We're so good in bed together because I love you and?"

"And I love you."

"Bingo! You get a gold star!"

I mumbled, "I'd rather have . . . ."

"I know what you'd rather have, Mister. That would be the same thing I'd rather have, and the sooner you get us to Las Vegas, the sooner we both get laid, so step on it!"

I stepped on it and we rolled into Las Vegas around seven-thirty, and I was immediately struck by how normal everything was. Until you've been through what we went through during the past week, you can't imagine how good it feels to drive through a town in which normalcy prevails—where buildings are still vertical, cars drive on the roads, and people walk on the sidewalks.

Around eight o' clock we were checked into the Comfort Inn north of town and were drinking margaritas at a Mexican restaurant called Viva Zapata's a few blocks up the road from the hotel. Well, more accurately, Kris, Bailey, and I were drinking margaritas. Kieley joined in the toast to better days with a glass of water. Even after deciding to leave the glamorous world of modeling, not worrying about every millimeter of change to her waistline was going to be a challenge.

Kristina, however, wasn't experiencing any such challenges. She was sucking up her fourth strawberry margarita when our dinners arrived. I'm no mind reader, but I had the distinct feeling both Kieley and Bailey were thinking Kris was overdoing the booze. Of course, Kris had no such concerns. Actually, she wasn't much concerned about anything.

Then, about halfway through our dinners, Kris made a gagging sound, got a strange expression on her face, and puked all over her plate. That pretty much ended dinner and we returned to the Comfort Inn so Bailey could put Kristina to bed.

The room Kieley and I were sharing was what passes for a suite in the world of Comfort and Holiday Inns. It was one long room with a miniscule divider between the sleeping area and a living area containing a couch and a desk.

Both of the rooms Kieley reserved were on the third floor, but across the hall from each other rather than adjoining. Suspecting that Kristina was in for a rough night, I thought the arrangement of our rooms might prove to be a blessing.

Kieley, on the other hand, was naturally worried about her friend. When I came out of the bathroom from brushing my teeth, I found her stripped down to her sleep shirt and sitting on the edge of the bed. The mattresses were the thick, extra comfy kind, making the bed too tall for her feet to touch the floor. So she sat there absentmindedly swinging her legs back and forth like a little girl.

I flopped down next to her and said, "Worried about Kris?"

Kieley turned and looked at me. "Kev, you wouldn't know this, but Kris doesn't drink. I've never seen her drink more than an occasional a glass of wine, let alone four margaritas."

Noting Kieley was concerned enough to keep track of

Kristina's booze consumption, I thought about the matter for a few moments before asking, "Kieley, it's none of my business, but do you know if Kris has ever had a problem with alcohol?"

She frowned at me. "You mean like alcoholism?"

I nodded and Kieley shook her head. "No. At least she's never said anything about it. I guess abstaining from alcohol could be a sign that she had a problem in the past, but it doesn't necessarily mean that."

I agreed with her. "No, it certainly doesn't."

Kieley looked at me again. "Did you see how pale she was?"

"It was so dark in there I didn't see that, but I did notice her breathing seemed irregular and labored at times."

"Yes, I noticed that, too. Kev, I'm really worried."

"What would you like to do?"

"I don't think there's anything we can do. I mean Bailey is with her and he knows she's not a drinker. So I'm sure he's keeping an eye on her."

"Do you think it would be helpful if you or I went over and talked to him? I mean just to tell him you noticed some things that concerned us?"

Kieley seemed to think about that, and then shook her head. "No, he's the specialist in handling emergencies. Let's leave it to him and try to get some sleep."

We assumed our usual sleeping positions, but Kieley didn't put her leg over mine. Instead, she said softly, "Kev, I was looking forward to making love with you tonight, but . . . ."

"I understand, Kieley. Just cuddle up and we'll save the love-making for another time."

"Really? You understand?"

"I do and even if I wasn't concerned about Kris, too, I respect your feelings. Just know I love you."

"Oh, I do, Kev, and I love you more every day."

NINE

Monday, August 22, 2022
Comfort Inn, Las Vegas, Nevada

I was having a restless night. When I woke up around three, I figured my restlessness was a holdover from the quakes. Then, as long as I was awake, I got up to use the bathroom. That's when I saw the note where it came to rest on the floor after being pushed under the door to our room.

Taking the note into the bathroom, I closed the door and turned on the light. After I read it, I knew disturbing Kieley was unavoidable. The time on the note was two-fifteen. Below that, it said:

Kieley and Kevin

Kristina is really sick. I am taking her to the hospital, which the desk clerk says is about ten miles from here. I will call you as soon as I have any word about her condition.

Bailey

Leaving the bathroom light on, I went back into the bedroom and awakened Kieley as gently as I could.

"What? What is it, Kev? Is something wrong?"

"I'm afraid so. Apparently we were right to be concerned about Kristina. Bailey took her to the hospital. He left us a note."

Hearing that piece of news woke Kieley in a hurry. I turned on a bedside lamp and handed her the note. She read it and said, "This is awful, and he didn't say which hospital he took her to."

"I think we can find out quickly enough. Hang on."

I picked up the bedside telephone and dialed zero. The guy at the registration counter downstairs answered after two rings.

"Front desk."

"A friend of ours staying here at the hotel spoke with you an hour ago or so about taking his friend to a local hospital. He left us a note saying you recommended one about ten miles away, but he didn't mention the name. Do you recall which hospital you sent him to?"

"Yes, sir. It was the Valley Hospital Medical Center. That's downtown at Twenty-Six Shadow Lane. Would you like the telephone number?"

"Yes, please."

"It's three-eight-eight-four-zero-zero-zero."

Scribbling the number on a pad, I said, "Great. Thanks for your help."

To Kieley, I said, "Okay, I have the hospital's name, address, and telephone number. What would you like to do?"

She frowned. "I want to know how Kristina is and if we can help, but I'm not sure of the best way to do that. Should we call the hospital, or go there, or what?"

Glancing at my watch, I said, "It's 3:07, so it's been a little less than an hour since Bailey wrote that note. It could take him half an hour to get her there and into the ER, so they're probably still trying to stabilize her and figure out what's wrong. Since it's unlikely she's been admitted yet, calling the hospital won't do much good. I think calling Bailey's cell phone is our best bet."

"Okay. My phone should be over there on the dresser." Kieley started to climb out of bed, but I stopped her.

"Stay put, I'll get it."

Handing her the phone, I said, "He may not answer if he's in the ER, but he'll see who's calling and know we found his note. I imagine he'll call back as soon as he can."

Kieley made the call, and from her tone of voice and what she was saying, I could tell she was talking to Bailey's voice mail. "Bailey, this is Kieley. Kev and I read your note and we're anxious to know how Kris is and if there's anything we can do to help. Please call or text me when you can."

She disconnected the call and slid off the bed. "I'm going to get dressed in case she needs us."

"Okay, I'll do the same."

She started for the bathroom, but stopped and ran back. Putting her arms around me and leaning her head on my chest, she said, "Kev, please hold me for a minute."

I did as requested. When Kieley finally stepped back, she said, "Thank you, Darling. I needed that. I'll just be a minute."

Slipping into a pair of jeans and a dark blue sport shirt, I took note of the fact it was my last clean shirt. I had a few clothes among the items we picked up at my place, but expecting to be gone a while, I packed most of my everyday stuff for the trip to Eureka, and now all of those things were ready for the laundry.

Since Kieley left the bathroom door open and I knew she could hear me, I said, "We need to get some laundry done. "

From the bathroom, she said, "I know. According to the motel guide thing, they have a guest laundry. I'll get some quarters later today and run a couple of . . . ."

"No you won't. They also have a laundry service bag in the closet. We'll load it up and put it out before we go to see Kris so they'll get our stuff washed and back to us later today."

She came do the door with a hair brush in her hand. "You're going to spoil me, Darling."

"What does money buy?"

Kieley looked at me for a second or two and caught my point. "You said money buys freedom."

"That includes freedom from chores when you've got bigger fish to fry. Besides, you could use a little spoiling."

Kieley smiled. "I'm not sure why you think so, but I'm not going to argue with you. I'll empty my suitcase into the laundry bag as soon as I get my hair brushed."

The bag was full to overflowing by the time we both stuffed our dirty clothes into it. Kieley filled out the laundry order sheet that went with the bag. "You don't want starch in your shirts, do you?"

"No, thanks."

"Okay, all done with the form."

"Thanks. I'll put the bag out in the hall."

As I closed the room door, Kieley was looking at her cell phone. I said, "Did we get a message?"

"Not yet. I was just looking to make sure the incoming text alert sound is turned on."

Suddenly the phone in her hand played a loud chime tone. It startled Kieley so much she nearly dropped the phone. After touching a couple of commands on the screen, Kieley said, "It's a message from Bailey. He says, 'Kris's blood pressure a little closer to normal; her breathing is better; and pulse is steady, but still too high. Admitting her to Valley Hospital. I will call when she has a room.'"

I said, "Sounds like they've got her stabilized."

"Yes. I'm sending a text to thank him for the information.

Anything you want me to tell him?"

"Maybe. Do you want to go to the hospital? If so, we should let him know we're coming."

"Do you think we can? I mean will they let us see her?"

"I think they will let you in. You and Bailey are as close to family as Kris has, unless her brother suddenly shows up, which I'm afraid is becoming less likely with every passing day. I'll grab your jacket for you, it's gonna be cool out there."

On the way out to the Jeep, I stopped at the desk to let the fellow know we'd left a large laundry order out in the hall. He promised to make sure it got picked up and returned to us when it was done.

Out in the Jeep, Kieley programmed the GPS for 26 Shadow Lane. By the time the engine was starting to generate a little warmth to heat the interior, she had the first driving instruction on the screen. It told us to head west on east Craig Road.

Valley Hospital turned out to be one of several clinics and medical facilities in a relatively small area of downtown Las Vegas west of I-15. We pulled into the hospital's parking lot around 4:45 and found a spot near the lobby entrance. Needless to say, the lot wasn't crowded at that hour.

I was afraid it would take a while for the woman behind the reception desk in the lobby to find Kris because they might still be in the process of admitting her. Surprisingly, their computer was on top of things and the receptionist said we would find Ms Kristina Bryant in the Cardiac Critical Care ward on the third floor and we should check in at the nursing station there.

We took an elevator up two floors, and then following the signs to Cardiology, we ended up at a nursing station just outside a pair of large wooden doors. There, a nurse explained Ms Bryant was considered a critical care patient and was only allowed family member visits. After explaining Kris's situation to the senior nurse on duty—a Ms Dillon—it was decided Kieley could be permitted a brief visit with the patient. I, on the other hand, could make myself comfortable in a waiting room adjacent to the nurses' station. I told the helpful Ms Dillon that was just fine with me.

I made myself comfortable in said waiting room while an orderly, or whatever they're called, escorted Kieley through the big wooden doors. No more than two minutes later, Bailey came through the same wooden doors and headed in my direction.

I stood and we shook hands. "I'm very grateful you brought Kieley here. Thank you."

"You're welcome, Bailey, but you've got that backwards. Kieley brought me here. I couldn't have kept her away even if I wanted to."

Bailey nodded and sat in the chair next to mine. I asked, "How's the patient doing? Have they figured out what's going on?"

"They've got her breathing easier and her blood pressure is down some, but her pulse is still too fast and a little irregular. The ER doctor said they're going to try getting her a few hours of sleep, and then a cardiac specialist will take over and start a series of tests like an echocardiogram and an MRI . . . stuff like that to see if they can isolate the cause."

"I'm sure as hell no doctor, but I'm wondering if stress could bring something like this on. If there was ever anybody who's been under a ton of stress, it's Kristina. And I don't mean just yesterday. Kieley and I have been with her since Thursday and Kris's world has literally been falling down around her since before we picked her up in San Francisco."

Bailey seemed to give that idea some thought. Finally, he said, "I think it might be helpful if you told her cardiologist that."

"Better yet, ask Kieley to do it. She's known Kristina a lot longer than I have, and her observations will be more meaningful. I know she'd be happy to do it. She and Kristina are like sisters, maybe even closer than sisters."

"All right, I'll do it. One of the nurses here said the cardiologist assigned to her case would be in around seven this morning." He looked at his watch. "That's less than two hours away. I'll ask the nurses to give the cardiologist a message to see us as soon as he can."

Standing, Bailey asked, "Do you think Kieley would be willing to stick around until then?"

"That's up to her, but I think she'll jump at the chance to do anything that might help Kristina."

"Good. Thanks, Kev. It's times like this when you discover how much friends are worth, even new friends."

"I know the feeling. Listen, if they're knocking Kris out, maybe the three of us ought to find their cafeteria, or whatever they call it here, and get some coffee . . . maybe even some breakfast between now and seven."

"I'd go for that."

The hands on my wristwatch were pointing to a few minutes before six when Kieley, Bailey, and I found a table in the Valley Hospital cafeteria where we could sit and drink our coffee. Kieley hadn't said much since leaving Kristina's room. Now, she leaned her head against my shoulder.

I said, "Seems like it's already been a long day and the sun isn't even up yet."

Kieley said, "It sure does."

"How did Kristina look to you?"

"She looks like somebody who belongs in a hospital bed." Looking across the table at Bailey, Kieley added, "In case you have any doubts, I'm positive you did exactly the right thing by bringing her here."

Bailey nodded. "That's what the ER doctor said." After a few seconds, he smiled and added, "I cheated a little, though. I brought her here code three. I'm not sure the Las Vegas P. D. would approve."

"Plus," I added, "If they stopped you, you might have had some explaining to do about what a car registered to the San Francisco Police Department is doing in Las Vegas."

"Actually, that would have been the easy part. I own that car now. At the end when they told us to evacuate, our captain realized two things. The department, as well as the City of San Francisco were out of business and none of us were likely to ever see our accrued vacation time, so he authorized bills of sale in the amounts of our accrued vacation time in exchange for some of the unmarked cars. That five-year-old Ford cost me six weeks of vacation time, or a little over eleven-thousand bucks."

"Still, it's not just any five-year-old Ford."

"That's true. It was also timely because my personal car is crushed under several tons of concrete in a downtown garage."

I was on my second cup of coffee, Bailey was getting some scrambled eggs and toast from the buffet, and Kieley's head was resting on her arms when a fellow in a white coat with a stethoscope hanging out of his pocket came into the cafeteria. He stood looking around the room for a moment, and then headed for our table.

He said, "Would you folks be here for Kristina Bryant?"

I said, "Guilty, Doctor."

"Good. I'm Ms Bryant's cardiologist, Mark Denton."

"Pleasure to meet you, Doctor. I'm Kevin Turner, and this is Kieley Bishop. I think she's the one you want to talk with."

Denton, said, "Good morning, Ms Bishop."

Kieley was sitting up again. My right hand happened to be resting on the table next to my coffee cup. She put her hand over mine and said, "Good morning, Doctor . . . I'm sorry, I'm a little out of it. What was your name?"

"Mark Denton."

Bailey showed up about that time and offered his hand. "Hello, Doctor Denton. I'm Bailey, Kristina's significant other. At least I think that's the current politically correct term for 'boyfriend.'"

Denton smiled. "Sounds right." Turning to Kieley, Denton said, "Ms Bishop, according to a message left for me at the cardiac telemetry nurses' station, you have some information that might shed some light on Ms Bryant's condition?"

Kieley cleared her throat. "Yes, doctor. Kris and I have been roommates for a couple of years, so I know her pretty well."

She coughed and cleared her throat again. I said, "Would you like more coffee or a glass of water?"

Kieley nodded. "Yes, water please, Darling. My sinuses are all messed up in this desert air."

"Okay, I'll be right back."

I found a stack of plastic cups for juice and water and filled one of them with chilled water from a cooler. When I got back to our table, Kieley was describing our adventures after we picked Kris up in San Francisco and headed south to LA.

When she finished the tale with our interrupted Mexican dinner the previous night, the doctor said, "So, if I understand what you're getting at, you are wondering if the extreme levels of stress Ms Bryant has experienced recently might have contributed to her heart problems. Is that correct?"

Kieley nodded and Denton said, "Under different circumstances, I would not expect stress to have such a debilitating physical impact by itself, but . . . but when you mix the death of her sister and the unknown fate of her brother with the chaos you've been through, I don't think we can scratch stress off the list of potential causes just yet."

Turning to Bailey, Denton said, "Mister Bailey, I suspect you also know Ms Bryant fairly well. Is there anything in your experience with her that makes you agree or disagree with that theory?"

Bailey thought about the question for a moment before saying, "Doctor, I'm a police officer—a homicide detective—so observing people is part of my job. When I first met Kris, I would have described her as a little high strung . . . or maybe nervous would be a better word. However, as we got to know each other, she began to relax more. I can honestly say that, before the quakes, Kris was perfectly normal in that regard.

"When I saw first saw her after four major quakes, Kris was worse off than she was when we first met. I noticed it right away, and it concerned me."

Denton said, "Mister Bailey, it's possible you will turn out to be an important part of her treatment." The doctor paused and looked Bailey in the eye. "I hope you'll think about that and all of its ramifications."

Bailey nodded and Doctor Denton said, "Well, I need to get back to my patients. Here's where we stand: Kristina will be in and out of tests most of the day. We're also keeping her slightly sedated to minimize the discomfort of all the poking and prodding we have to do.

"My suggestion to you folks is go get some rest and come back around five this afternoon. I'll be here until seven, so I can give you a report on the tests, and then you can spend some time with her. Ms Bryant will be tired, but I know she'll be glad to see you. Mister Bailey, Kieley, thank you for your input. You've made important contributions to Ms Bryant's recovery."

Standing, Denton said, "Do you two have business cards or something with numbers where we can reach you if we need to talk?"

I handed Kieley one of my cards and a pen so she could write her cell number on it. Bailey handed a card to the doctor, saying, "My cell number is on the back."

When he had my card with Kieley's cell number added to it, Doctor Denton said, "I don't want to give you folks false hope. At the moment Kristina is one very sick young woman. We are doing everything we know how to do for her, but until we get a handle on what's going on, her condition is precarious at best."

After the doctor left, we all stood and Bailey said, "I'm going out the emergency entrance because that's where my car is. I'll see you folks at the hotel."

Bailey walked off down a hallway and Kieley looped her arm through mine. "Let's go home, Darling."

I don't think it even occurred to her that "home" at that moment was a motel room in Las Vegas—a long damned way from any place either of us thought of as home before. Back in that motel room, I pulled the drapes together to close a gap through which bright sunlight was streaming and we climbed back into bed.

My last chore was to leave a three o'clock wake-up call with the desk. Kieley's last chore was to cuddle close and whisper, "Kevin, thank you for all you're doing to help me through this. I love you more than I ever knew was possible."

TEN

Thursday afternoon I woke up before the wake-up call and found myself looking into the prettiest pale blue eyes on the planet. Kieley said, "Good afternoon, Darling. I hope I didn't wake you."

"Just out of curiosity, how often do you lay in bed staring at me? It's okay, I'd just like to know what I'm missing."

Kieley grinned. "Not too often. Usually it's too dark to stare at you and actually see anything."

"Makes sense. Is my toupee on straight?"

"That's silly. You don't wear a toupee."

"Yeah, but I might need one someday."

"Darling, if there was ever a man who would never be caught dead with a hairpiece it's you. I don't think you have a vain bone in your body."

"Maybe, but you do."

Putting on a hurt expression, Kieley said, "I do?"

"Yes. You have a vain bone there," I ran my finger along her jaw, "And there," I slid my fingertip from her neck to her shoulder, "and . . . ."

Suddenly she said, "Now you've done it," and kissed me with enthusiasm.

"I did that? How?"

"Those weren't vain bones you were playing with, they were erogenous bones."

Love making for Kieley and me is usually a slow gradual thing, but this was certainly neither of those. Of course, the wake-up call came in at precisely the wrong moment. It rang unanswered for at least two minutes before Kieley grabbed the wireless handset, pressed a button that silenced it, and gave it a none to gentle toss in the general direction of the nightstand. I'd have let it keep ringing until hell froze over.

Laying with her head on my chest, she said, "That was rude. How's a girl supposed to have a decent orgasm with the damned telephone blaring in her ear?"

"I don't know. Perhaps you could ask Verizon."

"I'll do that. Are you aware there is no waiting period to get married in Las Vegas?"

I laughed. "Where did that come from?"

"It's perfectly logical." She held up her finger and counted the points off as she listed them. "We just made love, correct?"

"Correct."

Holding up a second finger, Kieley said, "Making love is also how to make babies, correct?"

"Is that how it's done?"

"Trust me, I read a book about it. All I have to do is stop using birth control and bingo, we have an offspring on the way."

"No kidding?"

"No kidding, but having a child out of wedlock is still frowned on in certain circles, so before I stop the birth control . . . " Kieley held up finger number three. ". . . the proper thing for us to do is get married. Make sense now?"

"I might have missed part of that. Go back to the making love part."

"We don't have time. We need to go see Kris and tell her we've set the date. When she hears that, she will get well instantly because she would never miss the opportunity to cry at my wedding."

"By all means. Incidentally, when is the date we set? I missed that part, too."

"Haven't you been paying attention, Darling? The date is the first day Kris is out of the hospital."

Thus having resolved all the matrimonial questions, we got out of bed and made ready to sally forth. When we arrived at Valley Hospital's Critical Cardiac Care telemetry ward a few minutes before five, Bailey was already there. He was sitting in the waiting lounge staring out a window when we joined him.

I said, "No Doctor Denton yet?"

"He's here. I saw him dash through a few minutes ago. He said he would be right back."

The good doctor was a man of his word and joined us in the waiting room a few minutes later. He also looked like a man who just spent nearly twelve hours making tough life and death decisions and doing his damnedest to help people get well.

Flopping into a chair, he said, "Well, the good news is I have no specific bad news for you. By that I mean we found no direct cause for Ms Bryant's symptoms. She does not have any kind of heart disease or defect we can find that would be severe enough to cause the symptoms we're seeing.

"Unfortunately, that good news is also not so good news because it leaves us with no tried and true course of treatment to cure her. The best news I have for you is we have stabilized her symptoms. Her vitals are almost exactly what they were at five this morning . . . not great, but not worse."

Bailey said, "Well, that's a better report than I was afraid we might hear."

Kieley said, "Yes, it is. Now, where do we go from here?"

Turning his head to look at Kieley, Denton said, "That's a good question. Given our test results, I'm leaning toward the idea you proposed—that extreme psychological stress is causing major recurring physical crises. With that in mind, I've asked the chief staff psychiatrist to speak with Kristina and see if that might be a possibility."

I asked, "Is your psychiatrist male or female?"

He looked at me for a moment before answering. "Doctor Felton is a woman. Do you think that matters?"

I nodded. "It could. I might be wrong about this, but some of what Kris has gone through might be better understood by a woman than a man." I looked at Bailey and said, "No offence intended."

Bailey shook his head. "None taken. In fact, I agree with you."

Denton said, "All right, then we're on the right track. I'll let you know what Doctor Felton thinks after her meeting with Kristina."

Kieley said, "Doctor Denton, I have a favor to ask of you."

Turning his attention back to Kieley he said, "If I can, certainly."

"Could you please break the rules for just a few minutes so Kevin and I can see Kristina together. We have a piece of good news for her. It might even help her get better."

The doctor said, "Oh? May I ask what your good news is?"

"Well, we haven't even had a chance to tell Bailey yet, so I'll kill two birds with one stone." Kieley looked at me and said, "Kevin and I have decided to get married and the date we've set is the day after Kris is released from your hospital so she can be my bridesmaid."

Denton leaned over and shook my hand. "Congratulations, Mister Turner. You obviously have excellent taste in women."

Bailey chimed in, "Yes, Kev, congratulations."

Sounding indignant, Kieley said, "Hey, how come he gets all the congratulations? I had something to do with this, too."

Doctor Denton laughed. "You are quite right, Kieley. Congratulations! I hope you and Kevin have a wonderful life together. As for your request, I'll grant it, but only for a minute or two. It's important we keep Kristina calm and relaxed. Also, remember she's sedated, so she'll understand you, but her response may not be as enthusiastic as you expect."

Kieley said, "I understand, Doctor."

As Denton stood, he looked at Bailey. "Will you be going in later?"

"Yes, Doctor. I won't stay too long."

"There's no reason to cut your visit short. I always encourage family members to stay with my patients as long as they want. Sometimes it's boring sitting there watching someone sleep, but when she wakes up and sees you in the room, I think you'll agree the time was well spent."

Looking at Kieley and me with a conspiratorial grin, Denton said, "Come on folks, I'll sneak you past the guards."

Kristina's room was darkened, and one of those mood channels was on the TV showing forest scenes and playing insipid elevator music. Kris was looking in the general direction of the screen with a vacant expression. She smiled when she saw us.

Kieley said, "Hiya, Girlfriend. Look who I've got here."

Kris said, "Hello Kevin. Thank you for coming to see me." At the same time she held her hand out to Kieley.

Kieley squeezed her hand. "I got special permission to bring Kev in with me for a minute because we have some news for you."

Kris looked from Kieley to me and back again. She was obviously sedated. Her words were slightly slurred when she said, "Well, don't keep me in suspense, what's the big news?"

Kieley looked at me. "You tell her."

I shook my head. "I think you should make the official announcement."

Kris said, "Well, somebody better tell me or I'll go back to watching that stupid tree show on the TV."

Kieley said, "All right, I'll make the official announcement. Kev and I have decided to tie the knot."

Kris clapped her hands together, although an IV in a vein on the back of her hand made the movement a little awkward. That's wonderful. I told you the other day I figured this time it was for keeps. Have you set a date?"

Kieley said, "Yes, and Kev is going to tell you that part."

"Well, it seems Kieley has someone special in mind to be her bridesmaid, and that special person is in the hospital at the moment, so we've decided our date will be the day after they toss you out of this place. That okay with you?"

"Oh, Kev, that's wonderful. I'm so happy for you guys I could cry."

Kieley looked at me. "I told you she wouldn't miss an opportunity to cry at my wedding."

I grinned. "Yes, you certainly did."

Kieley said, "This means you gotta do what that handsome cardiologist tells you and get your butt out of here. Okay?"

Kris held out her hand to Kieley again. "I will, Kieley, I promise, and thank you for waiting for me. I'll hurry!"

I said, "Kris, speaking of waiting, there's somebody outside waiting for me to get out of here so he can come in. I'm going to say goodnight and wish you a speedy recovery. Also, if you think of anything I can do to be of help to you, all you have to do is say the word."

Kris said, "Thank you, Kev. I think Kieley has herself a wonderful guy. Kieley, can you stay for just a minute?"

As I walked out of her room, Kris was holding Kieley's hand and speaking softly. Outside in the hall, the senior nurse I'd met the previous night was heading in my direction. With a smile, she said, "I was just coming to eighty-six you, Mister Turner."

"Gee, you guys run a tight ship."

She smiled again. "We try."

Bailey stood up as I walked through the big wooden doors and headed in his direction. I said, "Sorry to keep you waiting."

"You didn't. I'm just anxious."

"I don't blame you. Before you go in, though, one quick question."

"Sure."

"It looks like I'm gonna need a best man before long. Can I count on you?"

After a momentary pause, he smiled and said, "Sure. Be glad to."

It occurred to me to wonder why he had to think about it, if that's what he was doing. Bailey is a hard guy to read. "Thanks. I think Kieley and I are going to take off and get something to eat. Can we bring you anything?"

Bailey shook his head. "The boss nurse over there asked if I would like her to have a dinner tray for me sent up with Kristina's. I took her up on the deal. You guys go get something good to eat and I'll see you at the hotel."

"They have a continental breakfast. How 'bout we meet you there tomorrow morning, say seven-thirty?"

He paused again. "Sure, see you then."

I was just about to take a seat in the waiting area when Kieley came through the big wooden doors. I met her halfway and I gave her a hug because she looked like she needed one.

She said, "Thanks for going in with me, Kev. Did you see Kristina's face light up when we gave her the news?"

"I did. She seemed genuinely happy."

"She was. She is also scared out of her mind."

"How could you tell? They have her pretty doped up."

"Kris said so after you left. Bailey told her what happened at dinner last night, but she can't remember any of it after her first margarita. That just isn't like her."

"You know, that sounds like something else Doctor Denton might like to know."

"I had the same idea. I think he's gone for the day, but maybe I should leave him a short note. What do you think?"

"I think that's a good idea."

"Okay, I'll go write him a brief description of what she said to me and leave it at the nurses' station."

"All right, and when you're done with that, I'll take you out to dinner and we can make up for last night. I was reading about a casino not far from our motel that's supposed to have a highly rated Mexican restaurant."

Kieley smiled at me. "That sounds good. I'm actually hungry, which is an unusual experience for me."

It was nearly seven when we parked at the Cannery Casino Hotel about eight blocks west of the Comfort Inn on East Craig Road. The place has a surprisingly cozy feel about it, I suppose partly because it is ten miles or more from the big luxury casinos where the high rollers go to drop huge bundles of cash and the tourists go to watch and imagine they're high rollers, too.

Still, the Cannery has all of the flashing lights and jackpot sound effects designed to generate excitement and convince players the next roll of the dice or pull of the handle will make them rich beyond their wildest dreams. I handed Kieley a couple of silver dollars to put into one of those big super jackpot machines. She put the silver in her purse, instead. Smart girl.

We followed signs through the casino to the Casa Cocina Restaurant. It was a nicely furnished dining room without too many big screen keno displays on the walls. Strains of mariachi music drifted past our table from unseen speakers and the menu promised a tasty, if not authentic, south of the border experience.

While we were perusing that menu, we were visited by a waiter who asked what we wanted to drink. I looked at Kieley and she looked at me. Then, in unison, we said, "Diet Coke."

We both laughed and the waiter looked at us like he thought we were nuts. Maybe we were.

With our Diet Cokes in hand, we ordered a combination of small plate flavors that had my mouth watering. Our choices included shrimp ceviche, cups of albondigas soup, and an order of shrimp, steak, and chicken fajitas with flour tortillas. Splitting the ceviche and fajita orders gave us plenty to eat.

Kieley dug right in with me and as we ate, she said, "You know, I still feel funny every time I have anything but lettuce on my fork. I know I'll get over it eventually, but it will take some time."

I grinned at her. "Now you understand why it's so hard for people to lose weight. They have the same reaction to anything that isn't loaded with calories. Old habits are tough to change."

Later, as we finished dinner, Kieley said, "Sometimes I wonder about how my mind works."

"What's to wonder about? I think your mind works pretty darn well."

"Thank you, Darling, but it keeps wandering off in all directions, mostly to things in the future. It's like I want to start planning our future, but I can't. There are still too many unknowns and everything I think we ought to put on our future to-do list could turn out to be impossible and I'll end up being disappointed."

I reached across the table and took her hand. "I know, Kieley. It's not surprising that all we went through getting here is still impacting our lives, but it sure louses things up. It's like we can't escape that severe uncertainty. I feel like Old Man Fate is just around the next corner waiting to clobber us with some new crisis."

Kieley squeezed my hand. "Will there ever come a time when we can say to hell with everyone and everything and just do what we want?"

"We could do what we want right now, but that has consequences. Sometimes life seems like a long tightrope of compromises and we're constantly trying to maintain our balance by doing the right thing."

Kieley looked kind of sad. "I guess."

"I have a suggestion though."

Looking up with a hopeful expression, Kieley said, "What is it?"

"I think you've forgotten an important part of this marriage stuff?"

Obviously puzzled, she asked, "What did I forget?"

"A ring. You can't get engaged without a ring. I'm pretty sure that's a rule. So, I think after we take care of some business tomorrow morning, we should go out and correct that oversight."

Kieley grinned. "You did it again, Darling."

"What did I did again?"

"Made me ecstatically happy when I was feeling sad and low. Even if I had no other reasons, which I have many of . . . ." She shook her head. "No. Of which I have many, your ability to make me happy would be more than enough to make me love you."

ELEVEN

I got the idea Kieley might be feeling a little guilty about eating real food for dinner because, when we went through the buffet breakfast line at the hotel, she came away with a low fat yogurt and a hardboiled egg. I, however, was not suffering from any such guilt. I chose scrambled eggs, two strips of crisp bacon, and a slice of whole wheat toast. Hey, whole wheat is healthy!

Bailey had a waffle and two sausage links on his plate. He picked at the waffle, but didn't seem very interested in breakfast. Trying to engage him, I asked, "Are you headed back over to the hospital this morning?"

He nodded. "Yeah. After that I've got to find a Walmart or someplace where I can get some pants and shirts. I didn't bring much with me."

Kieley came to his rescue. "I saw a Walmart sign last night. It's a few blocks beyond that casino place where we had dinner."

I said. "Leave it to a woman to spot shopping opportunities. Go west on Craig Road about five miles. There's a Walmart superstore on the left."

"Thanks. Will you be coming by the hospital later?"

"This afternoon. I've got some business to take care of this morning . . . phone calls, mostly." I winked at Kieley and added, "After that we have a little shopping of our own to do."

Kieley grinned at my wink, and then said, "If it's okay with Kev, I'll try to be at the hospital a little after noon. You'll probably need a break from the tree channel by then."

Bailey grunted at her "tree channel" comment, but left abruptly a minute later. Something was definitely bugging Bailey.

When Kieley and I returned to our room, she busied herself unpacking the clean laundry we found waiting for us when we got back from dinner. I fired up my laptop and logged into my investment company's website.

Quickly comparing the numbers in my on-line account statements with the numbers in my head I verified that all seemed to be in order. I was moving on to the next item on my to-do list when Kieley asked a question. "Sorry to interrupt, Darling, but do you want your underwear and socks in the dresser or in your bag?"

I swiveled around in the Comfort Inn's desk chair to face her. "In the bag, please. Keeping my things packed makes me feel more mobile."

Frowning, Kieley unzipped my bag. "Does that mean we will be leaving Las Vegas soon?"

"The answer to that question requires answers to several more questions, some of which we can't answer right now, like how long will Kristina be laid up?"

Looking frustrated, Kieley asked, "Are there any questions we *can* answer now?"

"Probably. Here's one we can take a shot at. Sooner or later we probably ought to find a place to call home. Since we're starting with a clean slate, I guess we can go anywhere we want—at least anyplace that's still standing. Is there a place that especially appeals to you?"

Kieley had obviously given the question some thought already because she had an answer all ready for me. "Not in a big city. I did that before because I was already there and I thought I had to stay. Also, I want to live in California if we can."

"I'm with you on that, but finding a place in California that is still habitable after the past week could be a challenge."

"Do you remember that place where we stayed the second night of our trip?"

"Sure, the Benbow Inn."

"Do you think there's any place around there we could live?"

"Maybe. The Benbow Inn is in Garberville, but there are lots of small burgs in that area, or there used to be. If things have calmed down geologically, we might be able to find a suitable place. You think you would like living in the country?"

"Yes, I really do. Everything seems more real. In big cities all you see is concrete. Also, it was a good place because we were there together and . . . well, you know."

"I think I do, but tell me."

"Oh, you! You're making me think."

I grinned at her. "You bet I am. We're making some important decisions here."

"All right, I was going to say it's possible my impressions of that area are colored somewhat by the fact that my man was with me when I was there. That, however, does not mean those impressions don't count. If I ever go there again, my man will be with me then, too."

"Fair enough. How about Eureka? It's a little larger, and if most of the town is still there, it would make shopping and such a little less troublesome. To be honest, moving farther out into the hinterlands might be more than we're prepared to handle right now."

Kieley nodded. "Okay, a compromise. That works for me, but can we find out if Eureka is even still there without driving all that way?"

"I bet we can. Hang on a minute."

Opening a new browser window on my laptop, I Googled "Eureka, Ca Police Department." A few seconds later I was on the City of Eureka website Police Department page. There on the right side of the page was the department's non-emergency number, 707 441 4044.

I punched the number into my cell phone and after three rings, a pleasant female voice said, "Eureka Police Department, how may I direct your call?"

"Well, I'm not sure. I would like to speak with someone who can give me a brief idea of the conditions up there now."

"Yes, sir. I'll connect you with a Community Services officer. Please hold."

I held, and no more than five seconds later a male voice said, "Community Services. How can I help you?"

"Good morning, officer. We want to visit Eureka in a few days. Will you please give me an informal summary of conditions there?"

"Sure. Things are in pretty good shape right now. We have some damage along the waterfront and over on Samoa from tidal action. Also we have some older structures down in town, but all of our utilities are up and running and most of the roads are open and passable.

"We're still doing clean up, but that will be on-going. I don't see any reason you couldn't come on up. I suggest you make hotel reservations, though. Some folks who aren't able to return to their homes yet have moved into local motels temporarily. There are rooms available, but a phone call or two could save you some driving around. Does that answer your question?"

"It does and very well. Thank you, officer. I appreciate your help."

"You're welcome, sir."

I disconnected the call and said, "Things sound good there. They're still doing some clean up and he suggested we make hotel reservations before we get up there to save some driving around, but the officer said he could see no reason why we couldn't come on up."

"That's wonderful. I'm getting excited now."

Looking at my watch, I said, "Me, too. Now I need the routing number for your checking account."

She cocked her head to the side. "Why do you want that?"

"Because I'm about to make a telephone call for the purpose of arranging some electronic cash transfers and such. I thought it might be a good idea to put a few bucks in your account so you can pay off those credit cards and get out of debt."

Kieley looked down at my bag on the bed. "I've been trying not to think about that stuff."

"Why? Now is a good time for us to get back on the plus side of the ledger."

"I don't know. I guess I still feel a little strange about using your money to fix my mistakes."

"What mistakes? You used those credit cards to survive. You did what you had to do."

"I guess. I just don't think it's right . . . ."

"Kieley, are we getting married or not?"

She jerked her head up from stuffing underwear into my bag. "I thought we were."

"I am under the same impression, and when we get married all that money becomes OUR money. All we're doing is spending a little of your share to buy you some freedom. In this case, freedom from debt. Now, how much do you need to pay off your cards?"

Softly, she said, "About sixteen thousand."

"Okay, we'll round it off to seventeen so you'll have some extra. Now, give me your checkbook and I'll make my calls. While I do that, there are a couple of things you could do to speed things up."

That gave her spirits a lift. She liked doing stuff for us. "What do you want me to do?"

"First, look in the telephone book and find the closest UPS store and the nearest Bank of America branch. Also, find out what we have to do to get married in this town. Then find us the best jewelry store in town."

"Are you sure you want to give me all that money and a ring, too? We could wait on the ring, you know."

"No we can't, and I would pick out a jewelry store myself, but all I know about that stuff is it's shiny."

My first and most important call was to my investment manager in New York. He seemed very pleased to know I was still alive, saying it saved him a lot of damned paperwork. With such pleasantries out of the way, I instructed him to transfer seventeen thousand into Kieley's checking account.

Since I pay him to make good decisions for me, he advised against depositing the funds directly into Kieley's account. Instead, he recommended moving the funds into my Bank of America checking account, and from there into a new joint B of A checking account in both our names. She could pay off her credit card from the new account which, because it was also in my name, eliminated the need to submit an IRS Form 8300 to explain a transfer or transfers totaling more than ten thousand dollars within a 12 month period. I agreed to that and instructed him to also to do a one-time transfer of $40,000 and an ongoing monthly transfer of $10,000 into the same B of A account. We were going to need some spending money.

When we ended our conversation, I logged into my Bank of America account and was happy to see the total of $67,000 from all three transfers was already posted. That done, I asked Kieley to come over to the desk. I showed her the balance in the account and explained how we would open a new joint account at the Las Vegas B of A from which she could pay off her credit card.

She said, "I think I understand, but it sounds very complicated. Is it all legal?"

"It will be as soon as we get to the bank and set up the new joint account and make the transfer. When we walk out of the bank, you'll have a temporary checkbook for the joint account."

"Okay. Kev?"

"What, Kieley?"

"This is all happening so fast, I'm having trouble keeping up with it and I'm afraid I'm going to forget to say 'Thank you.'"

Grinning, I said, "Don't worry, I'll remind you. Come on, let's hit the road."

Our first stop was a UPS store on Craig. We came out with a snail mail address for Kieley and Kevin Taylor.

Afterward, Kieley said, "That was weird."

"What?"

"Signing my new name. I hope we don't get in trouble for using it before it's legal."

"People use aliases and DBA names all the time. Besides you needed practice signing 'Kieley Taylor.'"

With a little grin, she said, "It was actually kind of fun."

Our next stop was the Bank of America. When we came out, Kieley had a handful of temporary checks for our new joint account in her bag. While I was at it, I added her signature to the original account. For banking purposes we used her legal name for the time being.

Sitting in the Jeep, Kieley said, "Kevin, you know you don't have to do all this."

"Yes, I do. I don't expect anything to happen to me, but if it does, I want everything in place so you don't have to worry about anything. We can finish those arrangements after we're married and can meet with a lawyer."

"Kevin, I . . . I don't know what to say. I've never had this kind of responsibility in someone else's life before. I don't want to mess things up."

"You won't. Now where do we go to get a marriage license or whatever it's called in Sin City?"

"To the Las Vegas Marriage License Bureau, of course. It is in the Regional Justice Center at 201 East Clark Avenue."

Inside, the Las Vegas Marriage License Bureau reminded me a little of the Hollywood DMV office. We filled out an application form and stood in line waiting for our turn at one of ten windows. We handed in our form, presented our IDs, and a Visa Card to cover the $77 license fee. In exchange, the woman behind the counter gave us our license, saying it would be valid for one year. The process was considerably less complex than getting a driver's license.

Kieley looked a little shell-shocked when we got back to the Jeep. "You okay, Kieley?"

"Yes, it's just this isn't exactly what I expected when I pictured us getting married."

"Me, neither. I have an idea, though."

"What?"

"Let's get married twice. Once here in Vegas to cover the legalities and again when we settle in Eureka, or wherever we end up, for the memories."

Kieley leaned over and kissed my cheek. "I like your idea. I always knew you were a romantic kinda guy at heart."

"Now, speaking of romance, where is the jewelry store you found?"

Tapping an address into the GPS, she said, "It's in a shopping center on Las Vegas Boulevard."

I knew we were in high-roller country when I saw the center. It was called the Grand Canal Shoppes and you can figure the more unnecessary letters they use in the name, the higher the markup on the merchandise inside. Also, the center was nestled amongst some of the classiest hotels in town. Places like the Wynn, the Palazzo, and the Venetian want to see your Dun & Bradstreet score at the casino entrance.

Upon seeing the dazzling display of tasteless splendor adorning the Grand Canal Shoppes, Kieley, said, "Oh, oh. I think I might have overdone it. You said to pick out the best jewelry store in town. A jewelry store here is more likely to be the most expensive jewelry store in town."

"What the heck, it doesn't cost anything to look."

Inside, the center was designed to replicate Venice by someone who has never seen Venice. Being careful not to fall into a canal, lest we be run over by a passing gondola, we found a directory and followed its directions to a jewelry store named *Objets Brillants*, which Kieley translated with her high school French to mean "Shiny Objects," or something along those lines.

Surprisingly, the store was luxurious without being nearly as ostentatious as its neighbors. A fellow in a three-piece suit welcomed Mademoiselle and Monsieur and inquired as to how he might serve us.

I said, "We are here to look at bridal sets."

He was sizing us up to determine what sort of ring we could afford when I added, "We are particularly interested in non-traditional ring designs." I nonchalantly reached up with my left hand and rubbed my chin as I added, "Price is of less concern than selecting a unique design that my bride-to-be finds appealing."

Suddenly the salesman was all grins, saying, "Of course, sir. If you folks will please follow me, I can show you some stunning in-house designs."

I knew his sudden interest in pleasing us had nothing to do with anything I said. No, it had to do with the $15,000 Rolex Daytona chronometer strapped to my left wrist. It was a birthday gift from Uncle Jake the year before he passed away.

The salesman seated us at a table in a small but elegantly businesslike room and said, "Please excuse me for just a moment. I'll be right back with some designs for your consideration."

He left the room and Kieley looked at me. "What . . . ."

I held up my left wrist. Knowing our plans for the day, I swapped the relatively inexpensive Citizen watch I usually wear for the Rolex I brought from my safe at home. When she saw the big letters R-O-L-E-X on the face of the watch, she smiled and shook her head in what I took to be amazement at my technique for handling snooty sales people.

During the next hour the salesman showed us several dozen unique engagement sets. Then he and I both heard Kieley gasp. She was looking at a ring the salesman described as a central diamond accented by two sapphires and set in a sweeping yellow gold tone setting. Sinatra would have described a diamond that size as a "meatball."

She said, "May I please look at that one more closely?"

He handed her the ring and a jeweler's loupe, saying, "Certainly, and may I say you have excellent taste. This ring is a brand new creation from our top in-house designer. Only twenty will be made, so it will be forever unique."

It was then I remembered Kieley's birthday is in September, which makes her birthstone the sapphire. There was not only that coincidence, but the ring was exactly the right size to slide smoothly on and off her finger. She slipped it on and held her hand up so I could see the effect.

When I looked from her hand to her face, her eyes were sparkling just like the diamond. "Oh, Kevin, it's beautiful."

I said, "Yes it is. Would you like this one, or would you like to see more designs?"

"No, Darling, I love this one, but how expensive is it?"

The salesman looked at a handprinted card from his pocket and opened his mouth to speak, but I held up my hand to stop him. "Kieley, the price of the ring is of no concern. All that matters is you chose it. In fact, why don't you take a hike while I complete the transaction?"

Kieley stared at me as if she was planning to protest my suggestion. Thankfully, the salesman came to my rescue. "We have a new collection of charming vintage brooches on display in our grand viewing room. I'm sure Mademoiselle would find the display much more interesting than what remains to be done here."

One thing I can always count on with Kieley is she catches on quick. In a pleasant tone she said, "Why, yes, I would love to see the brooches."

The salesman said, "Of course." He stood, replaced the ring in its slot on the black felt sample board, and then led Kieley to the door, where he gestured to a woman who escorted her off down the hall to look at broaches.

When the salesman returned to the table, he got right down to business. Holding up the ring Kieley selected, he said, "Twelve thousand. Sixteen if you also want the matching wedding band. I recommend purchasing the band now, otherwise it might not be available should you decide you want it in the future."

I opened my wallet and handed him my American Express card and my driver's license. "We'll take both rings."

"Yes, sir."

Shortly after Kieley returned from brooch viewing, the salesman came back with my Amex card, driver's license, and some paperwork for me to sign. He also carried a small royal blue presentation box, which he opened to show us the rings inside.

Surprised, Kieley said, "You bought it?"

"Yes." With a grin, I added, "If you've changed your mind, now would be a good time to say so."

"No . . . no. I just thought it must be much too expensive for our budget."

Thirty minutes later, at one-fifteen, we parked in the Valley Hospital lot. Kieley was quiet all the way there from the shopping center. She did, however, have a tight grip on my right arm.

I said, "You're awfully quiet. Is everything all right?"

She looked at me with tears-streaks on her cheeks. "I'm sorry, Kevin. I'm just having trouble believing all this is really happening. It's like out of the blue all of my most precious secret dreams are coming true. I feel like a princess in a Disney cartoon."

"Good. I always wanted to marry a princess."

"Kevin . . . I . . . I saw the price of that ring at the bottom of the bill of sale. It was nineteen thou . . . ."

"You must have misread it." Holding up the little royal blue box, I said, "I found this in a package of Cracker Jack."

"Kevin, I hope you know I could have been all yours for a hell of a lot less money than you've spent on me since we got up this morning."

"Yes, but this price includes optional accessories."

Her cocked head puzzled look was getting a workout today. "What accessories?"

"Tears of joy and big smiles. Now, would you please stop fussing and answer an important question?"

A grin immediately teased me from the corners of her mouth. "What question is that, Darling?"

"Well, I realize this hospital parking lot is not the most romantic place on earth, but it might make a good story to tell our grandkids someday, so, Ms Bishop, would you please do me the honor of marrying me?"

The smile I was hoping for spread across her face. "Why, yes, Mister Turner, nothing would make me prouder and happier than to become your wife."

I took her left hand and slipped the engagement ring on her ring finger. She looked at it, and then looked at me. The tears of joy on her cheeks said all that needed to be said.

TWELVE

Wednesday, August 24, 2022, 1:30 P.M.
Valley Hospital, Las Vegas, Nevada

While Kieley checked in at the Critical Cardiac Care Telemetry nursing station, I settled into a waiting area chair and picked up a December, 2021 edition of PEOPLE MAGAZINE with the President on its cover. He had a Hubert Humphrey "Pleased as Punch" expression on his face, making him look dumber than he probably really is, although I'm not absolutely sure of that.

When I glanced up a second later, I was surprised to see Kieley striding briskly in my direction. She was carrying a piece of paper and she looked about as angry as I have ever seen her.

Judging by her demeanor, I thought I should prepare for action, so I stood up and said, "What's the matter?"

"Here, read this. I swear, if I ever see that man again, I'll scratch his eyes out!"

Dear Kieley,

Kristina is doing better and her doctor says she could recover entirely. Now that I know Kristina will be okay, I am leaving. I have no excuse or explanation other than I was not cut out to be tied down and I cannot handle having an invalid clinging to me.

I'll leave your boxes from my car at the hotel.

Bailey

Sighing, I looked at Kieley. She said, "How could he do this? I thought he really cared about Kristina. He's nothing but a damned coward."

I remembered suspecting Bailey was upset about something the last few times I spoke with him. That made me think his

121

leaving was not a spur of the moment decision. I said, "And this note reads like it was written by a man with a guilty conscience. If these are his true colors, I think Kristina is better off without him around."

"I wonder if he had the balls to tell Kris he was leaving."

Shaking my head, I said, "My guess is he expects you to do his dirty work for him."

"Kev, will you please help me? I don't know how to tell her about this."

I gave her a one-arm hug, still holding Bailey's note in my right hand. "I'll do whatever you need or want me to do."

She hugged me back and said, "Thank you, Darling. I think the first thing I need to do is find Doctor Denton and tell him what's going on. This news is not going to do Kris's condition any good. The doctor might have a suggestion about how we should break it to her."

"Good idea, and I think you need to do that quickly. Kristina may already be wondering why Bailey isn't there with her."

"Yes. I'll see if the nurses know where Doctor Denton is."

I walked to the counter with her. Kieley told the senior nurse, Ms Dillon, we had an urgent need to see Doctor Denton.

Nurse Dillon said, "I'm not sure where he is. The doctor might be having lunch in the cafeteria. I know he's in the hospital. I'm sure he'll be around soon."

I said, "Nurse, we just learned Ms Bryant is facing a new emotional crisis significant enough to warrant a discussion with Doctor Denton before we do anything else, and there is some urgency involved."

She was staring at me intently. When I finished speaking, she looked at Kieley for a moment, and then said, "I'll track him down for you. It will take just a minute."

Nurse Dillon was as good as her word and ten minutes later Kieley and I were sitting in the waiting area with Doctor Denton. He read what Bailey wrote, and handing the note back to Kieley, he said, "This surprises me. I had the idea Ms Bryant was quite important to Mister Bailey."

Kieley said, "So did we. Now we think he has put us in the position having to give her this very bad news."

Denton said, "You don't think he told Ms Bryant he was going?"

I said, "I'm guessing he didn't. Why else leave this note for Kieley? Obviously we are concerned about how the news will affect her emotionally and physically."

Denton nodded. "I share your concern."

Kieley held up Bailey's note. "In this note he seems to be indicating you gave him some good news about Kris. Is there something we haven't heard yet?"

"Yes. I should have realized you haven't yet heard about Kristina's interview with Doctor Felton, our staff psychiatrist, this morning. I also need to say her news isn't quite as rosy as Mister Bailey would have you believe from that note. Doctor Felton believes, as I do now, your idea Kris's episodes are brought on as emotional responses to trauma could very well be accurate.

"From what you've told me, I think it is safe to say there has been plenty of trauma in her life. At the root of the problem, however, is a physical weakness of some kind that leaves her vulnerable to these cardiopulmonary episodes."

I said, "Is there anything we can do to overcome that weakness by strengthening her heart?"

Denton shook his head slightly. "So far I don't know exactly where that weakness is. The human cardiovascular system is complicated. To find a recurring weakness in it could take 24-hour a day monitoring over a period of years to recreate the exact combination of conditions that would pinpoint the specific weakness.

"That leaves us with diet, light physical exercise, baby aspirin as a blood thinner, and maybe a beta-blocker to help control her blood pressure and help reduce the likelihood of further episodes. Diet is especially important. She really needs to put on a little weight. On the other side of the equation, of course, she needs to avoid stress."

I said, "And Bailey has provided us with one of the most stressful situations a person might ever have to face."

Denton smiled at me. "You ever consider becoming a doctor, Kevin? You might be good at it."

"No, I'll leave the doctor business to people like you who don't faint at the sight of blood."

Naturally, Kieley was most concerned with the immediate problem and cut to the chase. "Doctor, what should we do? We have to tell Kris something to explain Bailey's disappearance and I won't lie to her. If she ever found out we made up a story, Kris would run away from the only two people in the world she can count on."

Doctor Denton was quiet for several seconds. Finally, he said, "Well, Kristina is still under sedation and her vitals are within the normal range at the moment. I don't think there will ever be a better time to talk with her about this fellow Bailey. Say, is Bailey the guy's first name or his last name?"

Kieley said, "He swore Kristina to secrecy, but she told me. Now I feel like putting the truth up on billboards. Bailey is his last name. His first name is Horatio."

I muttered, "That figures."

Denton smiled, but said nothing about Bailey's name disorder. He did say, "Look, I can monitor Kristina's vitals remotely and I can hear what is said in her room." He quickly added, "We never eavesdrop on patients unless there is a medical reason.

"Anyway, how would it be if I monitored Kristina personally while you talk with her? That way we can act quickly if need be. Give me a few minutes while I set it up and have nurse Dillon stand by with a crash cart in case things go really badly. I don't think that will happen, but it won't hurt to be prepared. All right?"

Doctor Denton and I were both watching Kieley. She hesitated, took a deep breath, and said, "Yes, but I have one condition. I want Kevin in there with me."

Denton looked at me, and then nodded to Kieley. "I would want him there, too. Kevin, are you willing if I promise there won't be any blood?"

I couldn't help smiling. "For Kieley, I would even face a little blood." Then, looking at Kieley, I said, "You know, I hate to say this, but it might be an idea to remove that new piece of jewelry for this occasion. Seeing it could make Kris feel worse about the situation."

Doctor Denton put on a puzzled expression. Kieley answered his unspoken question by holding her left hand up.

He said, "Well now!" Then he gave me a wink and said, "Congratulations, Kieley."

A few minutes later Kieley, sans ring, and I walked through the big wooden doors and down the hall. When we walked into Kristina's room, she smiled. "I'm sure glad to see you guys. I've got no one to talk to. I think Bailey ran off with one of my nurses."

Kieley leaned over and gave Kristina a kiss on the forehead, and I said, "Hi, Kris."

She gave me a smile, looked back at Kieley, and frowned. "Something's wrong isn't it? I can always tell when you aren't telling me something. What is it? Did something happen to Bailey?"

Kieley looked at me. She was close to tears and I had the distinct feeling her eyes were pleading with me. Hoping I was reading her correctly, I said, "Kris, we do have some sad news. It appears Bailey has bailed out on us. He seems to feel he can't cope with your illness, so he . . . ."

At that moment Kristina threw us all a curve. "You don't have to sugarcoat it, Kev. I figured something like that was coming. Bailey isn't like you. He can't deal with emotional matters. I was surprised he stuck with me as long as he did."

Turning to Kieley, she said, "Don't look like that, Girlfriend. I know I should be mad at him, but I believe he really tried to do the right thing. Faced with physical danger, Bailey is as brave as the day is long. He just can't handle emotional situations."

Kieley shook her head. "Kris, you amaze me. I was afraid to tell you because we were worried about how it would affect you, and here you are, dealing with the situation better than I am."

Kris gestured to the telemetry monitor display and said, "Steady as a rock. You know why?"

"Why?"

"Because when I began to think Bailey might flake out on me, I remembered what you said a few days ago after you guys came back for me in San Francisco."

Kieley looked puzzled. Kris said, "You said we were like the Three Musketeers. We are always there for each other. I believed that, and it turned out to be true, didn't it?"

Grinning, Kieley looked up at the ceiling and said in a loud voice, "Doctor Denton, can you hear me?"

A tinny version of Denton's voice came from a speaker grill on the wall behind Kris's bed. "I hear you."

"My friend here is ready to leave your hospital. When can we pick her up?"

After a few seconds, the tinny Denton said, "How would tomorrow morning after breakfast be?"

Kieley gave Kris a questioning look and Kris said, "If I must stay for breakfast, I'll have a Denver Omelette with sourdough toast."

Denton laughed. "Your request will be sent to the kitchen. I'll stop by after breakfast with some instructions and to see you off. I'll be there around nine."

Kieley and I spent the rest of the day keeping Kris company and I noticed her becoming more alert as time passed. That, I concluded, was because they were reducing the level of sedation she was getting. Finally, after having dinner with Kris, Kieley and I headed back to the Comfort Inn.

The woman at the registration desk said some boxes were left for us that morning, and they were stacked in our room. With Kieley's help, I used a luggage cart to schlep the boxes down to the Jeep and went through the tedious process of repacking everything.

I noticed Kieley put her new ring back on the minute we walked out of Kris's hospital room. When we turned in for the night, I commented on that, saying it was good to see the ring back where it belonged.

She said, "I hope you know I'm never taking this ring off again. I already feel naked without it."

"Hmm. Do you feel naked now?"

"Yes, but that is because I AM naked. I'm surprised you didn't notice."

"Who says I didn't notice?"

"Kevin, can we talk for a minute?"

"You mean before I take advantage of your nakedness?"

"Yes, Darling, before that."

I sighed an exaggerated sigh. "If you insist."

"We did a couple of important things today and I think we ought to discuss them and how they will affect us."

"Which important thing do you want to discuss first?"

"What we, especially you, did for Kris. I know she came off like Bailey leaving didn't matter much, but I think you know better. I certainly do. The thing is, we now have to face the consequences of what we did."

"Consequences?"

"Yes. For instance, Kris has no immediate family, unless her brother shows up. That means we are now sort of stuck with Kris. I love her dearly and I wouldn't have it any other way, but I'm not sure how you're going to feel about having her around all the time."

"I'm not sure either, but that's how it is. You know, I could ask you the same question."

"Having her around isn't new to me. We were roommates, remember?"

"I remember, but you didn't have me around then."

Kieley was quiet for a moment, and then said, "That brings to mind a delicate subject, which I'm sure is why you said that. Can I ask you a question and get an honest answer?"

"Honest answers are my specialty."

"I'm serious about this. If I weren't in the picture and she was willing, would you sleep with Kris?"

"Probably not."

"Probably?"

"Kieley, the thing about hypothetical questions is, to answer them, we have to assume circumstances that sometimes cannot be imagined. For example, I cannot imagine you not being in the picture. You are an integral part of who I am. If we had never met, I would be a different person. Now, that guy might sleep with Kris, but the idea has no special appeal for me. Besides, you're a better kisser."

There was a smile in her voice as Kieley said, "Okay, I get the point. No more hypothetical questions."

"Tell me, did your confidence in me really need that booster shot?"

She didn't say anything right away, and then, "No, not really. I guess a girl just likes to hear she's special to the man she loves."

"Fair enough. Now let's get to the real question."

"All right. What do you think the real question is?"

"How does having Kris with us affect our plans?"

"Yes, you're right, that is the real question, and my answer is we ought to do exactly what we talked about this morning, except we need to make sure Kris has good medical care nearby. We also have to make supporting her recovery our responsibility."

"Do you think that will work? Isn't she going to feel like a fifth wheel?"

"Oh, maybe at first, but come on, Kev, look at her. How long do you think she has to be someplace before every guy in town is lined up around the block? Just because she doesn't get you all hard and excited doesn't mean she won't have that effect on other guys."

"I suppose, but just to set the record straight, I did not say she doesn't get me all hard and excited."

"Oh? Then she DOES excite you? Let's see."

Before I could stop her, Kieley was checking for the aforementioned condition. She said, "Well, hell. At the moment nobody is giving you a . . . No wait. Oh, oh. Now, is she doing that or am I? And it better be me, Mister!"

Two hours later I managed to convince her she was solely responsible for instigating the activities leading to her dramatic discovery. Her final comment on the matter was, "Damn! We must remember to do that again sometime."

THIRTEEN

Thursday, August 25, 2022, 9:00 A.M.
Valley Hospital, Las Vegas, Nevada

The hospital had some paperwork pertinent to Kristina's release which required our attention, so we applied a divide and conquer strategy to arranging her getaway. I went to the business office while Kieley made sure the staff had Kris ready to go and to hear Doctor Denton's final instructions.

In the business office, the social worker—a term no longer reserved for those receiving government assistance—had enough paper stacked in front of him to fill three large shredders. Fortunately, he was a very organized fellow and things moved right along.

His first step was to determine who was financially responsible for Kristina's care. He looked relieved when I said I was. He didn't care about my relationship to the patient, just so long as somebody was responsible.

Next he summarized Kristina's bill. The total cost of ER treatment, tests, three days and nights in Critical Cardiac Care, three days of cardiac telemetry, medications, emesis basin, plastic storage container, non-slip socks, facial tissues, and other assorted sundries was $112,582.34. Kris's health insurance required a ten-percent copay, which brought the responsible party's share to a whopping $11,258.

His third step was to inquire how we planned to make the copayment. Removing my checkbook from my inside jacket pocket, I said, "Personal check okay?"

That made him deliriously happy because it would be no skin off his nose if my check bounced higher than a kite. In that event, the matter would be handed over to a collection service. His responsibility ended with printing my California driver's license number on the back of the check.

First, though, he examined the check and my ID with great care, and then asked, "Is this your current address?"

"It might be."

I was having some fun with him. He jerked his head up. "Might be?"

"Yes, if that last earthquake the other day didn't knock my house off the top of the hill, it is my current address. If the quake did knock my house down the hill, you'll have to go find the house at the bottom of the hill and see what street it landed on."

Bean counters take this sort of stuff very seriously and I had thoroughly confused him. Feeling only a little guilty for upsetting his applecart, I helped him out of his dilemma. "Don't sweat the small stuff, Jack. The check is good."

The fellow shrugged, diligently signed my receipt form in two places, and used a giant electric stapler to secure the stack of receipts, forms, and other paperwork. Finally, he instructed me to show the receipt on top of the stack at the nursing station. I hurried to the elevator before the guy remembered he hadn't charged us for any hospital air Kris may have breathed while in her cardiac telemetry room.

On the third floor, Kieley was sitting in a waiting area chair, Kristina was sitting in a wheelchair parked next to Kieley, and a patient escort—at least I think that's what wheelchair pushers are called nowadays—was standing behind Kristina's wheelchair, looking like Dale Earnhardt awaiting the green flag at Daytona. All three of them waved in my direction.

Nurse Dillion and I joined the happy little group about the same time and I handed her the stack of papers in my hand, saying, "The assistant bean counter downstairs said I should show you this stuff to spring our gal."

Nurse Dillon smiled at my attempt to make light of something they all took very seriously and looked at the receipt. "It seems Ms Bryant is officially sprung." She turned to Kristina and said, "I won't say it's been a pleasure having you visit us because I'm certain you would argue that point, but I am glad things turned out well and you can be on your way."

Kristina said, "Thank you for all you've done, Nurse Dillon. I will always be grateful for your help."

Nurse Dillon handed Kris her paperwork, the patient escort released the wheelchair brakes, and we were off to the elevator like a herd of turtles. Earlier, when Kieley and I arrived at Valley Hospital, we left the Jeep in a loading zone in front of the entrance so it was only a short trip to the curb from the lobby.

At the Jeep, Kris bailed out of the wheelchair like she was rocket propelled and took her official seat behind mine. As we drove out of the Valley Hospital parking lot, Kris said, "Kevin, did you pay this copay for me?"

"Yup. Otherwise they were going to make you wash dishes in the cafeteria for the rest of your life."

"Thank you. I don't know when or how I can pay you back, but I will, I promise."

"Don't worry about it, Kris."

"I am worried about it. I know how much photographers make, even the best ones like you, and it's not enough that you can afford to be spending $11,000 bailing me out of the hospital."

I saw Kieley raise her eyebrows at the size of Kris's copay. I said, "But I am no longer a photographer. I'm beginning a new career as a professional husband."

A confused voice came from the back seat. "A professional husband? That sounds like fun, but surely it doesn't pay very well."

I looked at Kieley and winked. She turned around, held up her left hand, and said, "It must pay pretty well if he can afford this."

"Oh, Kieley! It's beautiful! When did you get that?"

"Yesterday. Kevin took me to this classy jewelry store and we spent an hour and a half looking for just the right ring."

"You sure found it! I love the design. It's not ostentatious, but it just oozes class."

I said, "So does the girl wearing it."

Kris agreed. "That's for sure. Gosh, I'm so excited for you guys. It's none of my business about the money, but I'm glad things are going well for you."

Changing the subject, I said, "Kris, before I point us toward the hotel, are there any stops we need to make for you."

"The only things I need are a prescription the doctor gave me, some baby aspirin, and some clean clothes. I only took a couple of tops and two pairs of jeans from our apartment. I've been handwashing the shirts out overnight, but I really need to do some laundry."

"Kieley, where can we go to solve Kris's wardrobe dilemma?"

"I know just the place. Turn south on Las Vegas Boulevard. I noticed a Nordstrom yesterday near that center with the gondolas where we picked out my ring."

Kris said, "Gondolas? Aren't they some kind of Italian boat?"

Kieley said, "In this town they're transportation in high-buck shopping centers."

Softly, Kris said, "Kieley, I hate to rain on the parade, but I'm pretty sure I can't afford Nordstrom or gondolas."

Kieley looked at me and said, "Kev, can she afford Nordstrom's?"

"She can and so can you if you see something that strikes your fancy. Are you up to some shopping, Kris?"

Sounding a little panicky, Kris said, "Physically, yes, but really, I can't afford . . . ."

Kieley interrupted her. "Kris, if Kev says you can afford Nordstrom's, you can afford Nordstrom's. Just let it go at that. Okay?"

I pulled up near the outside entrance to Nordstrom's store in the Fashion Show mall. "Kris, my briefcase is on the floor behind Kieley. Would you please pass it up here?"

I opened the case and handed Kieley a stack of one hundred twenties. "Will that be enough to get things rolling?"

"Sure, but why cash instead of a credit card?"

"Because you aren't Kieley Turner quite yet. I hope to fix that small oversight tomorrow, but in the meantime a place like Nordstrom is sure to check your ID against the card for a large purchase and call it in if the information doesn't match."

"I take it you aren't going shopping with us?"

"Nope. I'm gonna find a drugstore or someplace where I can pick up Kris's prescription. Do you have it handy, Kris?"

Kieley reached into the pocket of her jeans and came up with a prescription. She said, "This is for something called Metropol, or something like that. Doctor Denton called it a 'beta blocker' for treating high blood pressure, angina, and other heart problems. He said it was 'just in case.'"

"Anything else?"

"Just the baby aspirin."

"Okay. Kieley, call me when you're about done and I'll pick you up here."

"Okay, Darling. I promise we won't keep you waiting too long."

"There's no need to hurry. I don't know how long it will take a drug store to fill this prescription."

I found a CVS, where they filled Kristina's prescription without any fuss. They had Metoprolol in stock, and all I had to do was present Kris's insurance info, sign for the drug, and pay a copay. Done.

The best part was CVS stores are all over the west, so as long as we had the prescription number and there were refills on it, we could get them almost anywhere we went. At least anyplace there was a CVS still standing.

By four o'clock we were back at the hotel, where I was treated to an impromptu fashion show, which included a couple of skirts and tops for Kristina and a sweater for Kieley. After I judged the shopping excursion a success, Kieley went across the hall to help Kris stuff her old wardrobe into a laundry bag and fill out the form.

When they came back, I said, "It might be a good idea to call the desk to let them know we've got laundry to go."

She said, "Actually, I think I'll go down to the lobby and tell them in person. I could use a cup of coffee, and they've always got coffee on in the breakfast room.

I said, "As long as you're going . . . ."

Kieley smiled. "Yes, Darling."

Kris said, "I'll go with you, Kieley. You're going to need a couple of extra hands."

With genuine Comfort Inn mugs of fresh coffee in hand, we settled down and began a discussion of our immediate plans. I sat on one end of the couch, Kieley sat in the swivel desk chair facing me, and Kris sat at the other end of the couch.

I started things off. "Kris, Kieley and I have made some plans, and since you are part of those plans we want to share them with you."

Kris said, "Kev, I will be eternally grateful to you for all you've done, but I don't expect you to adopt me like a lost puppy. You two are starting a new life to together and you don't need me complicating things."

I looked at Kieley. "She was your friend first. You want to straighten Kris out on a few points?"

In a vehement tone Kieley said, "Yes, I certainly do. Kris, Kev and I discussed this at length last night." She glanced at me and grinned. "And we agree you are part of our family. Now, if you honestly don't want to hang with us, that's your choice, but we certainly aren't going to abandon a member of our family in a strange city with no money and nobody to turn to for help. That just isn't going to happen. Do you understand what I'm saying?"

Even from the other end of the couch I could see tears in Kris's big brown eyes. When she didn't answer Kieley right away, Kieley repeated the question. "Do you understand what I'm saying, Kris?"

"Yes. Of course I want to stay with you, but . . . ."

I said, "Good. That's settled. Now, have you ever been up to Eureka in northern California?"

Kris shook her head. "Well, Kieley and I were there just before the first quake and we both like the area. It's a relatively small town on the coast with a lot of trees and a decent climate. We thought it might be a good place to start a new life, so we called up there and talked to the cop shop to find out if the place was still standing. They told us the town is in pretty good shape after the quakes and tsunamis. How does that sound to you?"

"It sounds like heaven. I never want to live in a big city again."

Kieley said, "You and I agree on that one, Girlfriend. I said the very same thing to Kev yesterday."

Kristina frowned. "But, can I find work in a small town like that? I don't have much experience at anything besides modeling and it doesn't sound like Eureka is a town with lots of modeling jobs."

Kieley said, "Kev, the answer to that question is kind of up to you."

Kris looked at me. "Why is it up to you, Kev?"

"I guess because I'm the one with twenty million bucks in the bank."

Kris's reaction was a lot like Kieley's when I told her about the money. "You have what?"

"Twenty million. That's twenty followed by six zeros and two commas. One day when we have nothing else more important to talk about, I will tell you how I happen to have it, but what's important for now is the money is legit and safely invested to give us a very comfortable monthly income for life. Bottom line: you don't have to work unless or until you find a job you really want to do."

"That's wonderful, Kev, but it's your money."

"In twenty-four hours it will Kieley's money, too. Come hell or high water, Kieley and I are getting married tomorrow, and when we say 'I do,' that will make her a full partner in twenty-million bucks."

Kieley said, "Not really, Kris. I mean, yes, legally in a community property state like California, I guess it will be partly mine, too, but I trust Kev to make the financial decisions for our future. One decision he already made and I support a hundred percent is you will always have a place in our home. I don't mean you're stuck with us when you find some handsome prince charming, but until then, you are Sister Kristina."

I laughed. "Just what we need, a nun in the family!"

Kris said, "Are guys sure? I mean, I never ever want to do anything to come between you."

Faking a hardboiled attitude, Kieley said, "Yeah, well, we talked about that, too."

I cringed because I knew what was coming, but Kristina bought into it hook, line, and sinker. "You did?"

Kieley was laying it on thick now. "You bet we did. I hate to tell you this, Sister, but Kev says I'm a better kisser and you don't turn him on at all, not so much as a twitch, and I intend to make sure things stay that way!"

Kristina caught on to the gag. Looking at me with a hurt expression, she said, "Not so much as a twitch?"

Kris was wearing a loose camisole top with string straps. She used a finger to flick one of the straps off her shoulder, and then leaning over, she exposed herself clear down to her belly button, Kris said, "Even now?"

My discomfort with staring at Kristina's boobs must have been obvious. Kieley found the situation hilarious and Kris joined her in a laughing fit. I stood up and leaned on the edge of the desk. Suddenly, Kieley realized things had gone too far and I wasn't happy.

"Kev, I'm sorry. I was just trying to put Kris at ease with the situation. I didn't mean to upset you."

Kristina also got serious. "I'm sorry, too. Kev. I was just teasing you a little."

"No, Kris, you were teasing me a lot. That goes for you, too, Kieley. Looking at Kris's boobs is great fun, but not conducive to maintaining the kind of relationship we were discussing. I was brought up believing two things about women. One, they are to be respected and protected above all else, and two, I'm a one-woman-guy. Kieley, you are that one woman and I don't see that commitment as something to joke about."

I was just realizing I sounded too much like a Baptist preacher when Kris abruptly jumped up and ran out of our room. I heard the door to her room across the hall slam a second later.

Kieley was staring at me as if I'd turned into someone she didn't even recognize. Softly, she said, "Kevin, I didn't realize our teasing was that offensive to you. I'm really sorry I upset you. I promise it will never happen again."

Ashamed of my behavior, I was at a loss for words, and when I didn't respond, Kieley hurried over to me. In a tone of voice that included some panic, she took my hands and said, "Kevin, please. Forgive me. Yell at me, slap me . . . punish me any way you want, but please don't stop loving me."

Kieley put her arms around me and held on for dear life. I said the only words I could think of to say. "Kieley, I could never stop loving you."

"Oh, Kevin, I'm so sorry I hurt you. You mean everything to me. I just . . . just love you so much!"

I led her over to the couch and we sat. I felt her sobbing in my arms. Gently taking her face between my palms, I looked down into her eyes. "It's okay, Kieley. I'm partly to blame. I overreacted. We'll make it past this."

"Kevin, I feel like I just came very close to losing you. And when I realized that, I felt all hollow and empty, like there was nothing left inside me. I never want to feel that emptiness again. Never."

"If I have anything to say about it you won't feel it again and neither will I."

We heard a door close out in the hallway. I wondered if it was Kris's door.

Kieley wondered the same thing. "Kevin what about Kris? Should we talk to her?"

"To be honest, I don't much feel like it at the moment, but this can't be doing her emotional state any good. Would you please see if you can catch her?"

"Yes, Darling."

Kieley opened the door to our room and looked up and down the hall. She said, "I don't see her, but the laundry bag isn't out here anymore. That isn't a good sign."

I joined her at the door. "Come on, let's find her."

When we got to the elevator, it was on the first floor. I said, "I'll take the stairs and meet you in the lobby".

I don't think I've ever gone down two flights of stairs any faster. When I came out of the stairwell into the lobby, I saw Kris. She was about ten feet ahead of me and leaning against the wall. Her backpack and carry-on were on the floor and she was gasping for breath.

She turned toward me and cringed when I put a hand on her shoulder. "It's all right Kris. Come on, let's sit somewhere."

Kris didn't argue. I picked up her bags and she leaned against me heavily as we walked into the lobby. The desk clerk looked at Kris and said, "Is she hurt? Should I call 911?"

Easing Kris down onto a loveseat, I said, "Thanks, but not yet. Let me see how she is before we call for help."

Kieley finally got the elevator down to the lobby and came running after us. "Are you all right, Kris?"

Kris looked at her and nodded slowly. Kieley gave me a

questioning look.

I said, "I think we need some aspirin."

Kieley turned to the desk clerk. "Do you have any plain aspirin down here?"

"Yes, I think there's some in a first-aid kit in back. I'll get it."

What he came back with was a full three-hundred-twenty-five milligram Bayer aspirin. I said, "Water." While Kieley went to a soda machine and bought a bottle of water, I used the blade of my pocket knife to split the aspirin tablet in two.

Recalling what little cardiac first-aid I knew, I said, "Kris, I want you to chew this tablet. Don't just swallow it, chew it first. Do you understand?"

"Yes."

"Kieley has some water for you to help the powder go down, but you have to chew it before you swallow. That gets the medicine into your system faster."

She made a face at the aspirin's bitterness, but she chewed the tablet thoroughly before swallowing it. I said, "Good. Now we need to get the other half of the tablet in you, only this time, hold the chewed up tablet under your tongue for a minute or two."

As she took the other half of the pill from the palm of my hand, Kris made a face and said, "I must have REALLY pissed you off for you to be this mean to me."

I couldn't help smiling. "Just be grateful there's no castor oil in the first aid kit."

Leaning over my shoulder, Kieley said, "Kris, will you listen to me while you chew up the rest of the pill?"

Kris nodded and Kieley said, "Kevin was angry with both of us for teasing him the way we did, and I don't blame him. He said he forgives us, though, and I promised we wouldn't be so . . . ." She finished in a lower tone so the desk clerk wouldn't hear. "We wouldn't make so many sex jokes."

She looked from Kieley to me, and said, "Gosh I didn't think my boobs were that awful to look at."

I said, "Never mind your damned boobs. How does the rest of you feel now?"

"Tense and kind of nervous."

"Any tightness in your chest?"

"No."

"Kieley, how are you at taking a pulse?"

"I learned how in a high school first-aid class, but I need to see a watch with a second hand."

I held up my left wrist so Kieley could see my watch and she started counting to herself. When she got to twenty-eight, Kieley stopped counting and said, "About one-twelve, but steady. I didn't feel any of the atrial fibrillation Doctor Denton warned us about."

"Good. We'll check the pulse again in a while and see if it slows some. It should."

Turning to Kris, I said, "Here are our options: The man over there behind the counter has offered to call 911 for us. Do you want to go back to the hospital, or up to our room?"

"I don't want to go back to the hospital."

"All right. Rest and when you feel like going up to the room, say the word. In the meantime, concentrate on breathing normally."

"I'll try."

After a few minutes, Kris nodded to me and I helped her to her feet. She leaned against my shoulder and we started toward the elevator. Kieley picked up Kris's bags and trailed along behind. I thanked the desk clerk for his help as we passed him.

When we got back to our room, Kris sat on the couch and Kieley said, "Kris, what did you do with the paper laundry bag we put out into the hall?"

"I emptied it back into my backpack."

"Is it okay with you if I put your stuff back into the laundry bag again?"

Looking kind of defeated, Kris nodded and handed Kieley her room key.

Kieley went to take care of the laundry and I said, "Kris, where were you going when you left your room?"

She shrugged. "I don't know. Away . . . away from you and Kieley before I ruined your lives."

"I thank you for putting our welfare ahead of yours, but as a survival technique, that sucks."

Kris looked away. "You're still mad at me, aren't you?"

"Not at all. I just think it's time you started thinking like the intelligent woman you are instead of seeing the dark side of everything. Yes, right now the world doesn't appear to be treating you fairly, but if you look at things another way, you're standing at the end of a rainbow looking at the pot of gold. I'd say the second view is better than the first, wouldn't you?"

She shook her head. "I don't understand what you mean about a rainbow and a pot of gold."

"I mean you have won the hearts of two people who think you're pretty damned special and want to help make your life better, but Kieley and I can't do it all for you. You have to do your share."

"How? I mean . . . I don't know . . . ."

"Part of your share is gratefully accepting what we do to help you and making the most of it."

Kieley came back into the room at that point, but said nothing. She just stood there watching Kris.

"I really am grateful, but . . . ."

"But nothing. Let me show you what I'm talking about. How much do you owe on your credit cards?"

"I only have one card left and it's at the limit, about nine-thousand. Why?"

"Because Kieley is prepared to sit down at my laptop over there and arrange a transfer of nine thousand dollars into your checking account so you can pay off the card and be out of debt, no strings attached."

Kris started to say something, but I cut her off. "Hear me out, Kris. I did the same for Kieley and she owed a lot more than you do. Now, paying off your card is the small part of this. The big part is you standing up and saying, 'Thank you, Kieley and Kevin, I appreciate your help.'"

"Now, can you do that or will your pride or lack of confidence or whatever is going on in your head keep you from accepting our help?"

Kris looked down at the floor and Kieley came over to where I was sitting and cuddled close. She and Kris both wore expressions of pain and fatigue.

I said, "Kris, you don't need to put that much thought into this decision. Is your answer yes or no?"

She looked at me and looked at Kieley, and then slowly stood up. Still a little shaky, she walked toward us and stopped a foot or two away. Kris took a deep breath and said, "Thank you, Kieley and Kevin. I really do appreciate what you're doing for me."

I said, "Good job! I not only love you, I'm proud of you."

Kris gave me a sort of sheepish grin and said, "Thank you, Kev."

"You're very welcome. Kieley, would you please log into our B of A account number one and set up a transfer into Kris's checking account?"

"Okay, as long as you're here to answer my dumb questions."

"I'll be right here exploring dinner choices."

After our business was completed and we made a medium gourmet veggie pizza from Round Table disappear like magic. It was nearly ten p.m. and we were all full and exhausted. I stood up, stretched, and said, "Ladies, I'm going to bed. Kristina, you are welcome to sleep in here tonight if you want to. That couch opens up into a bed, which explains why it is so damned uncomfortable to sit on."

"Thank you, Kevin. I would like that, but will my being here disrupt your . . . ah . . . privacy?"

"Kris, I am going to assume you are no longer a virgin and are knowledgeable about the process by which two people make love. Is that a safe assumption?"

I was surprised when Kris actually blushed. After a second, she answered in a quiet voice. "Yes, Kev, that is a safe assumption."

"So if Kieley and I make love tonight and you hear us, which you undoubtedly will, may I also assume the fact that your best friend is experiencing the most incredible climax imaginable will not shock you?"

Kieley was looking at me with a shocked expression on her face, but Kris grinned and simply said, "Touché!"

Sometime later Kris heard exactly what I warned her she might hear. Hell, people clear out in Winnemucca must have heard Kieley. What's more, I'm pretty sure I also heard a quiet giggle coming from the couch just as the big moment arrived. I gave Kris credit for having the last laugh . . . or giggle.

FOURTEEN

I awoke Friday morning harboring an intense dislike for Las Vegas, Nevada. For some, Las Vegas and its desert environment are heaven on Earth. For others, like me, Vegas is an abrasive town that wears us down like a piece of gritty sandpaper until our nerves are raw. I'd had enough.

Sitting in the Comfort Inn's breakfast room for what I sincerely hoped might be the last time, I watched Kieley and Kris put away small bowls of instant oatmeal with a little strawberry jam mixed in. My plate still held half a toasted bagel and a plastic tub of cream cheese. I was pretty sure my appetite would improve proportionately to the distance we put between us and Las Vegas.

When Kieley finished her last spoonful of oatmeal, I said, "Would you mind looking something up on your magic cell phone"

Picking up her phone, Kieley said, "I'd be happy to. What do you want to know?"

"Where do you get married in this town if you don't want Elvis impersonators riding animatronic swans participating in the service?"

Kieley made a call. I heard her say, "Yes, please. We have our Clark County license and we want to get married in a simple civil ceremony without Elvis impersonators, pink Cadillacs, or animatronic swans. Can you please suggest a place where we can do that?"

She listened for a few seconds, and then said, "That's great. Do we need an appointment or anything?"

After another pause, Kieley said, "That's what we'll do then. Thank you very much."

I said, "That all sounded positive, who were you talking to?"

"The Marriage License Bureau. There is a judge on call right there in the Clark County Regional Justice Center who will perform simple civil ceremonies for a small honorarium. If we give them a call fifteen minutes before we show up, we might not even have to wait."

"Terrific! Now can you find us a paralegal service close to that Marriage License joint?"

While Kieley tapped my request into her phone's Internet browser, I swallowed some coffee and looked at Kris. She was in a cheery mood and was the very picture of good health. "What are you so damned happy about?"

Kris said, "I'm alive and with my family. I think those are two very good reasons to be happy. Now tell me what you're so damned grumpy about."

"I can't tolerate people who smile before noon. They should be . . . ."

Kris crossed her eyes and stuck her tongue out at me. She looked so silly I couldn't help laughing. Kieley looked up and giggled. Kris said, "That always works."

Kieley said, "Found it. There is an outfit called Las Vegas 24/7 Paralegal Services. They're at 500 South Third Street, which appears to be about two blocks south of the Marriage License Bureau."

"Ah ha! Things are getting better. Kieley, are you still up for the idea we discussed about having two weddings?"

"Absolutely."

Kristina had not yet heard about my two-for-one marriage system. "Two weddings?"

Kieley explained the logic. "A wedding should be a special occasion, but everything here is so commercial and cheesy, Kev came up with the idea of two weddings. How did you say it, Kev? One here in Vegas to cover the legal technicalities and another one for the memories when we're settled in our new home?"

I laughed. "Damn, you do listen to what I say sometimes."

"Darling, I listen to what you say all of the time."

"I guess I'd better watch what I say then."

"Yes, I would highly recommend that. For example, you didn't think I was paying attention when you asked me to marry you and look at the trouble that got you into."

"Yeah, now I'm stuck with the prettiest, sexiest, charmingest, and most caring woman on the planet. It will be tough, but I can do it."

Kris ginned. "Ah . . . is charmingest a word?"

"Didn't I just say it?"

"Yes, you did, but . . . ."

"Then it's a word."

Kris laughed. "The way you two kid each other, you ought to be on TV. You're always cracking me up."

I mumbled, "Yeah, we're a regular Mary Tyler Moore and Dick Van Dyke."

Kris looked at me with a puzzled expression. "Who?"

Didn't you ever watch reruns on TV when you were a kid?

Kris started to say something and I stopped her. "Kris, if you ask what reruns are, so help me, I'll smack you."

Looking excited, Kris said, "Oh boy! Do you have whips and handcuffs, too?"

When I didn't reply immediately, her smile faded, "Oh, Kev, I'm sorry. I . . . ."

I turned to Kieley. "Where does she pick this stuff up? From hanging around with you?"

Kieley could tell from the tone of my voice I was kidding. "No, she used to date a cop, remember?"

"Oh, yeah. How could I forget Horatio?"

Kieley changed the subject. "Okay, oh great leader, what is our itinerary for the day?"

"Hey, who died and left me in charge?"

"You're just a born leader, Darling."

"Swell. Before I can make a suggestion, I need one or two more answers. Kieley, would you please ask your amazing mystical cell phone what is the best route from here to Eureka and what is the mileage for that route?"

Kieley's fingers tap-danced on her phone's screen and, after a few seconds, she said, "According to Google maps, the best route is up US Highway 95 to Reno, and then US 395 from Reno to a place across the California border called Susanville. From Susanville, we take California State Route 44 to Redding, and from there, California 299 to Eureka."

She held the screen up so I could see the route, saying "The total distance is 779 miles and Google says the driving time is 13 hours and 15 minutes. That, of course, assumes no delays due to road conditions."

"Got it. Okay, here is my suggestion. We go back to the room and you two get your finances in order electronically by paying off those credit cards. After that we check out of this dump, get hitched, and go to that paralegal joint, where we get a simple will drawn up. Finally, we fax a copy of the will and marriage certificate to my investment people in New York. With luck, we can get all that done before noon. Now, please do a time and mileage calculation from here to Reno."

After only a few seconds, Kieley said, "It's 439 miles and about seven hours."

"Perfect. If we head north on US 95 and don't encounter any big problems, we ought to be in Reno around seven tonight. I feel confident in that time because Highway 95 should have little or no quake damage. We spend the night in Reno and head northwest into California and toward Eureka in the morning. Hopefully the route will be clear as far as Susanville. From there I have no idea what we'll encounter. How does that sound?"

Kieley said, "Reno is more than halfway, so we might make Eureka by tomorrow night."

I said, "Maybe, but I don't want to count on it without knowing how the roads are. We might be able to find out how things are beyond Susanville from Caltrans, the California Department of Transportation. They used to have a website and an 800 telephone number for road conditions, but with all that's happened, there is no guarantee their information services will be up to date, or even working."

Kieley looked at Kris. "What say you, Sister Kris?"

"I'm not looking forward to another long road trip, but if that's what it takes for us to get to this Eureka place, let's go."

I was pleased to hear Kris use the word "us." I hoped it might mean she was accepting her role in our family.

Kieley said, "I vote with Kris. Let's get the heck out of Sin City."

I said, "Good, we have a plan! Let's go back to the room so you guys can do your banking."

Kieley nodded enthusiastically. "Good idea. That will definitely be a feel-good thing."

"After that, we can carry our stuff down to the Wrangler and . . . ."

Kris interrupted. "Wait. What about my clothes we sent to the laundry last night? When will they get back?"

Kieley said, "The bag says they guarantee delivery by one o' clock, so we'll just swing by here on our way out of town."

I added, "And when we check out, I'll tell the desk clerk we'll be back for the laundry and ask him to hold it at the desk."

With the bill paying ceremony over, it didn't take long to pack our gear. Kris went back to her room and grabbed the outfits she picked out at Nordstrom. Down in the lobby we got a small break. While I was settling up with the desk clerk for our rooms, the hotel's laundry service showed up with Kris's clothes.

Finally, I asked the clerk to see if he could get us a reservation at the Reno Comfort Inn and guarantee it for a late arrival. He did so and wished us a pleasant trip.

Ten minutes later we were rolling south on Interstate-15 toward downtown Las Vegas. Kieley placed a call to the marriage license bureau and requested a judge to perform our civil service. She was told to check in at Window Number One when we arrived.

We parked in a city parking structure across Third Street from the Clark County Regional Justice Center. Making sure we had our license and the wedding band that went with Kieley's engagement ring, we headed for the Marriage License Bureau with Kristina, our designated witness, in tow.

Once we met the judge, the marriage process took less than five minutes. After he pronounced us man and wife, I slid the ring on Kieley's finger, we kissed, thanked the judge, and made tracks to the paralegal office down the street.

Creating a last will and testament took a little longer than getting married. It was ten-thirty-five when I signed my new will naming Kieley Bishop Turner sole beneficiary in the event I died. The next step was faxing a copy of our marriage certificate and the will to my financial management company.

When we returned to the Jeep and I said, "Kieley, how do you feel right now?"

"Like I just rode down the Matterhorn at Disneyland backward. Are we really married?"

"Ask our official witness."

Kieley looked back over her shoulder and said, "What about it, Kris? Did you witness a marriage or a three-ring circus?"

"I'm pretty sure it was a marriage, but it's not official until I cry, and I'm saving my tears for your next wedding."

I said, "Hopefully, to the same guy."

Kieley leaned over. "Absolutely to the same guy. Now kiss me again, only this time do it like you mean it."

When we were still kissing after about fifteen seconds, Kris said, "I'm sorry guys, but no matter how we stack stuff, there just isn't enough room in this vehicle for . . . ."

Gasping for breath, Kieley said, "Don't bet on it, Sister Kris."

I was tempted to show Kris how wrong she was, but time was a wasting, so with everyone belted in, we headed north on US Highway 95. At the north end of town, I took the West Azure Drive off ramp and we filled the Jeep's tank at an Arco station.

Before getting back on the highway, we pulled into a Farmer

Boys Restaurant drive-thru, where the girls ordered southwest chicken salads and I got a charbroiled chicken club sandwich and an order of fries. Kieley informed me the fries were not a healthy choice and I would have to eat them all by myself. I set the cardboard fry container on the console, and soon noticed the number of fries in the container was decreasing at a rate somewhat greater than I was consuming them. There also seemed to be a lot of giggling going on.

Back on the road, we made good time and with virtually no traffic, I even had a chance to take in some of the countryside. The most remarkable scenery consisted of huge housing developments on both sides of the freeway. There were a few scrawny trees among the houses, but mostly what we saw around the houses was rocky caliche soil. Well, at least they didn't have to waste much time mowing lawns. Still, out among the Sidewinders and Gila Monsters seemed like a strange place for home sweet home.

The housing tracts went on for miles, and then they suddenly ended. After that there was one puny golf course, and beyond that nothing for miles until we passed Creech Air Force Base.

Kieley did some arithmetic and determined that, even with the gas and food stop, we averaged forty-three miles per hour since we left downtown Sin City. And now, with nobody around but Wiley Coyote, I stepped a little harder on the gas, holding the speedometer at seventy-five.

Kieley did the math and figured if we kept that speed up, we could hit Reno by 6:30, which was half an hour earlier than I hoped. That was, of course, assuming Old Man Fate wasn't hiding behind a sand dune waiting to ambush us.

The next bit of excitement we encountered was the town of Tonopah. Mostly, Tonopah consisted of some gas stations, a couple of motels, a few storefront casinos, and a quaint five-story brick hotel built in 1906. According to a sign we passed, the population of Tonopah is 2,478. I think they counted half the population twice.

I was also surprised to learn the elevation was over six thousand feet. I had no idea we climbed that far. Kieley got her trusty cell phone calculator out and figured we covered 211 miles since leaving Las Vegas and our average speed for that distance was a hair over 59 miles-per-hour.

Kieley said, "It's sure nice to be driving on good roads for a change."

"It sure is." Glancing into the rear view mirror, I saw Kris leaning on the boxes to her right and she was sound asleep. In a quieter tone, I said, "Looks like our economy class passenger is missing all of this beautiful scenery."

Kieley looked over her shoulder and frowned. "I wonder. Kris? Kris, wake up."

After a few seconds, Kieley's tone of voice turned urgent. "Pull over, Kev. Kris isn't waking up."

One good thing about being out in the middle of nowhere is you have plenty of room to stop off the road if you need to. I pulled off and Kieley ran around to Kris's side of the car. Opening the door, she shook Kristina. Kris's arms flopped limply.

"Kris, come on, wake up!"

Looking over Kieley's shoulder, I said, "She's breathing." I held my left wrist out so Kieley could see my watch and said, "Check her pulse?"

Fifteen seconds later, Kieley said, "It's about fifty-six. That's way too low, Kev. We have to wake her up!"

Kieley put her hands on Kris's shoulders and shook her vigorously. "Come on, Kris. Kris! Wake up, girl."

Finally, Kris's eye lids fluttered and she looked at us in surprise. "What's wrong?"

Kieley said, "We're worried about you, Kris. You appeared to be sleeping, but we couldn't wake you. How are you feeling?"

"Kind of groggy."

Kieley gave me a questioning look. I said, "Let's find out our options. Can you Google 'urgent care Tonopah, Nevada'?"

Nodding, she said, "Okay," and went to work with her cell phone again.

I thought about other possibilities and something occurred to me. "Kris, did you take your baby aspirin this morning like Doctor Denton prescribed?"

Kris didn't have to think about her answer. A sheepish expression appeared on her face. "No. In all the excitement of checking out, I forgot. The bottle is right here in my purse. Should I take one now?"

"I don't know if that has anything to do with the immediate problem, but it sure couldn't hurt."

While she took her baby aspirin with water from a bottle left over from lunch, Kieley reported her findings.

"I found a couple of places offering urgent medical care. One of them is right on the highway at the other end of town."

Kristina was looking a little panicky. "I think I'm okay. Really. I didn't sleep well last night. That's probably . . . ."

Looking at Kieley, I asked, "What do you think?"

"We passed a supermarket with a drugstore at this end of town. I think we should go back there and get a couple of things."

Kris asked, "What things?"

"A blood pressure cuff and a large cup of coffee. The cuff will give us a better idea of how you're doing, and the coffee will pump a little caffeine into you, which might help counter whatever conked you out."

I said, "Sounds like a good idea to me. Kris, what do you think?"

"I think I'm okay now. I don't want to mess up our trip."

Kieley said, "You aren't messing it up, Kris. Come on, let's go back to that store."

I found the market, a Raley's, and suggested Kieley take Kris in with her while I topped off the tank at a Shell Station up the road couple of blocks. Thirty minutes later we were in the market parking lot encouraging Kristina to drink her coffee. I needed no encouragement to drink the cup Kieley brought for me.

Unpacking the blood pressure cuff, Kieley said, "This is made by the same company that makes the ones they use at Valley Hospital. I hope that means it is accurate."

She loaded the gizmo's battery compartment and wrapped the cuff part around Kris's upper arm. When Kieley pressed a button on the box attached to the cuff by a couple of rubber hoses, the cuff began to inflate. A few seconds later, the cuff deflated and Kieley read the numbers on the display.

"Blood pressure is 125 over 80. According to the chart that's slightly elevated. The pulse is a little better, though. It's up to 63. Maybe that coffee is working."

I added a few numbers of my own to the conversation. "According to the GPS, it's 228 miles to Reno. At the speed we've been going out here, that's a little over three hours. Also, there is one good-sized town on our route about an hour and a half ahead. It's larger than Tonopah and might be a better choice for medical care. I'm thinking we'd be better off to keep going. What do you think, Kris? Are you up to going on?"

"Yes. We should keep going."

"Kieley?

"It's a risk, but it might be worth taking. If Kris is up to it, let's go."

I said, "Kristina, would you please try something for me?"

"Of course, Kev. Anything you want."

"Please keep an eye on your watch, and about every fifteen minutes take your blood pressure. Did you see how Kieley did it?"

"Yes. I'll just leave the cuff thing on. That will help me remember."

"Good idea. The reason is I think having a job to do will help keep you alert. Just sing out your blood pressure and pulse when you take it. Okay?"

"I feel a little silly, but if it means we can keep going, I'll do it."

"Good. Let's get back on the road."

The rest of the trip went smoothly. Kris sang out her blood pressure and pulse every fifteen minutes and at the outskirts of Hawthorne, Kieley said, "The numbers are in the normal range now. Unless you have another reason to stop, I'd say keep rolling."

I said, "Kris, how are you doing back there? Are you up to finishing the trip?"

"Yes, absolutely. I could use a restroom, though. That coffee went right through me."

I found a Chevron Station where I could fill up the Jeep's tank while Kieley and Kris used the restroom. When she got back, Kieley handed me a small paper sack, saying, "It's not much of a wedding gift, but it's from the heart."

I opened the bag and found a box of Brown Sugar Cinnamon Pop-Tarts. Leaning across the console, I kissed her. "Thank you, Kieley. From the heart is the best gift a person can receive."

Kieley smiled warmly. "And you've given me so much from the heart. I have a lot of catching up to do. Like when we get to Eureka, we're going to get you a wedding ring. With all that's been going on, that never even occurred to me. Like I said, I've got some catching up to do."

As I slipped the Jeep into gear and left the Chevron Station, Kieley said, "Kris, are you all buckled in back there okay?"

"Yes. How much farther is it and do I have to keep taking my blood pressure?"

Kieley said, "Your blood pressure and pulse have been normal for a while, so I think you could take a break from the BP monitoring. It's only about two hours to Reno. Is that right, Kev?"

"Sounds right to me. The GPS says 125 miles, so we should make Reno around eight-fifteen or so."

Our GPS began playing freeway roulette as we drew closer to Reno. About the time US 95 crossed US 50, the GPS shunted us onto Nevada Route 439, which took us north to Interstate-80. There, we turned west, paralleling the Truckee river and climbing through a mountain pass that led us down into the suburb of Sparks.

Just east of Sparks we got a déjà vu sort of shock. The eastern end of Sparks is a light industrial area very reminiscent of what we saw passing through Bakersfield on our way to meet Bailey in Buttonwillow. The destruction here was not as bad as it was in Bakersfield, but it was clear California shared its earthquakes with this part of Nevada.

I'd just spotted a yellow blinking light marking a detour sign when Kieley said, "This doesn't look good."

A nervous voice from the back seat said, "What is it? What doesn't look good?"

Kristina was at a disadvantage scenery-wise because her view out the right side of the Jeep was entirely blocked by boxes clear to the roof. Her view out the windshield was also limited by the front seat headrests.

As I slowed to follow the detour off the freeway at Sparks Boulevard, I said, "It's just a little quake damage they haven't repaired yet, like we saw in Bakersfield."

"I thought they didn't have earthquakes here. I don't like this! What if they have another one?"

I sighed and Kieley looked at me. I think she realized I was tired from a day of driving and not in the mood to deal with Kris's quake paranoia. She said, "Relax, Girlfriend. This is old damage from a few days ago, probably last Tuesday, and this is Friday, so the damage is nearly a week old. It just takes a while to repair highways."

Just like our experience in Bakersfield, getting to our destination in Reno required some zigging and zagging, but we finally got to the Comfort Inn and Suites across Interstate 580 from-the Reno-Tahoe International Airport.

Kieley and Kris got out to stretch their legs while I went in to get us registered. The hotel had a variety of rooms available, and I deliberately chose two adjacent rooms with one bed each. On this particular night Kris would have to make do with a connecting door.

After bringing our gear in, we walked to a nearby Denny's for some dinner. I'm not a huge Denny's fan, but it was the closest eatery, so in we went. At that point I'd have settled for Golden Arches. Well, maybe not.

Later, when Kieley climbed into bed and draped her right leg over mine, she whispered, "Thanks for getting us our own room tonight, Darling."

"I hope Kris isn't too unhappy with the arrangement."

"She isn't, at least she said she wasn't. I think she was probably too tired to care."

"What do you think we should do about her condition? I'm asking because this is the largest town with the most medical options we're going to see on this trip."

"I wish I knew how to answer that question. Unfortunately, we can't rely on Kris for much help. She's so intent on not messing up our trip, she's downplaying how poorly she feels. On the other hand, her blood pressure and pulse numbers today settled down into the normal ranges."

"Yeah, I know, but if something happens on the road it could trigger an episode out in the boondocks and we would be hard pressed to do anything about it."

"True, but her episode today happened under perfectly calm conditions. I don't know what the trigger could have been."

"How about all the running around and excitement this morning? It might have been a delayed reaction to that."

Kieley was thoughtful for a moment, and then said, "I suppose that's possible. I just don't know."

Using a Nevada-style metaphor, I said, "You know, we could adjust our plans a little to cover our bets."

"What do you mean?"

"We could simply stay here a while and get her in for a check-up. It would give us a chance to see how she responds to a more normal and relaxed routine."

Kieley propped herself up on her elbows. "You'd do that for Kris?"

"Wouldn't you?"

"You know I would if it's the best thing we could do for her."

"All right, let's find out. You want to call Doctor Denton in the morning, tell him what happened today, and get his opinion?"

"Yes, I'll do that. If he thinks a check-up would be a good thing, he might suggest someone here in Reno for Kris to see."

"If he recommends seeing someone, we'll stay here for a few days and see how Kris does, and then adjust our plans accordingly."

"Thanks, Kev. Kris may not like delaying our trip to Eureka, but I would much rather be safe than sorry." After a short pause, Kieley asked, "Darling, how do you feel about tonight?"

"You mean about traditional wedding night activities?"

Kieley smiled. "Yes. I want to feel us together more than ever, but I also want our first time as husband and wife to be special. I'm not sure either of us are up to 'special' tonight."

"I think you are right."

"I love you with all my heart, Kev. Today I did the smartest thing I have ever done in my entire life; I married you."

"And I'm sure glad you did because I think it was a pretty smart move for me, too. Sleep well, my love."

FIFTEEN

Saturday, August 27, 2022, 7:30 A.M.
Comfort Inn, Reno, Nevada

In my dream, the coffee smelled so good it woke me up, and then I realized the dream was sitting on the edge of our bed. The dream said, "Good morning, Darling."

"Good morning. You're up early . . . or did I oversleep?"

"A little of both. It's seven-thirty."

I sat up and took a swallow of the coffee Kieley brought me. "Then, I guess I should get up and get going before all the best worms are gone."

"All right. I'll look in on Sister Kristina while you do that."

When I returned to the bedroom from my shower, Kris and Kieley were deep in a serious discussion. Still in her sleep shirt and with tousled hair, Kristina was sitting in the desk chair. She was not happy. "No! I do not want to stay here. I'm fine!"

Kieley was standing a few feet from the desk. "You weren't fine yesterday out in the desert. We just don't want you to have a worse episode a million miles from anyplace we can get help."

Tears were pooling in Kris's eyes. "No! Please don't do this, Kieley! I'm okay!"

Kieley noticed I was out of the bathroom. "Kev, ..."

Handing my empty coffee cup to Kieley, I said, "Would you please make me a refill?"

She looked at me questioningly for a second, and then realized I was trying to defuse a tense situation. Taking my cup, she said, "All right, Kev."

Sitting on the edge of the bed, I looked at Kris. She glared back at me, her big brown eyes daring me to tell her we needed to stay in Reno for the sake of her health. I said nothing.

Finally, my silence wore her down. "Kev, come on. I'm really all right."

"Kristina, right now it would not be too difficult to convince myself I don't give a flying fig what happens to you, and it appears that would be just fine with you."

The tears were back almost instantly. "No! I don't want you to feel that way. Can't you understand? I . . . I . . . I . . . ."

Kristina was gasping for breath again and Kieley was at her side in an instant. "Breathe slowly, Kris. Lean back and relax." Looking at me, Kieley said, "Find the blood pressure cuff."

I remembered seeing it on the backseat of the Jeep when we carried our bags in. "It's in the Jeep. I'll be right back."

When I got back to the room, Kris was stretched out on the bed. Kieley took the cuff and quickly wrapped it around the upper part of Kristina's left arm. After the cuff took its reading and deflated, Kieley read the numbers. "Eighty over 60 and 58. Way too low!"

I asked, "Nine-one-one?"

"Let's give it five minutes. Kris, can you hear me all right?"

Kris's eyes were wide open as if she knew something bad was happening to her, but she couldn't tell what it was. With tears streaming down her cheeks, Kris said, "Yes, Kieley."

"You have to relax and take slow even breaths. Fight the urge to gasp. Remember what Doctor Denton told you."

"I'm . . . I'm so sorry, Kieley . . . ."

"Kris, you have nothing to be sorry for. Kev and I love you and we're going to get you well, but you have to help. Okay?"

"Yes."

"Good. Now, concentrate on relaxing and slowing your breathing. Take normal breaths."

After a very few minutes, Kieley's instructions began to show results. She said, "You're doing good, Kris. Keep it up. I'm going to check your BP again."

The new set of numbers were much closer to normal. Kieley said, "Eighty-nine over 60 and 66. Better! Good work, Kris. Keep it up . . . breathe slowly . . . take even breaths. Remember not to gasp."

Kris turned her head slightly to look at me. "Kevin, I . . . I really want you to care . . . ."

"I do, Kris. I absolutely care what happens to you. Kieley and I want you to beat this thing. We know you can. You're proving that right now by getting your blood pressure and pulse back to normal."

From the corner of my eye, I saw Kieley nod. She said, "Kev, would you please keep Kris company for a few minutes? I'm going to try calling Doctor Denton. Maybe he can recommend a cardiologist in Reno."

"Good idea. While you do that, I'll entertain Kris with tales of your misspent youth."

"Ha! Don't believe a word of it, Kris."

I sat on the edge of the bed again and took Kris's hand. She squeezed and I squeezed back. She looked at me with a timid smile.

I said, "Actually, Kieley's youth wasn't all misspent, just the parts of it she spent hanging with me; but you can forgive her for that. She was in love."

Softly, Kris said, "Yes, I know. I was at her wedding. She married a really terrific guy."

Kieley spent quite a bit of time on her cell phone. When she finally ended the call, she said, "Success!"

Sitting next to me on the edge of the bed, Kieley said, "Thanks to Nurse Dillon, I actually got to talk with Doctor Denton. He knows a fellow here at something called—she looked at a note in her hand—the Renown Regional Medical Center. He gave me the doctor's name and number, and suggested we call today for an appointment. What do you think?"

I said, "Kris?"

Kris looked from me to Kieley. "Could you please make an appointment for me to see him?"

Kieley said "I will. While I do that, Kev can take your blood pressure again."

I did as requested and the numbers were 94 over 68 with a pulse of 70. Kieley was apparently on hold and leaned over to read the screen.

"Good. Go get dressed, Kris."

Getting off the bed slowly, Kris looked at me and said softly, "Thank you, Kev."

Kris went into her room and Kieley finished her call. "We have an appointment to see a Doctor Brewer at eleven. He'll meet us in his office on the third floor of the hospital building. He said Doctor Denton called him about Kris and is faxing her test and lab results. As we expected, he asked if Kris could be in town for a few days, so we'll need to keep our rooms."

"Good work, but I've got a better idea about lodgings. On the way into town I saw a sign for a Hilton Homewood Suites here. Homewood is my favorite home away from home. I suggest we look up the number and see if we can get a two bedroom suite. It would be more comfortable and a maybe little more like a home for Kris."

"Wonderful idea, Kev. Shall I call right now so we'll know we have a place to stay tonight?"

"Well, yeah, but I could make the call. You don't have to do all the work, you know."

"But I really like doing the detail stuff. I think I'm pretty good at it, too."

I smiled. "You are without peer when it comes to math and details. Have at it."

"Okay, but I've got one more little thing to do first."

Kieley walked over and kissed me. "That's a thank you for being so good with Sister Kristina."

"With incentives like that, I can be even better."

"Don't go getting too good with Sister Kris, Mister."

Of course, that's when Kris walked in. Kieley smiled in celebration of her excellent timing and sat down at the desk with her phone and the Reno yellow pages.

Kris watched her for a second, and then looked at me. "What did Kieley mean by that?"

"She made you an appointment with a colleague of Doctor Denton's for eleven o' clock. He's going to look into your problem. That means we'll be here for a few days more, so she's making us a reservation at the Hilton Homewood Suites."

Kris looked at me for a second. "Okay, don't tell me what she meant by that. I bet she was just making sure her new husband behaves himself."

"Why, how did you guess?"

"Because that's what I would do if you were my new husband."

"Go pack your bag, Sister Kris."

"Yes sir, Brother Kev."

It was 10:45 when we pulled into the parking lot at Renown Medical Center in downtown Reno. If their building was any indication, they were doing all right for themselves. Renown built a very modern twelve story building with lots of curves and angles. I kept looking at it, trying to decide if I liked the style. To my eye, the individual pieces of the design were interesting, but as a whole they didn't seem to work together. I finally decided it didn't really matter whether I liked it or not.

Doctor David Brewer was located in the physicians' office wing on the third floor. Figuring the doctor didn't need my help, I suggested Kieley go in with Kris while I waited out on a couch in the hall.

I'd been sitting there daydreaming for about twenty minutes

when my brain sent me an urgent message. The exact text of the message was: "Oh shit!" Then the rest of me felt the rolling motion of an earthquake and agreed wholeheartedly with my brain.

I stood with some help from the wall behind me and lurched across the hall to Doctor Brewer's office door. I got there all right, but it took a few moments for me to find a footing secure enough to push the door open.

For some reason I expected the doctor's office to be larger instead of a single small room. Kieley and Kris were sitting slightly to my right in front of the desk to my left. The wall beyond them was covered with a large bookcase and books were flying around like they had wings.

Holding onto the door-opening lever, I leaned into the room and yelled to Kieley who was closest to me. "Grab my hand! Kris, grab Kieley's other hand!"

It took Kris a second longer to understand than it did Kieley, but she grabbed onto Kieley and I pulled them toward me and the door. Then I saw the chain break as a large book flew from the bookcase and smacked Kris alongside her head.

Kieley turned to see what happened to Kris, but I jerked her into the doorway. "Kieley stay here in the doorway and hang onto the door knob. Don't let go! I'll get Kris!"

Picking up a small book that landed nearby, I opened it and jammed half of the book's thickness under the office door as a doorstop, making it a lot easier for Kieley stay in the relative safety of the doorframe. I took a quick look around to get an idea of what was going on in the office. I saw three things of note. First, Kris was on her hands and knees about three feet in front of me. I yelled, "Kris, crawl to Kieley, hurry!"

Seeing that she could make it on her own, I decided to deal with the second thing I saw. The movement of the quake had broken the floor-to-ceiling metal bookcase loose from whatever held it to the wall. It was teetering back and forth, and if it fell, the bookcase would land right on Kris and the third thing I saw, which was a middle-aged man in a white lab coat. He was still in his desk chair and staring at the teetering bookcase as if it were the eighth wonder of the world.

Using the chairs Kieley and Kris were sitting in seconds earlier for some added support, I got to the bookcase before it toppled and leaned into the thing to help keep it upright. I yelled, "Doctor, get to the doorway." he looked at me, but didn't seem to understand what I was saying.

Still trying to keep the bookcase vertical, I gestured toward the doorway with my head and yelled, "Go to the door. Now! Move, damn it!"

The last thing I saw before the bookcase won the battle in which we were engaged was the doctor working his way along the wall opposite me toward the doorway. Then half the medical knowledge in the western world landed on me.

The next thing of which I became aware was the ugly green and brown hallway carpet. I was lying face down on it. I evaluated other observations as they occurred to me.

The shaking stopped—a good thing. My head hurt like hell and there was what seemed like quite a bit blood around me on the ugly carpet—bad things. Kieley was holding my hand and saying something about hanging on—sort of a good thing.

Doctor . . . whatever-the-hell-his-name-was seemed to be busy wrapping gauze around my head, which could have been either good or bad depending . . . depending on something I couldn't recall at that particular moment.

Next I noticed there seemed to be a lot of people in the hallway. One of them was Kris. She was much more vertical than the last time I'd seen her, and she also had gauze wrapped around her noggin. Maybe it was the latest fashion.

Doctor what's-his-name said, "That will stop the bleeding for now. Let's get out of this building. There will be more compete first-aid available down on the street."

Kieley said, "Come on, Kev. I'll help you up."

I'd gotten as far as my knees when the doctor guy offered me his hand. That was good, because as weak as I felt, I couldn't give Kieley much help in getting me completely vertical.

Then we joined a crowd in the stairwell. Doctor whose-it had his black doctor bag in one hand and was guiding Kristina down the stairs with the other hand while Kieley made sure I was making it all right. Another small shaker hit between the third and second floors, but fortunately it stopped before the people in the stairwell panicked and trampled each other to death.

I can honestly say I was never so happy to see daylight as I was when we stepped out of the lobby and onto the sidewalk. I got my bearings, and remembering where we parked the Jeep, I said, "Kieley grab Kris's hand and let's get to the Jeep. Being around this crowd is dangerous."

Fortunately, we were forced to park far enough from the building that falling debris landed short of the Jeep. I unlocked the doors and we helped Kris into the back seat.

I looked at her. She had a pretty good-sized lump on the side of her head, but otherwise, she seemed to be doing at least as well as I was, maybe better. I said, "How are you feeling?"

"I'm fine. Kieley and I want to know how you are!"

Kieley was looking closely at my head where the bleeding had been. "Yes. I was sure you were dead when that bookcase landed on you."

Kris said, "We were trying to pull you out from under it when a hospital security guy came along and helped us get you out."

Kieley eyes flashed anger as she said, "Yes. That doctor is the most worthless person in an emergency I've ever seen. And you saved his life for crying out loud. We asked him to help get you out, but he was still hanging on to the doorframe for dear life."

Kris added, "And that was after the quake finally stopped."

Looking back toward the hospital, I said, "Speak of the devil, here comes doctor worthless now."

He yelled, "Why did you run off? I want to take a closer look at that head wound."

"All right, look."

He gave me an odd expression, set his doctor bag on the ground, and carefully lifted the gauze he'd wrapped around my head out of the way a little so he could see the wound clearly. He said, "Good. The bleeding has stopped. We probably ought to clean the wound and apply some antiseptic. Is that okay with you?"

"Can you do it here?"

"Sure, but why not over there where the paramedics and supplies are?"

"Because there are going to be more aftershocks and around people is the last place we want to be when the shaking starts again."

He looked a little pale. "Oh. Okay, I've got cotton swabs, antibiotic, and more gauze. If you'll sit facing out in the driver's seat, I'll get you fixed up."

I sat. He pulled on a pair of purple gloves went to work. I noticed Kris, and especially Kieley, watched him like a hawk. I think if I'd said ouch they both would have brained him.

The doctor asked me a few questions as he worked. "Are you having any dizziness or lightheadedness?"

"I'm a little lightheaded, but that is to be expected, isn't it?"

"Yes. Your pupils look equal, but you still might have a slight concussion." He held up the index finger of his left hand. "Can you follow my finger with your eyes?"

He moved his finger from left to right and back a couple of times. I successfully followed it with my eyes. He stopped moving his index finger and held up three fingers. "How many fingers do you see?"

"Three."

"Well, you really should have a CT scan to check for physical damage to your brain, but you seem to be all right. If you experience any of the problems I mentioned, see a doctor pronto."

He finished wrapping the gauze and appeared to be admiring his work as he said, "Now I need you to come back with me so they can fill out the paperwork for your treatment."

"So they can bill me?"

Doctor jerk said, "Well, most insurances cover emergency . . . ."

Looking as fierce as I ever saw her, Kieley interrupted him. "Look, asshole, this man saved your lousy life while you were frozen with fear back there in your office. Do you have some forms to fill out so he can bill you for that emergency treatment?"

Kris added, "Yeah, and even though you're a coward, your life is still probably worth a little more than a dribble of Neosporin and some gauze."

"Listen, you can't . . . . "

I think he was about to say something inane, like she couldn't talk to him that way, but he thought better of it and walked away.

Kieley wasn't done with him yet. "Hey, doctor asshole, aren't you even going to thank the man for saving your sorry life?"

He stopped and looked back over his shoulder at us. "Thanks for saving my sorry life."

I was about to say something clever like "Think nothing of it," but another aftershock hit at that precise moment and Doctor Brewer landed on his butt in the middle of the parking lot. I was pleased because I remembered his name. That had to mean I was doing better.

I looked at the other two members of our little family. "Damn! Remind me to stay on your good sides. That was a conversation Doctor Brewer will not soon forget."

Kieley and Kris grinned, sharing an enthusiastic high-five. My wife said, "Nice going, Girlfriend!"

I said, "Okay, now let's concentrate on getting someplace safe and figuring out what to do next."

Coming into the hospital parking lot, I noticed a small park across Mill Street on a narrow triangle of land created by nonparallel streets. We piled into the Jeep and I pulled across the street and into the little park. Not surprisingly it was pretty much deserted.

We got out of the Jeep and sat at a picnic table next to the parking area. Kris said, "Well, that was certainly a lot of fun!"

I felt bad about forcing her to see the doctor in the first place. "Kris, I'm really sorry. Our intention was to help, not put you through more stress."

Then Kieley said something strange. "You know, maybe we did help, after all." Turning to Kris, she said, "How are you feeling?"

"I'm fine. Why?"

"Because you just went through a pretty heavy earthquake and a lot of chaos, but you're as calm and collected as if nothing happened."

Kris gave that a few seconds' thought. "You're right. I wonder what the difference is?"

Kieley said, "I think I know. This time you were focused on Kev just like I was. Remember, we were really worried that he was badly hurt?"

"Yes! You're right. I didn't think about myself until later, after we knew he was going to be okay and we were all safe."

"Swell! I'll make sure a ton of bricks lands on my head every time there's a crisis so you . . . ."

Kieley said, "Kev, be nice. This is important. Now that we have a clue, how do we use it?"

Trying to be helpful, I said, "It sounds as if the anticipation of what could happen is worse than the actual event. But what set off the episode this morning?"

Kieley said, "Stress from anticipating something bad. Kris, you were worried about us and delaying our trip to Eureka, right?"

Kris nodded. "Yes. That is exactly what was upsetting me. I remember what I was thinking when it started. I was thinking I made Kevin mad at me by being foolish. You guys are my family. The last thing I want to do is hurt either of you or make you mad at me."

Kieley said, "Kris, I think I'm beginning to understand this. Think back to that Saturday we met you in the city."

"Oh, I remember that day very well."

"What do you remember about it specifically. What is the most vivid image of that day in your memory?"

"That's easy. I remember watching you guys drive away after we finished packing your stuff. I've never felt so completely alone in the world as I did then . . . alone and terrified. I hadn't heard from my brother or Bailey. It was like you two were my only friends in the whole world and suddenly you were gone.

"And then you called and said you were coming back for me. I felt . . . I actually felt the fear leave me. I was going to be safe with Kieley and Kevin!"

Kieley summed the situation up. "So next to being hurt in an earthquake, your greatest fear is being alone in the midst of all the chaos, isn't it?"

The tears were back in Kris's eyes. "Yes. I know it's selfish, but I think I fear losing you two even more than the earthquakes."

Kieley looked at me across the table. She was sending me a mental message. Hoping I'd gotten her message right, I said, "You know, we've been calling you 'Sister Kristina,' but that's more than a joke. People don't necessarily have to have the same birth parents to feel true kinship. In fact, I think people who aren't biologically related are sometimes closer than those who are. What I'm trying to say is Kieley loves you, and so do I. We will never leave you behind again. Ever."

Kieley opened her arms and Kris almost fell into them. Kris said, "Thank you . . . both of you. I know having me along isn't easy, but maybe we can fix that."

I said, "Now that doctor Kieley Freud has us on the right track, I'm pretty sure we can. Next, I'm going to fix something else. I'm hungry."

I reached into the brown paper bag I brought from the Jeep and pulled out the box of Brown Sugar Cinnamon Pop-Tarts Kieley bought for me in Hawthorne. As I opened the package, I noticed I was the center of attention.

Ripping open one of the stay-fresh foil packets inside the box I said, "Would either of you care for a Pop-Tart?"

Kris looked at Kieley. Kieley said, "You know, Kev, I don't believe I've ever had one."

"You are missing one of life's great pleasures. Here."

Kieley slid a Pop-Tart out of the packet and looked at it. Then she broke the pastry into two pieces and handed half to Kris. Kris stared at the Pop-Tart like it was something from another planet. "Aren't you supposed to toast these things?"

I said, "That's what Kellogg's tries to tell us, but they don't know what they're talking about." I took a bite out of the Pop-Tart in my hand, and held it up. "This is how to eat one of these."

Kieley cautiously bit into the half Pop-Tart she held. After a moment, she said, "This really isn't bad." Turning the box around so she could see the nutritional information panel, she added, "It has an awful lot of calories and not much nutrition, but as a sweet treat, it's pretty good."

Gaining her courage from Kieley, Kris tried a bite of hers. "Yes, it is tasty. Are the other flavors this good?"

"I've tried a couple of flavors, but I stick with the brown sugar cinnamon. The others taste too sweet. I think of Pop-Tarts as the ultimate road trip food. They're easy to eat on the road without making a mess, and they're guaranteed to stay fresh for two hundred years."

Kieley raised an eyebrow at me. "Two hundred years? Are you sure about that, Kev?"

"Well, maybe not quite that long, but I'll bet they'll outlast a Twinkie."

SIXTEEN

Saturday, August 27, 2022, 1:30 P.M.
Pickett Park, Reno, Nevada

As another aftershock shook our picnic table, Kieley reached across the table and grabbed my hand, but I was watching Kris's reaction. She was holding onto the edge of our table, but her expression just showed surprise, not panic.

I said, "You know, I could get tired of all this shaking. After a while it gets on a person's nerves."

Kieley agreed. "That's for sure."

Kris suddenly grinned and I said, "What are you smiling about?"

"I was remembering Doctor Doofus landing on his butt in the parking lot. That picture pops into my mind every time we have another little shake."

Kieley laughed. "Maybe Doctor Brewer accomplished something worthwhile after all. Speaking of doctors and such, what do we do now?"

I looked from her to Kris and back to Kieley, who said, "I'm damned if I know. Any suggestions?"

Kris said, "Maybe we should forget about doctors for now and get on with our trip. I have a lot more confidence in my ability to control what's happening to me."

Kieley looked at Kris. "And you're doing a good job of it, too. I think that aftershock a minute ago scared me more than it did you. The thing we have to keep in mind is what Doctor Denton said about there being something physical underlying the emotional problem.

"The thing we figured out a few minutes ago might be what triggers your episodes, and that's a big step in the right direction. The concern is we still don't know what is actually happening during your physical reactions."

Kris nodded. "Yes, I know that, but Doctor Denton also said it could take a long time to figure out what the physical problem is. Do we really want to spend all that time here, and do we want anything more to do with Doctor Doofus?"

I threw my two-cents' worth in. "I know I sound like a chiggered up CD repeating myself, but it seems to me we need more information before we can decide what we want to do and where we want to do it. What concerns me most right now is the strength of the quake that hit while we were in the hospital."

Kieley frowned. "I didn't think it was as strong as some of the others we've had."

"That's true, but remember where we are." Pointing toward the mountain tops we could see to the west, I explained, "Assuming that quake was on the Fortuna Fault like all the others, there is now a massive mountain range between the fault and where we are. For us to feel the quake that strongly here, it must have been an incredibly strong on the other side of those mountains."

Kieley picked up my train of thought. "So there might be a lot of new damage in California—new damage that could keep us from getting to Eureka."

"Yes. In fact, I suppose it is possible Eureka isn't even there anymore."

Kris asked the big question. "So how do we get the information about what's happening on the other side of those mountains?"

I said, "We had a plan before we saw Doctor . . . What did you call him, Kris?"

Kris grinned. "Doctor Doofus."

"Right. We had a plan before we saw Doctor Doofus, and even though we probably have no intention of seeing him again, I suggest we go ahead and check into the Homewood Suites, assuming they're still in business after that last shaker. We can use the place as home base for a day or two while we do some research to find out what awaits us on the other side of those mountains.

Kieley agreed. "That makes the most sense to me. We don't need to go charging off into the unknown without some idea of what we're getting into."

Kris said, "It's okay with me."

Grabbing the leftover Pop-Tarts, I followed Kris and Kieley to the Jeep. After keying the Homewood Suites' address into our GPS, Kieley studied the display for a moment and said, "It's south of here, down past the airport. The total distance is only four-point-eight miles down I-580, but traffic conditions on the freeway are red. It looks like our best bet is to turn south off of Mill onto Kietzke Lane. It goes directly to the hotel."

"Got it. Are you buckled in back there, Sister Kris?"

"Yes, sir. Ready for takeoff."

As we inched our way along the frontage road that parallels the freeway, Kieley was looking intently at the Reno Tahoe International Airport on the other side of the freeway. I was wondering what she found so interesting about the place, when she said, "That's not the airport where they have the Reno Air Races, is it?"

I said, "I don't think so. They have them out at an old Air Force Base north of town. This one is their big passenger airport. Why the interest in the air races?"

"Because I was there two years ago doing a layout for some men's magazine. The things I remember most were the noise and the guys who race the planes. They are all absolutely crazy and horny as hell. Airport security had to rescue me from them a couple of times."

"Now don't you miss modeling?"

I sensed Kieley looking at me. "Not one iota, whatever an iota is."

From the backseat, Kris weighed in on the subject. "I'm with you on that, Kieley. I did a shoot at an airshow once. It was someplace down by San Jose and it was just like you said. I envied women in the old days who kept their hats in place with six-inch pins. At least they had a weapon to defend themselves."

It was about three o'clock when we finally arrived at the Homewood Suites, a rather bland looking tan stucco building bordered on the east by light industry and on the west and south by upscale housing developments with names like South Meadows, Mountain Gate, and Golden Hills. We could see some light damage here and there, but the hotel looked all right.

Inside, the two women behind the registration desk were talking about was how terrible the quake was. I restrained myself from telling them they didn't know the meaning of terrible.

As we slogged through the registration chores with a sluggish computer, the gals behind the counter suddenly found something new to talk about. One nudged the other and gestured to the front windows. They both stared for a long moment, so I turned to see what was holding their attention.

They were staring at Kieley and Kris. Now, both of the women behind the counter were attractive enough to be noticed in a crowd, but they were in awe of my wife and Kristina. It often works like that. It seems pretty women always notice other pretty women, but these two were so distracted I had to ask for my credit card, which was still in their card reader.

Kieley and Kris met me outside the entrance and I made a show of putting an arm around each of them as we walked to the Jeep. In doing so, I provided the two gals behind the counter with enough scandalous excitement to keep them distracted all afternoon.

In our suite, I told Kieley and Kris about the incident. Kris seemed fascinated, but Kieley wasn't impressed, or at least she didn't let on if she was. Personally, I thought it was pretty impressive that just making an appearance was enough for them to bump a major earthquake from the top topic of discussion.

Our suite consisted of three main rooms, a central "living room" with a bedroom on each side. The bedrooms each had a bathroom, and the living room featured a kitchenette alcove. The layout seemed efficient and actually quite cozy for a hotel. Kieley and I grabbed the bedroom with a king bed, leaving Kris with two queen beds.

We stashed our bags and gathered in the living room. Kieley fiddled with the flat screen remote trying to find us some news of the latest shaker and got nothing. After the same result from each of the bedroom sets, she called the front desk.

"We have three TVs in this suite and none of them are working. Is your satellite system down or am I doing something wrong?"

After listening for a moment, she said, "I see. Any idea when your system will be back up?"

She concluded the conversation by saying, "Okay, thank you."

Dropping the hotel's wireless telephone handset back on its charging cradle, she said, "Satellite system is down. They have a repair call in, but there is no guarantee when the system will be back up."

Nodding, I said, "I bet the quake knocked their dish off-axis. It's an easy fix for a tech with the right gizmo, but I bet every dish in town is out of whack. Let's fire up my laptop and latch onto our own satellite."

I set my laptop on the living room coffee table and when it finished booting up, I turned the keyboard over to Kieley. It was already clear to me that her skill with electronic devices was an added bonus I hadn't really figured on before we were married.

The word "married" lit up in my brain like a neon sign. Kieley and I were really married. When did that happen? Yesterday? Yes, yesterday. It seemed like weeks ago. Apparently time flies when you are not having fun, too.

My little trip down memory lane was interrupted when I heard Kieley say, "Eureka!"

I asked, "Exclamation or location?"

Kris said, "Both! Come see what Kieley found."

Kieley was sitting in the middle of the couch where she could reach the laptop. Kris was sitting on Kieley's left side, so I flopped down on her right side.

Kieley said, "It's the CalTrans website you were talking about the other day. I asked it for conditions on US Highway Three-Ninety-Five in California and it gave them to me. It says this information was current as of two hours ago. That was just before the last quake. I'm hoping they update conditions soon, but we'll have to wait and see."

I said, "Nice work, Kieley. How about opening a new tab and looking for a cable news headline webpage?"

"I was just going to do that, but I wanted you to see the CalTrans page."

Feeling as though I just told Emeril Lagasse how to fry green tomatoes, I said, "Sorry. I'll try to be more patient."

Kieley said, "Oh, hush. When I need an apology from you, Mister, I'll let you know."

Kris giggled, and I said, "Just so you know, I saved a Google map of our route to Eureka the other day. It's in the 'Other' bookmarks category and the file name is 'LasVegas_to_Eureka'."

"Good, I'll load it into a third tab so we can refer to it for the highway numbers."

Soon Kieley found a live streaming report from Las Vegas on the Headline One Network website. They were showing Las Vegas Boulevard and much of it was in shambles. One view showed the replica Statue of Liberty at the New York-New York Hotel and Casino. It was tipped at an angle and was buried to its hips in rubble. A scene from PLANET OF THE APES popped into my mind. The rest of the report showed many more pictures that were just as disturbing.

A view of Valley Medical Center popped on the screen during the Las Vegas report. Watching intently, Kris said, "That's the hospital where I was, isn't it? I hope Doctor Denton got out before the earthquake came."

Next came a video shot over San Francisco after EQ-5, the buzzword-name reporters were using for keeping track of the quakes. At least the woman doing the voiceover claimed the vast area of devastation was San Francisco, but you couldn't prove it by me. She was explaining that none of the five bridges spanning San Francisco Bay were serviceable. As she said that, a view of a single Golden Gate Bridge tower thrusting up out of the water at an odd angle flashed on the screen. According to experts the reporter quoted, the size of the bay was reduced by one-third just due to the rubble thrown into it by the quake.

The next H-O-N feature story showed an animated map of Los Angeles County that moved the coastline nearly seven miles east, past Santa Monica to Interstate-110, roughly between Inglewood and Compton. While no accurate death toll was available yet, estimates for LA County were at the two-and-a-half million mark. Estimates for the entire state amounted to nearly ten percent of the California's former population of almost forty-million.

Aerial footage of Anaheim popped on the screen, clearly showing only one spire of Disneyland's Cinderella Castle still standing. The Matterhorn was nowhere to be seen.

H-O-N's blonde talking head filled the screen next, saying, "Another area especially hard hit was California's north coast. The small towns of Eureka and Arcata are now on the list of communities obliterated by the California earthquake storms."

On hearing about Eureka, my first thought was Old Man Fate did it to us again. Our future home was gone before we could even get there. Suddenly Kieley closed the laptop. I looked at her and she fell into my arms. "God, it's awful!"

I held her and Kris put a comforting hand on Kieley's shoulder. I said, "Let's call it quits for a while. I'll see if I can scrounge up some coffee. There's a Keurig coffee maker and some K cups in the kitchen.

Kris jumped up. "I'll go."

"Thanks, Kris."

Kieley leaned back on the couch. "I don't mean to be such a baby about all this, Kevin, but it's so overwhelming. What started out for us ten days ago with you saving me from a bucking bridge has turned into a monster devouring millions of people!"

"That pretty well describes it, and you're right, it is hard to imagine anything that destructive."

In a sad soft voice, she said, "I guess we have to find another new home town."

"Yes, I guess we do, but there is one bright side to all this bad news. At least we weren't already in Eureka when the quake hit it. It seems like we got out of Las Vegas just in time, too."

"I know, Kev. I'm just getting tired of being at the whim of Mother Nature. It's like she's following us around just to mess things up."

"Or maybe she's trying to point us in a different direction. We've had one close call after another. I think if Fate or Mother Nature or whoever is running things wanted us dead, we'd be long dead by now, but we aren't and that tells me something else is going on here as all of this applies to us."

Kieley looked at me with a little smile tugging at the corners of her mouth. "That's another thing I love about you, Kev. The world is falling down around us and you can still find a bright spot in it all the tragedy."

Kristina arrived with a tray. "Here we go. Kieley, the cup on the napkin is decaf. Kev, you get the regular in the cup closest to you, and the third cup is hot cocoa, which is for yours truly. Did I get it all right?"

I laughed. "Don't worry, I'll see you get a big tip for excellent service."

Sitting on the edge of the coffee table so she could face us, Kris said, "The only tip I need is a place where we can go in this world that won't fall down on top of us."

Kieley said, "Kev has a theory about that. He thinks God is trying to point us in a different direction than the ones we've picked. Tell her what you said about us surviving all these close calls, Darling."

I shook my head slightly. "I'm probably way off on this, but I just have the feeling if Mother Nature or Fate or whatever wanted us dead, we'd be dead by now. We just haven't picked the right place for us yet."

Kris nodded slowly. "Okay, if that's what is happening, where do we go from here?"

Shrugging, I said, "We go with the flow, and before you ask, I have no idea which direction that might be. Right now, I think our best bet is to relax a little and think things through. Answers will come to us. I don't know if they'll be the right answers, but short of just giving up, that's our only choice."

Kieley looked at Kristina. "What do you think about that, Kris?"

Kris grinned at her. "Don't ask me! I'm the nutcase, remember?"

"Kris you are no more a nutcase than Kev or me. I'm serious, what do you think?"

Kristina thought about her answer for several seconds, and

then she said, "I think . . . I think we do what Kevin said; we think it all through again and come up with a new direction and see what happens."

Kieley looked at me. "I vote with Kris. Kev, we go with your theory. Now, while we're relaxing, I want to take a look under that gauze you two are wearing."

As we drank our coffee, Kieley examined the wounds Kris and I sustained at the hospital during "EQ-5." Her diagnoses was Kris could throw her gauze away in the morning, but I needed to wear mine a little longer to protect.

Kieley asked me if the cut was painful. I said, "Not really. One more hole in the head doesn't amount to much in my case."

She kissed my cheek and said, "I happen to like your head just the way it was, without any extra holes."

Kristina changed the subject on us. "I think that Pop-Tart thing is making me hungry. Anybody else ready for dinner?"

Kieley said, "I could eat something, but I'm too lazy to go out looking for it."

I said, "There's an advertising sheet over there on the table from some outfit called 'Grub-Getter'. They deliver from restaurants in the area."

Kris brought the card back to the couch and read off Grub-Getter's list of eateries. We agreed Chinese sounded good, but P. F. Chang's was closed because of quake damage, so we had to settle for Panda Express.

While we were waiting for our food, Kieley said, "Anybody mind if I take a shower?"

Kris said, "Not at all. In fact, take one for me while you're at it."

Kieley stuck her tongue out at Kris, and then winked at me. After Kieley left the room, I moved my laptop to the desk in our bedroom and plugged it in to catch up on its charge. That done, I closed the open tabs and disconnected from my satellite connection. Before closing the Caltrans tab, though, I reloaded it and saw the page had not updated. I had a bad feeling there might not be anyone left to update it.

My computer chores done, I wandered into the bathroom. Speaking loudly to be heard over the shower, I said, "You need any help in there?"

The shower stopped a moment later and the glass shower door slid slowly open to reveal a dripping Kieley. Her bright blue eyes looked at me through the steam, and my eyes were immediately drawn to her small firm breasts and flat belly. My reaction was instantaneous and I knew she sensed it. Kieley didn't say a single word. She didn't have to. Her message was clear: We would be a little late for dinner.

SEVENTEEN

The way things turned out, Kieley and I were also a little late for the Homewood Suites breakfast buffet. Kris already had a table for us when we finally got there. "My goodness, don't you two look happy! Reno must really agree with you guys."

Kieley looped her arm through mine and leaned against me. "Girlfriend, I assure you it is not Reno making me smile like this."

Kris gushed, "I so happy for the two of you, I could bust. Kieley, you have to know I'm jealous. I only hope I can find someone who makes me smile the way you're smiling right now."

I said, "You will, but looking for that guy is a waste of time and can get you into trouble. Fate will bring you together. All you have to do is keep the door open. Like when I called Kieley from Eureka to offer her a job, I had no idea we would be married less than two weeks later. The only thing I knew when I made that call was I had loved Kieley for a long time, but that time hadn't been the right time for us."

Kieley said, "And when my cell phone rang that morning and I saw it was Kev, my heart nearly stopped. If you remember, Kris, you and I were both pretty low then, but seeing Kev's name in the caller ID made me happier than I'd been in months. I think that's when I began to realize I never stopped loving him."

"You guys! It's like a fairy tale. I can't wait for your 'official' wedding so I can cry my eyes out for both of you."

Kieley smiled. "I wouldn't be surprised if I do a little crying, too."

I smiled. "Dang! My Kimberly-Clark stock will go through the roof!"

Kris said, "Of course, the big question is still where are we going to cry all those happy tears of joy? Anybody have any great ideas this morning?"

I answered her question with a question. "Well, there are lots of possibilities, but are any of them places we want to live?'

Kris threw the conversation right back into my lap. "It might help if we knew what some of those possibilities are."

"Pick a compass direction."

Kieley joined in. "Ah, how about north?"

"We might be safe in eastern Oregon or Washington, but that's pretty barren country. Idaho is greener, but that's a long way from anywhere any of us have ever called home.

Kris asked, "Anything to the east of Reno?"

"Just more of what we saw coming up from Las Vegas; desert, rocks, and mountains covered with more rocks. There is an entire country beyond that, but again, I'm not sure any of us would be happy so far from where we grew up."

Looking a little sad, Kris said, "The thing I miss most about San Francisco is the water . . . the bay and the ocean."

A thought occurred to me. "Kris, would you settle for a great big lake instead of an entire ocean? I mean a huge lake surrounded by trees and mountains."

Kieley said, "That sure sounds good to me."

I was liking my idea even better now. "It so happens we have exactly that less than fifty miles from where we're sitting."

Kris looked puzzled. "Where?"

I could tell from her expression Kieley knew where I was thinking about. She removed all doubt by saying, "Lake Tahoe."

Kris knew about Lake Tahoe, too. "Yes! We've been there. Remember, Kieley? We spent a weekend at that casino with Bailey and that guy . . . ."

Kris stopped mid-sentence and suddenly looked like someone who just let a very large cat out of the bag. Kieley smiled at her. "It's okay, Kris. Kev knows I didn't join a convent while we were apart."

Kris quietly said, "I'm sorry."

Kieley said, "Do you have a particular area of the lake in mind, Kev?"

"Again, we don't know how badly the area was effected by the quakes, but all things being equal, I've always liked the north end of the lake, like around Crystal Bay and Incline. It's quieter and hasn't been all built up with a casino or a motel on every corner. What do you think?"

"That would be nice, although remember, there's snow up there in the winter. Kris?"

"Are you guys sure you want me and my big mouth living in the same house with you?"

I said, "No. Actually, I was going to get a place with a doghouse in the backyard for you."

Kieley quickly said, "Kev, you don't mean that! Come on, Kris, snap out of your funk. Everything is okay."

Kris looked across the table at me for confirmation I didn't mean what I said. "Of course I was kidding, Kris. Sometimes when you say something as silly as what you just said, I assume you're kidding, too. So next time you make a silly comment, be kidding and save all this fuss."

Still looking a little glum, Kris said, "Okay, Brother Kev."

Kieley said, "Okay, how do we go about finding out if Lake Tahoe is a place for us to settle?"

She already knew the answer to that. Sometimes I think Kieley makes a point of making me look smarter than her. That's a sure sign of someone with a lot of love and a lot of confidence.

I said, "We could go online and find a realtor at North Shore we can call. If anybody knows what's going on up there it would be somebody in the real estate business."

Kieley said, "Okay, as soon as I change the dressing on your head, I'll go online and find a Lake Tahoe real estate agent who is open for business on Sundays."

As we left breakfast, I got the idea Kris was still a little glum. I put my arm around her. "Kris, despite how the world around us looks lately, this is a good time in our lives. Yours, too. We want you to enjoy it with us."

"I'll try. It's just that you guys are being so special to me and I'm afraid I'll do something dumb and mess things up just like I almost did."

Kieley was walking on Kris's other side. "Kris, honestly, there is nothing you can do to mess things up for Kev and me. Nothing."

As we passed through the lobby, Kris looked out the front doors and said, "I feel like stretching my legs a little. Would it be okay if I took a walk around the hotel while you guys look for a real estate company?"

Kieley looked at me and I shrugged. I didn't like Kris being too far out of sight. She was going through an emotional time, and emotions were what triggered her heart problems. On the other hand, she needed her space, too.

Finally Kieley answered her. "Sure, take a walk. Do you have your cell phone?"

"Yes. I'll even turn it on."

"Good. If you're not back and we decide to go somewhere, I'll call you."

Back in our bedroom, I powered up the laptop. While it was booting, Kieley rewrapped the head wound I acquired saving Doctor Doofus from his own damned bookcase. While she was wrapping and taping, I got the definite impression something was on her mind. I said, "Okay, Missus Turner, what's goin' on in your head?"

She looked at me for a long moment. "Kev, are you still okay with me having dated other guys while we were apart. There were only a couple and . . . ."

"Kieley, I'm fine with it. I dated too, you know."

"I know, I just . . . ."

"You just what?"

"I don't know." after a pause, she said, "Yes, I do know. Listen, Kev, I dated three guys for short periods of time while you and I were apart. We fooled around a little and I slept with two of them, once each."

"Kieley, you don't have to tell me all . . . ."

"Yes I do. I need you to know some things."

I closed my mouth, thinking the details of her sexual adventures with other guys were the last things I wanted to hear. It turned out, though, she wanted me to hear something else.

"The part you need to know is each of those two times I . . . I was with one of them, I felt bad. Somewhere in the back of my mind I felt like was cheating on you. I know that sounds silly, but I'm sure they sensed it, too. They walked away thinking I was little Miss Frigidaire with a cute butt.

"And in case you're wondering, this all happened before I was raped. The rape had nothing to do with my lack of enthusiasm in bed at that time. After I was . . . assaulted, though, I decided I had bigger problems than whether or not some guy was interested in me."

I started to speak, but Kieley interrupted me again. "Just one more thing. Do you remember that night in the airport Holiday Inn, our first night back together?"

I smiled at the memory floating through my mind. "I'm not likely to forget that night in this lifetime."

Nodding, Kieley said, "Me, neither. That's because I learned an important lesson that night. I learned the only kind of sex worth having is about love. When I got off that plane, my interest in sex was down to less than zero, but the minute I saw you, I immediately wanted you emotionally and physically. I wanted to be close to you in every way a woman can be close to a man, and I wanted that because I suddenly realized I still loved you and I would always love you."

When I didn't say anything after several seconds, Kieley's voice filled with emotion. "For cryin' out loud, Kev! I just poured my heart out and told you about some of the most painful moments in my entire life. At least say SOMETHING!"

"Okay. I just wanted to make sure you were through telling me stuff."

Kieley glared at me. "I'm through, damn it!"

"All I've got to say is I thought you were going to tell me something I didn't already know." I paused for a second, and then added, "Well, the part about the refrigerator with a sexy ass was kind of interesting."

In a tone dripping with exasperation, she said, "Kevin!" Then she suddenly put on a sly smile. "Actually, I do have one more small confession."

"Let me guess. You and Kris have been lovers."

Kieley looked totally surprised. "What on earth makes you think that?"

"You are too close for just roommates. You share the kind of closeness only lovers share."

"All right, suppose Kris and I did make love. Does that change your opinion of me?"

"Only to the extent it tells me you have excellent taste in women." After a moment, I said, "Did you?"

Kieley grinned. "Did I what? Make it with Kris?"

"Yeah."

Her grin turned evil. "Oh, maybe a dozen times. Why? Do you want to play too if we ever do it again?"

"Even though the idea has considerable appeal, I can honestly say no."

Kieley looked genuinely surprised. "Why for heaven sake? I can't imagine any man turning Kris away. She's beautiful!"

"Yes, she is, but that has nothing to do with it."

Kieley gave me her cocked-head puzzled look. "Then why?"

"Because I'm pretty sure you would not like sharing me."

Kieley looked thoughtful for a moment, and then said, "I just stereotyped you, didn't I?"

"Sort of, but that's okay."

"No, it isn't. I was so astonished hearing a straight guy say he didn't want Kris, I lost track of who you are. I forgot for a few seconds you aren't like any other man I ever met. You . . . you love with your heart and your mind, not just with your . . . well, you know.

"And now that my mind is straight on all that again, I definitely do not want to share you with any other woman, even Kris." A tear started down her cheek. "You are my man, and I know seeing you making love to another woman, even with Kris, would hurt. It really would."

"It might seem strange thing to say, but it makes me feel good to hear that."

Kieley leaned into me and wrapped her arms around me. "Please be patient with me, Kevin. I'm still learning how to love you."

"Just like I'm still learning all the little nuances involved in loving you the way you need to be loved. All those things might take a lifetime to learn."

Kieley looked up at me with moist blue eyes. "Yes, but what a wonderful way to spend a lifetime."

She was back at the laptop and just starting to scroll through North Shore realtor listings in Firefox when Kris joined us. She took one look at Kieley, and then looked at me. Finally, looking back at Kieley, Kris said, "You look like you've been crying. Are you okay?"

Kieley gave her eyes a wipe, sniffed, and said, "Yes, I've been crying. And yes I'm okay. In fact, I'm wonderful. Kev and I just had something amazing happen to us."

Kris looked at me again. When I didn't say anything, Kris said, "Kieley, you have to tell me what amazing thing happened."

"What happened is something I thought was impossible. The more we learn about each other, the more in love we seem to be. I could not have imagined loving Kevin more, but I really do."

Kris turned from Kieley to me again. She was still confused, but it wasn't something Kieley or I could explain to her. With luck she would learn it on her own someday.

Wiping a tear from her cheek and looking back at the monitor, Kieley said, "How does North Shore Real Estate and Property Management sound? They have a nice website, and it says they're open on Sundays."

"Give them a call."

"What do you want me to ask them?"

"Two questions: First, how much damage did the area sustain from the quakes? If they did okay, ask about homes for sale in the Crystal Bay and Incline areas. If she has some, find out if we can come up this afternoon and take a look."

Kieley keyed a number into her cell and Kristina stared at me. I stood up and gestured for Kris to follow me into the bedroom, where I said, "Something is puzzling you. What is it?"

"I . . . you two really don't have any secrets from each other, do you?"

"If we do, they are unintentional. Why?"

"Then . . . Then you know about Kieley and me . . . I mean about . . . the relationship we had before."

I was surprised Kris came up with that particular thought. Either she and Kieley had some sort of nonverbal communication going on, or that part of her relationship was already on her mind for some reason. "If you mean that you and she were lovers, yes. What about it?"

Looking a little astonished, Kris said, "And you don't care?"

"Of course, I care. Kieley and you are the two most important people in my life, but the part I care about is you two finding a way to help each other through what must have been some really tough times, especially for Kieley."

Kris nodded. "Yes, they were tough times. I don't know if I would have survived those times if it wasn't for Kieley."

"Are you afraid you've lost her now?"

Her answer was vehement. "No! Kieley and I will always . . . ." Kristina paused as if trying to decide how to end her sentence.

I offered a suggestion. "Have a special loving relationship?"

"Yes." Kris stared at me for a minute, and then said, "You understand that, don't you? You really do."

I shook my head. "I can't feel what the two of you feel, but I can certainly feel the love in the way you treat each other."

Kris took one step toward me, and then another, and then she ran into my arms. I held her for several moments, and when I looked up and saw Kieley in the doorway. I continued holding Kris and said to Kieley, "You heard?"

Kieley nodded and joined our hug. What we were doing was reassuring Kris she really was a member of our family.

Turning back to the matter at hand, Kieley told us she received positive answers to her questions and made an appointment for us to meet an agent named Tracy Bingaman at two. Considering it likely we would need to spend a few days looking at homes if we liked the area, I suggested we check out of the Homewood Suites and make a reservation in Crystal Bay or somewhere nearby. With her usual efficiency, Kieley got us a reservation for the Tahoe Regency Hotel at Crystal Bay.

By eleven we were checked out of the Homewood Suites and

on the road again. Our route took us south and east on Interstate-80 to Truckee, and then southeast to the community of Crystal Bay. In all, the trip was only forty-some miles, but took us about ninety minutes, mostly due to detours around damaged sections of I-80.

Rolling along the lakefront, however, I saw very little quake damage. The Nevada side of North Shore looked just about like it did in photos made back when Frank Sinatra owned a piece of the Cal-Neva Lodge and Casino. I wondered if Sam Giancana's ghost still haunted the casino.

It was only around twelve-forty when we arrived at the Tahoe Regency Hotel, so we decided to check in and grab a bite of lunch. Kieley and Kris went into the coffee shop to find us a table, and I went to the desk and checked into our suite.

My companions completed their scrutiny of the menu and ordered something called the Buffalo Bomb salad and I asked for a Club House sandwich on white. Different sandwiches require a specific bread to be done right, like a Reuben goes on marbled rye. A club sandwich is not a club sandwich unless it's on white bread or white bread toast.

We were just starting on our lunch when a cell phone began playing *I Just Called to Say I Love You*. The tune told me the ringing cell phone belonged to Kris.

With a puzzled expression, Kris looked at the screen, shrugged and touched the answer button. After listening for a moment, Kris smiled and said, "Hello, Doctor. I'm surprised and happy to hear from you."

After another pause, she said, "We're just having lunch in Crystal Bay at Lake Tahoe. We came up here to look at houses . . . yes, I think so. Hang on for just a moment."

Kris looked at us and enthusiastically said, "It's Doctor Denton! He's in Reno and wants to know if we'll be here for a few days."

Kris's enthusiasm told me she was more than a little pleased to hear from the doctor. I said, "Yes, I expect we'll be here for a few days."

She repeated what I said into the phone and listened. After a pause, she said, "We're staying at the Tahoe Regency." After another, longer pause, Kris said, "I think that would be very nice. Let me ask Kieley and Kev."

Looking up at us again, Kris explained, "Mark says the Valley Hospital he was at in Las Vegas had to shut down because of quake damage, and he came up to Reno to escape the destruction and chaos. He offered to buy us dinner here tonight. Would that be okay?"

I nodded and Kieley said, "I think that would be very nice. Ask him if six o'clock would be okay. Oh, and ask him if he wants us to make him a reservation at the hotel."

Sensing that the conversation we were witnessing was somewhat private, I looked at Kieley and turned back to my club sandwich and fries. Kieley grinned at me and stole a French fry from my plate.

Kris disconnected the call and sat there for several seconds looking a little starry-eyed. Turning toward me, Kieley said, "Brother Kev, I believe our little sister might have a crush on a certain handsome fellow of the medical persuasion."

I turned to Kris. "Is that so, Little Sister?"

"No! His folks have a place up here, so he was headed there when he remembered we came up to Reno. He was just checking on his patient."

Kieley smiled. "Sure he was, Girlfriend." Kieley looked at me. "I think little Sister is trying to one-up me by catching a doctor."

"And here you are, hanging around with an unemployed photographer. Too bad."

"Quit it, you guys. He's just a good doctor checking on his patient. That's all!"

Kieley and I both nodded knowingly and turned back to our lunch. Just as we were finishing up, an explosion of thunder shook the rafters and everyone in the room ducked. I guessed the mass reaction was because they were afraid one of California's earthquakes had found Crystal Bay. Instead a very wet rainstorm found it. The parking lot was already developing lake-sized puddles when we made a dash for the Jeep

Promptly at two, we walked, or more accurately, ran into the North Shore Real Estate and Property Management Company's office at 22 Nevada State Route 28. Tracy Bingaman turned out to be an athletic brunette with an earthy tree-hugger look about her— an unlikely type to find in a ritzy resort area real estate office.

After determining we planned to spend the night, and since there was darn near as much water in the air as there was in the lake, she recommended we discuss our housing needs so she could prepare a list of likely places to look at in the morning.

She took copious notes on a yellow legal pad as Kieley led the discussion of features we wanted in our new home. The first requirements were a minimum of three bedrooms and two baths, although more of both would be desirable. Next came a quiet location off the main highway and a lake view.

I mostly kept quiet and let Kieley do the talking. She was doing a good job of describing the sort of house we needed. The last items on her list were a natural gas stove and heating, modern insulation, and a plowed street in winter.

Tracy Bingaman's next question concerned our price range. Kieley looked to me for the answer to that one. I said, "Well, I wouldn't mind keeping the price around a million, but it seems unlikely we'll find what we're looking for at that price."

I was pretty sure Tracy Bingaman had noticed my Rolex and Kieley's ring by that time. Relators, just like the Grand Canal Shoppes jewelry salesman in Las Vegas, learned early in their careers how to separate the serious prospects from the window shoppers. A few well-placed clues were usually all they needed.

Ms Bingaman said, "You might be surprised. Your timing is perfect. You're here at the peak of a buyer's market. A lot of the property up here is owned by people in California and many of them are very anxious to get the money out of their summer places here so they can rebuild their primary homes . . . somewhere. Sadly, we are also beginning to hear about foreclosures and estate sales. I think we can certainly find what you're looking for at a price in the neighborhood of one-point-five million."

Next, she cast her line into the water again to fish for a little more information about our situation. "Financing, however, can be a little tougher. Real estate loans are difficult to come by right now because banks are being extremely cautious. Many of them have taken a bath on properties in the worst hit areas of California with no hope of collecting on their investments and no possibility of selling the property. As a result, we're doing some very creative financing."

I said, "No financing, creative or otherwise, will be required. This will be a wire-transfer cash transaction."

Tracy Bingaman's jaw literally dropped and she got as excited as relators selling snooty properties allow themselves to get. "Good! You're my kind of customers, Mister and Missus Turner. Assuming we don't float away overnight, I'll have homes for you to look at by nine tomorrow morning."

The rain slacked off a little before we left Ms Bingaman's office, so I suggested we drive around the area a little to get a better idea of what it's like. Kieley and Kris thought that was a grand idea, so we followed Nevada State Route 28 further east across the northern end of the lake. That took us into Incline Village.

There, Kieley raised a very reasonable question. "Where the heck does a person buy groceries around here?"

The answer to that question showed up a moment later when we turned into a shopping center boasting a Raley's market, along with an Ace Hardware, a bank, a pet store, an Italian seafood restaurant, a flooring and window store, a real estate office, a gym, an urgent care facility, and a few boutique shops.

Other necessities were just across the highway, including a Seven-Eleven and a Starbucks. We also passed several high-buck restaurants offering a variety of international cuisine. Noting these, Kieley said, "Those are the kinds of places that want twenty-five bucks for bean salad out of a can with dressing out of a bottle. I have a feeling we'll be doing a lot of home cooking. Just wait until you taste Kris's spaghetti sauce."

I said, "Sounds good to me!"

Kris piped up to say, "It's an authentic old-world recipe from my dad's grandmother. I like it with some al dente penne pasta and hot garlic bread. Mmm!"

Kieley said, "All this talk about food is making me hungry. I should have made Kris's dinner date for earlier."

"It's not a DATE!"

EIGHTEEN

Sunday, August 28, 2022
Tahoe Regency Hotel, Crystal Bay, Nevada

I pulled up to the Tahoe Regency's entrance and unloaded our bags. Then I gave Kieley the keys to our room and a few bucks for the bellman, saying, "With all of our worldly possessions in the Jeep, I'm going to park and lock it myself instead of using valet parking. Shall I meet you at the restaurant?"

Kieley said, "Okay, but Kris and I might take a few minutes to freshen up."

"Oh, maybe I should . . . ."

"You're fine, Kev. I really like that corduroy jacket and those slacks. Go ahead and get us a table so we don't keep Kris's date waiting."

"He is NOT my date!"

I parked the Jeep and went in search of the Tahoe Regency's fine dining restaurant. It turns out the place is called Reggie's . . . or more correctly, Reggie's at the Regency. The ambiance, however, was much nicer than the name would make you think. There was a decidedly woodsy feel about the place with knotty pine paneling and paintings of the lake in rustic frames on its walls.

I told the hostess I expected to meet someone, and she immediately led me to the table at which Doctor Mark Denton was seated. He stood and we shook hands.

"Good to see you again, Mister Turner."

"Please call me Kevin or Kev, I answer to either."

"I'm Mark."

The ladies will join us shortly. They went upstairs to gussy up a bit. We got a little soggy in the rain earlier."

The cocktail server showed up next, asking if I would care for a libation. I decided I would imbibe for a change and asked for a

Glenlivet rocks.

When she went off to get my drink, Mark asked, "How is Kris doing?"

"You'll be a better judge of that than me, but I would say she's doing better. We had a couple of rough incidents, including a strong shaker while she and Kieley were in seeing Doctor Brewer, but if anything, those experiences have made her stronger and more able to cope with stress. The human mind is amazing."

Denton smiled. "Are you sure you don't want to be a doctor? You certainly have the right nature for it."

"I'm not sure Doctor Brewer would agree with you."

Denton laughed. "Yes, I heard there were some tense moments during that quake. Just between you and me, I think Dave was a little embarrassed about you saving his life. We doctors like to think we're the only ones with that ability."

It was my turn to laugh. "Just don't be surprised if Kris slips and calls him 'Doctor Doofus'."

At that moment there was a distinct hush in Reggie's ambient noise level. I saw Mark's eyes go a little wide and I knew what was happening. I confirmed it by turning and watching my wife and Kristina make their grand entrance, only it was a little grander than I expected. Apparently they held out on me during their Nordstrom fashion show after shopping in Las Vegas.

Kieley was wearing a snug fitting black cocktail dress that showed a lot of leg and a whole lot more cleavage than I knew she had. Kristina took a more elegant route in a long fitted dark blue gown with a split in the skirt so she could actually walk in it and show off a shapely leg at the same time.

We could actually hear "Oohs" and "Aahs" from neighboring tables. For a moment I thought the room might actually give them a standing ovation.

Doctor Denton and I rose to the occasion and held the appropriate chairs for our ladies. As Kieley sat, I leaned over and whispered, "Holy Shit!"

Kieley gave me a pleased look. Mark complimented both girls on their beauty before the cocktail gal showed up again and asked for their drink orders. I looked at Kris with a raised eyebrow. She grinned at me and said, "A Virgin Mary, please."

"Kieley, what would you like?"

She smiled at me charmingly and said, "Something festive. Surprise me, Darling."

I had a selection in mind that was just made for such occasions and allowed me to show off a little. Turning to our cocktail server, I said, "The beautiful lady to my right will have a Mai Tai made with Appleton Estate Reserve, blended, and served with a pineapple spear garnish, please."

"Yes, sir. Right away, sir."

The conversation was at a low ebb because Doctor Denton seemed to have lost his voice. I thought that might be a good time to find out if I was right about where the gowns came from, so I looked at Kris because she was the easier of my two companions out of whom to wrangle a confession. "Tell me, Ms Bryant, did that elegant frock just get off the boat from Paris or Las Vegas?"

She looked at me a little nervously, but Kieley came to her rescue. In a tone of voice fairly oozing sophistication, my wife said, "Kevin, Darling, don't you agree life would be a terrible bore without a few surprises now and then?"

I smiled and shook my head. "What some dames won't do to grab a little attention."

Without missing a beat or losing her sophisticated tone, Kieley said softly, "Call me a dame again and you will require Doctor Denton's surgical skills to remove my salad fork from your left ear."

Kris giggled and Kieley lost it. They were both laughing their heads off and Mark joined in. I looked around and noticed that people at the closest tables to ours were also smiling. They didn't know what the joke was, but if those two gorgeous women found it funny, it must be hilarious.

I said, "Okay, you two look absolutely ravishing and you'll get no complaints from me about the price of the ravish."

Kieley smiled a soft smile. "I knew you would feel that way, especially when you saw Kristina. Isn't she beautiful in that gown?"

"Yes, she is, although I'm not sure how she can walk in it."

Kris grinned. "That is a secret men are not meant to know, but simply to enjoy."

Our drinks arrived. I raised my Scotch and said in a voice loud enough for those at the nearest tables to hear, "To the two most beautiful women in this or any other room."

In addition to Mark Denton, a fellow at one of the nearby tables raised his glass to join in my toast. Kieley said, "Thank you, Darling."

Kris looked at me and said, "Yes, thank you, Kevin." Then she turned to our host and said, "And thank you, too, Mark. It's really good to see you again under happier circumstances and without a stethoscope around your neck."

Doctor Denton finally found his voice. "It certainly is. This is turning into a very special night. I had no idea I would be dining with a princess. You are absolutely amazing!"

I smiled at Kieley. "So are you, Missus Turner."

Denton heard the 'Missus Turner' part and said, "Missus? Did you two already tie the knot?"

Holding up her left hand so he could see her wedding and engagement rings, Kieley answered his question. "Technically, yes. There were some legal matters that needed our attention and they required we get married in order to settle them, so we did it before leaving Las Vegas. We are planning to do it again, though."

Mark looked confused, but Kris explained it to him. "The way Kev explains it, the civil ceremony in Vegas was for the technicalities. The next one is for the memories."

"Under the circumstances, that makes a lot of sense. I hope I'm around for the next one."

Kris smiled softly and just a little coyly. "I hope you are, too."

Our little dinner party continued on in the same fashion until about nine, when Kieley and I excused ourselves. Offering my hand to Denton, I said, "Mark, this has been a pleasant surprise and a delightful evening. Thank you."

Mark shook my hand. "It was my pleasure. I hope we'll get to see more of each other. I'm seriously thinking about opening a private practice here, but that gets kind of involved and complicated, so it may take a while."

I couldn't help noticing Kris's smile grow larger with every word Mark said about opening a practice. Knowing full well what her response would be, I said, "Kris, I hope you don't mind us deserting you."

She looked up at Denton with soft eyes and said, "Not at all. I mean, how could I be any safer than with my own personal cardiologist?"

Kieley also shook Mark's hand and said to Kris, "You have the room key, right?"

Kris looked at Kieley for a couple of seconds, and I got the idea some nonverbal communication was taking place. Then we walked to the elevator and rode it up to the second floor.

In our room, I hung my jacket in the closet and pulled Kieley into my arms. "You know, I have photographed you in hundreds of settings and in all kinds of light, but you have never looked more beautiful than you do right now."

We kissed an unhurried kiss, and then Kieley said, "I think maybe there is one photo you made that comes a close second to the way I feel right now."

"Oh?"

"Yes, the one Kristina no doubt pointed out to you on my nightstand in San Francisco. I can hardly wait until we have our own nightstand so I can put it back where it belongs."

"You know, my first thought when I saw what had become of that photo was how good it felt to know I was part of the last thing you saw every night before you went to sleep. I hoped you would put it on our nightstand someday."

Kieley kissed me again and began undressing for bed. I did the same, saying, "That was one hell of an entrance you two made at dinner. How did it feel to have everyone in the restaurant admiring you?"

"It was kind of fun, but the real question is how did it make you feel to know everyone in that restaurant was admiring your wife?"

I grinned at her. "I was the proudest, happiest fellow in the place."

"Good! That's the only opinion I care about." After a momentary pause, she said, "Well, I'm also a little interested in what Mark Denton was thinking when he saw Kris tonight."

I laughed. "I wish I'd had a camera to capture his expression. His eyes were big as saucers and he was completely awestruck. Kris had him hook, line, and sinker from that point on. If, that is, she wants him."

Kieley grinned at me. "IF she wants him? I have never seen her look that starry-eyed before. It was like he was the only man in the room."

"I hope she isn't riding for a fall."

Kieley gave that idea a moment of thought, and then said, "I don't think so. In case you didn't notice, Doctor Denton is kind of shy. It took a drink and a half for him to tell Kris she looked like a princess and that she was amazing.

"My impression of him is he's not a worldly kind of guy, and the thing Kris needs most in her life is a man who is down to earth and honest. I'm withholding judgement on the question of whether he would make a good husband for her, but he's definitely on the plus side right now."

I went into the bathroom and brushed my teeth while Kieley finished undressing down to her undies. When I came out she was holding up two clothes hangers. One had a black lace nighty on it and the other had absolutely nothing on it.

"Hubby, here are your choices for my sleepwear tonight.

Which one appeals to you the most?"

I was about to say the empty hanger, but the sound of the suite's hall door opening interrupted me. Kieley grabbed a short black robe out of the closet and headed to the other room. In case Kris had invited Mark in for a nightcap, I stepped back into my Dockers.

When Kris saw Kieley, she ran over and hugged her. The smile on her face told me what I most wanted to know.

I got the next hug, and then we sat to talk. Kieley said, "Well, Girlfriend, since you have now tested both candidates, is Doctor Denton as good a kisser as my guy?"

Kris saw me smiling at the question and said, "Well, I'm not sure."

"Not sure? Didn't he kiss you goodnight?"

"Well, he sort of did. I got a terrific hug, and then a very proper little peck on the cheek. In case you didn't notice, Mark is kind of shy."

I asked, "Is shyness on the plus side or the minus side?"

Kris grinned. Actually, she hadn't stopped grinning since she came into the room. "For now, it goes in the middle, but I'm hoping he gets over his shyness quickly. He did hold my hand when we went for a walk around the casino. That's a plus."

The inquisition continued with Kieley asking, "Do you have plans to see prince charming again anytime soon?"

"Well, kind of. He said he likes Italian food and I told him about my spaghetti sauce, so he invited us all up to his folks' home at Incline for an Italian dinner, at which I agreed to be the official spaghetti sauce maker."

Kieley said, "Oh. That's good. You'll get to meet his folks, too."

For the first time since she came back to the room, Kris looked a little sad. "No, I won't. Mark's folks are gone. They both died a few years back. He inherited the summer house up here."

Kieley asked, "So when is this spaghetti feed?"

"We didn't set a date because I didn't know when we would all be free."

Smiling, I said, "Ya know, Sis, you don't need us there as chaperones. Kieley and I could be busy or something."

"Yes, I do need you there as chaperones. I'm afraid Mark will insist on it."

Kieley gave Kris a questioning look with a slight smile. "Do you think that's for propriety's sake or because he's afraid to be alone with you?"

I thought Kieley was kidding, but something about her

question made Kris look sad again. I said, "Whatcha thinkin', Kris?"

"I don't know the answer to Kieley's question, and that worries me."

"What worries you about it?"

Kris added thoughtful to her sad expression. "What worries me is I think he might actually be afraid to be alone with me. I mean he may think I'm a different kind of woman than I really am."

Kieley said, "I think I know what you're thinking, but so Kev understands, what kind of woman might Mark think you are?"

"Maybe a . . . maybe he thinks I'm too experienced."

Nodding, Kieley said, "You were going to use a different word, weren't you?"

Kris nodded and I was puzzled. "I'm not following this. What word were you going to use?"

Looking me in the eyes, Kris quietly and simply said, "Slut."

I had the feeling she said the word for its shock value, and it worked. "That's nuts, Kris!"

Kieley filled in the blanks for me. "Kev, it's not as crazy as you think. Some guys, especially, guys like Mark who haven't been around much, get strange ideas about women in professions where they use their beauty and their bodies—dancers, actresses, models, and like that—to make a living."

Nodding slowly, I said, "Oh. Well, I guess I can see that, but it's certainly a prudish point of view."

Even from across the room I could see the sheen of tears in Kris's eyes. "All right, we definitely know you are not a slut or anything like that, so how do we go about straightening out the good doctor's thinking, assuming he actually thinks something along those lines? Would it help if I spoke to him?"

Almost simultaneously, Kris and Kieley both said an emphatic "No!"

I almost laughed. "Well, I guess we can rule that option out."

Kieley said, "I know Kris appreciates your willingness to help, but if Kris's concern is valid, the only way to change Mark's opinion is show him the truth over a period of time. He has set the boundaries of their relationship. If Kris wants to make something of this, she has to carefully stay within those borders and be very patient."

Nodding my understanding, I said, "I can see that. I'll tell you this, though, if any other guy ever called either one of you a name like that, I wouldn't hesitate to knock him into the middle of next week."

Kieley smiled at me and Kris said, "I know you would come to our defense like the knight in shining armor you are. It feels really good to know you are in my corner."

We all turned in a few minutes later, but it seems our conversation with Kris cooled some of the ardor Kieley and I were feeling when she came in. As we snuggled into bed, I muttered, "Slut, indeed!"

Propping herself up on her elbows, Kieley said, "Remember, Kevin, you knew me intimately before I became a model, so your impressions of me are different than someone who meets me or Kris for the first time now. Also, Darling, we don't know for sure Mark thinks that about Kris. We know he's shy, so maybe she's reading more into that than is real. I hope so."

Kieley was quiet for a while and eventually laid her head on my chest. Finally, she said softly, "Kevin, may I ask you a question?"

"You may ask me any question any time and get an honest answer, but if you ask what I think you're going to ask me, you'll also get smacked."

"I'm serious, Kevin."

"So am I. Ask your question."

"Kevin, have you ever thought of me as a . . . as too experienced?"

"Never, and you just earned yourself a smack on your cute little butt. Now, get back to being the confident self-assured woman I fell in love with. If you have to worry about something, worry about Kristina, but not us."

NINETEEN

I woke up to Kieley whispering in my ear. "Darling it's six-thirty Monday morning, the Twenty-Ninth of August and I love you and I want you so much I will start screaming if you don't wake up immediately and make love to me."

After letting that sink in for a few seconds, I mumbled, "Sex before seven a.m. costs extra."

Kieley's hand slid down my stomach and found me just as her lips found mine. That got my attention and by seven Kieley was collapsed on top of me trying to catch her breath. I was in roughly the same condition.

Between gasps, I said, "Darling, you said you were going to start screaming if I didn't wake up and make love to you, so I did and you screamed anyway."

She covered my face with little kisses. "I didn't say I would not scream if you made love to me, did I?"

"Actually, no, you did not say that."

A voice from the bedroom doorway said, "I have a question."

Kieley lifted her head and looked at Kris. "It better be a damned good question, Missy."

Kris thought for a second, and then said, "Well it seems like a good question."

Kieley sighed. "Okay, Kris, what's your question?"

Grinning like a playful ten-year-old, she literally skipped across the room and landed facing us in a kneeling posture on the foot of the bed. She was clearly getting a big kick out of tormenting us.

I mumbled, "We probably could have heard you from where you were."

"I wanted to be sure. Here's my question: If I hear you making love and Kieley screams a bunch of times, does that mean you're all done and I can come in, or is there likely to be more lovemaking?"

Kieley groaned, and I said, "This is why locks were invented for bedroom doors."

Paying her back for previous sins, I got out of bed still naked and walked to the bathroom. Passing within inches of Kris, I gave her a solid swat on the butt. Kris yelped and I closed the bathroom door.

When I finished my shower and returned to the bedroom, Kris was off creating mischief elsewhere and Kieley handed me a cup of coffee. "I think you should know your little sister paid you a very nice compliment while you were in the shower."

I was immediately suspicious. "Do I want to know what she said?"

"It was really very nice, Darling. Kris said she hopes Mark Denton is as . . . I believe the term she used was hung . . . yes, that was it. Kris said she hopes Mark Denton is as well hung as you are. Now, wasn't that nice of her?"

Stepping into my shorts, I said, "Kieley, if you don't get your little sister under control, she is going to drive me to drink."

She frowned at me. "Is that anyway to talk about Kris, especially after she said something really nice about you?"

Kieley's early morning requirements put us a little behind schedule, so I ordered a light breakfast—yogurt and fruit for Kieley and Kris, and a bagel with cream cheese for me—delivered by room service.

The suite had a sort of breakfast bar with stools, and I noticed Kris kept peeking at me over the top of her coffee cup. Finally, I said, "Kris, do you have something on your mind, or are you just making more comparisons between me and Mark Denton, like how well we're . . . ."

Kieley said, "Uh, uh, uh. You be nice, Kevin! Kris loves you and only has the nicest things to say about you."

Kris and I ended that conversation with me saying, "Ha!," and her giggling.

About five minutes after nine, we trooped into the North Shore Real Estate and Property Management Company's office, where Tracy Bingaman was waiting for us with a list of six homes she felt met our requirements.

A few minutes later we trooped back out of the office and found seats in Ms Bingaman's Chrysler Pacifica van. Then we were off on our house hunting adventure. By two p.m. we'd seen all six homes on the list.

We also returned for a second look at one place—number four on the list. It was plain to see Kieley was enthralled with the home, and after all, she was the one I wanted most to please.

Back in the agency's conference room, Ms Bingaman stepped out to find some coffee and give us an opportunity to talk about the homes we saw. Kieley reassumed leadership of the Home-Finding Committee, asking, "Okay, did either of you see anything you really, really liked?"

Almost in perfect unison, Kris and I said, "Number four."

According to Ms Bingaman's fact sheet, the fourth house we looked at was a new four bedroom, four bath thirty-six-hundred square foot, two-and-half-story home on a hill above Crystal Bay. Its most attractive features included a great room plus a large family room with a deck of its own and a large bedroom/office, all with lake views. In fact, there were terrific views from every room in the house.

The great room featured a rugged granite fireplace and a cherry wood staircase. The extensive use of exposed woods in almost every room gave the place a look that made me think of the Craftsman Style houses that were so popular early in the Twentieth Century.

The master bedroom was on a level of its own for privacy from the other bedrooms on a lower level adjacent to the family room. That arrangement would require Sister Kristina to climb at least one flight of stairs before barging in to interrupt whatever might be going on in the master bedroom.

All of the appliances were built-in and included. There was also an extra tall three-car garage with a space for four more cars out front. The place was clearly designed for entertaining.

Another selling point was the home's location on a lot adjacent to Forest Service land, which meant nobody was going to build another home right next door and block any of the views. The price on the listing was $1.9 million. I also noticed the house had been on the market for more than eight months and the price had already been reduced once.

Kieley agreed house number four was the perfect home for us, but was concerned about the nearly two-million-dollar price tag. I said, "It has also been on the market for eight months and the price has been dropped at least once during that time. With the earthquakes and all, the builder might be a little more eager to deal by now."

When Tracy Bingaman returned with a tray of coffee cups, she asked, "What do you think? Did we find the right house today, or do we continue the search tomorrow?"

I said, "We might have found it. We kind like the fourth house you showed us."

"Oh, yes, the four bedroom on Tuscarora Road above Crystal Bay. It is a stunning house in a fabulous location."

"Setting all the adjectives aside, what sort of an offer do you think the owner would accept?"

Tracy consulted her listing book and said, "Well, the last offer they had was $1.7 million, and they rejected it, so . . . ."

Interrupting Ms Bingaman, I asked, "When was that offer made?"

She checked the date in the listing information and said, "Two months ago."

"How close is the agency handling the place? Do they know the area?"

"Oh, yes. Tahoe Development built the house and they're handling the sale. Their office is just over on the California side near Dollar Point."

"All right. Please write up a first and final offer for $1.5 mill cash out the door with closing, including payment in full, before end of business tomorrow."

Ms Bingaman looked at me like I was nuts. "Mister Turner, that's two hundred thousand below the offer they just rejected. I doubt very much . . . ."

I interrupted her. "Correction, that is two hundred thousand below the offer they rejected before five colossal record-breaking earthquakes destroyed the State of California. Ms Bingaman, the first of those quakes practically killed my wife, and we rode out the next four sitting virtually on top of the fault. Now the Fortuna Fault is going to help pay for our new home."

Shaking her head, she said, "Okay, I'll write it up, but . . . ."

"Thank you, Ms Bingaman. We'll enjoy your coffee while you prepare the offer."

Tracy Bingaman disappeared for a short time, and came back with a typed offer for Kieley and my signatures. I pushed the sheet over to Kieley, and said, "Ladies first."

Kieley read the offer, kind of gulped, and looked at me. I smiled and she signed. Then I signed the offer and slid it across the table to Ms Bingaman. "Fight the good fight, Tracy."

She looked at the offer, shook her head, and said, "I'll do my best."

Kieley held up crossed fingers and said, "Gosh, I hope they

accept it."

Kris said, "Me, too. That is such a beautiful house. I'm afraid I would spend all my time sitting on the deck working on my tan and looking at the lake."

Laughing, I said, "No problem, Sister Kris. Didn't you see that room with all the workout gear?"

She glared at me. "I saw it."

"Heck with that stuff, you might even develop boobs as big as your sister's."

Kris stuck her tongue out at me, and Kieley said, "I wonder how much they would want for the furnishings. They were good quality, and even if they aren't the style we end up with, they would save us the fuss of having to furnish the house before we could move in."

I smiled at Kieley. "One thing at a time, Darling Wife. One thing at a time."

My supreme confidence was beginning to slip a little when a clock somewhere in the building struck the three o'clock hour. I needn't have worried, though. Ms Bingaman walked back into the conference room a short time later and set a piece of paper in front of me.

Shaking her head as if she couldn't believe the news she brought us, Tracy said, "They accepted your offer, Mister Turner. They accepted it and actually thanked me for the deal! Moreover, the agent said for an extra ten thousand they'll throw in all the furnishings, including the decorator items."

Winking at Kris, I asked, "The workout gear, too?"

She nodded. "Yes, everything in the house."

"Please tell them we accept their generous offer."

We spent the next two hours working out details and timing. Kieley wrote Ms Bingaman a thousand dollar check for earnest money, and the agency contract person went to work typing the contract of sale.

We agreed to meet at the North Shore Title Company two suites down the hall from the real estate office at ten the next morning to finalize everything. I got the escrow account information and the exact amount of the purchase to pass along to my financial management folks for a wire transfer in the morning.

While we were doing that, Kris excused herself. When Kieley and I came out Kris was leaning on the Jeep and talking on her cell phone. To Kieley I said, "Care to place a small wager on who she's talking to?"

Kieley laughed. "Is there any doubt?"

"I wonder if we're having spaghetti for dinner."

"Could be."

Kris spotted us and said into the phone, "Here they come now. I'll ask and call you right back."

"Hi, guys! Do we have a new house?"

Kieley said, "We should have the keys in less than twenty-four hours. How's Doctor Denton?"

Kris looked at Kieley. "How do you know that's who I was talking to?"

I said, "Was she right?"

Looking a little sheepish, Kris nodded and I said, "Elementary, my dear Kris. The two of you have become, as they say, an item. Now, pray tell, what are you supposed to ask us?"

"Mark invited us on a sunset dinner cruise tonight. He said the food is good and the scenery is really pretty. Would you guys like to go?"

I looked at Kieley and she gave me an almost imperceptible head shake. I nodded and said, "No, Kris, we have other plans tonight, however, you are free to go with Mark if you want to."

She almost looked as if she was going to cry. "Don't you remember? He's afraid to be alone with me!"

I said, "It's not likely you'll be alone on a cruise ship. Please get him on the phone for me, Kris."

Now Kris looked terrified. "Kevin, what are you going to do?"

"I'm going to get you an invite on that dinner cruise that doesn't include us."

"No!"

Kieley handed me her phone. "It's ringing."

Mark answered and I said, "Hi, Mark, this is Kev."

"Hi, Kev, what's up?"

"Kris was just telling us about your kind invitation for a dinner cruise on the lake tonight."

"Yes, I think you would really enjoy it."

I glanced at Kris. She still looked ready to burst into tears. "I'm sure we would, Mark, but Kieley and I spent the day buying a house here and we have some planning to do because we expect to clear escrow tomorrow."

"Wow, that's terrific. Congratulations!"

"We're pretty excited about it, but as I said, we have some planning to do tonight. Kris, however, needn't be tied up and I'm prepared to make you a deal."

Sounding a little suspicious, he said, "Ah, what kind of deal?"

"I'll trade you a dinner cruise with Kris for a helping hand with moving into our new home on Wednesday. What do you say?"

I could hear the smile in his voice. "I say great!"

"All right. We're just headed back to the Tahoe Regency. We should be there in a few minutes. Can you pick Kris up there?"

"I can and will."

"We're in suite Two-Fifty-Two. See you soon."

I handed Kieley her telephone and Kris threw her arms around me. "Thank you, thank you, thank you, Kevin."

She punctuated her thanks with a kiss. Kieley said, "All right, that's enough of that. You got an entire doctor all your own to kiss, so stop kissing on my guy!"

Not looking in the least contrite, Kris said, "Yes, Sister Kieley."

We hadn't been back in our room for more than a few minutes when Mark knocked on the door. Sounding like a teenager getting ready for the prom, Kris yelled from her room, "Please tell him I'll be right out."

Kieley grinned at me and I opened the door. Mark stood there with a silly grin on his face. It seemed everybody was grinning, so not wanting to be a party pooper, I grinned, too. "Come on in. Kris is just about ready."

Speaking in a low voice, presumably so Kris wouldn't hear him, Mark said, "Thanks for this chance to take Kris out on a real date. I owe you."

I smiled. "All you owe me is a hard day's work on Friday. Oh, and please bring Kris back in one piece. We'll need her help on Friday, too."

After Kris and Mark left, we decided dinner was in order, so we went down to the hotel coffee shop and ordered dinner. Kieley still hadn't kicked the salad habit and ordered a plate of rabbit food and I ordered a ham steak and eggs.

Back in our suite, I flopped on the couch and Kieley promptly flopped into my lap. "You know, Kev, if I had a big brother, I would want one just like you. Kris was near crisis stage tonight, but you solved all of her problems and set her up with a dream date."

"Hell, that wasn't hard. I mean, look at her. Kris is drop-dead gorgeous. If Mark wasn't already following her around like a lovesick puppy, guys would be lined up around the . . . ."

Kieley laughed. "You didn't think I would remember saying those same words when we were talking about our move to Eureka, did you?"

"I thought you might. Listen, Dearest, we need to do some

planning."

"I know. Should I get a pad or something to write on?"

"No, I like you where you are and I think we can address the first item of business without taking notes."

"What's the first item of business?"

"Your birthday present."

Kieley was genuinely surprised. "My birthday present!? Kevin, you bought me a beautiful ring, clothes for Kris and me, and spent a million-and-a-half on a new house for us. All this is way more than enough for my birthday."

"Well, the present I have in mind is something practical. We're about to be going in six directions at once with the move and all, and that poor little Jeep only knows how to go one direction at a time. We need to get it a stablemate."

Kieley's eyes lit up. "A car? For me?"

"You do have a driver's license, don't you?"

"Of course, but it is a California license."

"That will do for a little while. We'll get Nevada licenses when we're settled into the house."

"After seeing how you handled that real estate deal, I can't wait to see how you deal with a car salesman. I was sure we were going lose that house, but you knew exactly what you were doing. I'd trade a cute butt for that skill any day."

"Not on your tintype, Dearie. You keep your cute butt. I'll take care of the deals."

"All right, if you insist. What kind of a car do you think we should get?"

I was stroking her back and Kieley stretched like a cat. "Oh, that feels so good."

"What we get is up to you, although, I reserve the right to veto any thing exotic or strange, like a Yugo."

Pressing herself closer to me, Kieley said, "You aren't much help. How 'bout a Ferrari?"

"Show me a factory authorized Ferrari repair shop listing in the North Shore telephone book and I'll consider it."

"In that case how would it be if we got something useful, like another Jeep?"

"That makes sense, but I wouldn't object to you having something sporty like a Challenger or a Camaro."

"I'm really not into sporty these days. I'm feeling very domestic, so I like the Jeep idea . . . what the hell!?"

The jolt that hit us darn near dumped Kieley off my lap and onto the floor. I yelled, "It's another damned quake!"

The shaking stopped and I was thinking it had been a relatively minor quake, until I remembered where we were. A quake felt that strongly up here, must have been incredibly intense on the other side of the Sierras.

Kieley said, "Kris! Do you think she's all right?"

I looked at the time. It was a few minutes after seven. "Mark said the boat left Tahoe City at six-thirty. Try calling her. I'll get our coats in case we need to . . . ."

An aftershock hit and threw me into the wall near our bedroom door. I just kept going in the same direction, and after a few more cushion shots, I was at our closet door and the aftershock ended. I grabbed our jackets and ran to the living room.

Kieley was getting up from the floor. "Are you okay?"

"Yes, I just got caught off guard. I'm okay, but there is no cell service right now."

"Come on, let's go get Kris."

"You think she's in trouble?"

Handing Kieley her jacket, I said, "So far we've survived by sticking together. This might have been a reminder we should keep it that way."

Slipping into her jacket, she slid the cell phone into the jacket's inside pocket and I made sure I had a room key in my pants pocket. Then we were off. The elevator was just a few doors down from our room, but the stairs were at the end of the hall. I grabbed Kieley's hand and we ran for it.

We made it down the stairs before the next aftershock came along. It was minor and we kept going. The lobby showed only a few signs of the quake—stuff on the floor and a swaying chandelier. We hurried out to the parking lot, stopping only long enough to grab a brochure for West Shore Cruises out of Tahoe City.

According to a rough map on the brochure, Tahoe City was around the west side of the lake. I pointed the Jeep in that direction while Kieley entered West Shore Cruises' address into the GPS.

Kieley said, "We're headed in the right direction. Stay on North Lake Boulevard for another eight-point-five miles. God, I hope Kris is okay and the boat didn't tip over or something."

"I think boats on the water do better in earthquakes than people on supposedly solid ground. She's probably fine. We're just going to make sure."

TWENTY

The address of the West Shore Cruises dock turned out to be a strip mall built around a CVS and a supermarket. The mall stores back right up to a bluff above the beach and the cruise line's dock extends from the base of the bluff below a parking lot at the north end of the mall.

We had to determine that much by moonlight because there were no lights anywhere in the mall. There were, however, several small lights out on the cruise line's dock. The way they were moving around, the lights looked like fireflies, but they were more likely flashlights or cell phones. Something out there was attracting quite a few people.

We hopped out of the Jeep and briskly followed directional signs down a stairway leading to the cruise line's dock. I got the idea the lake was quite shallow along this section of shore because the L-shaped dock extended at least 150 feet out into the lake to reach water deep enough to accommodate the 60-foot cruise ship.

Just as we reached the dock, two Placer County Sheriff's deputies ran past us. Looking out maybe fifty feet beyond the short section of the L-shaped dock, which extended to our right, I could now make out a large dark shape in the water. It was the cruise ship and it appeared to be hard aground.

Between the ship and the dock, there was a lot of splashing going on. A flashlight momentarily illuminated someone in the water. Apparently passengers on the boat were swimming ashore.

Kieley asked the obvious question. "Why don't those people stay on the boat until someone comes out for them? Aren't they safe there?"

An eruption of flame from the far side of the ship answered her question. I put the obvious conclusion into words. "The damned cruise ship is on fire. Do you see Kris out there anywhere?"

"Not yet."

The ship spewed another eruption of flame and the reflection off the water also lit our side of the scene. Kieley yelled, "There! Kris is still on the boat. I was afraid of that. Kev, Kris doesn't know how to swim!"

I made a face at Kieley, and then handed her my wallet, cell phone, and car keys. It didn't take Kieley more than a second to realize what I was up to. She simply said, "Please bring her back safe, Kev."

I said, "You hang onto this railing in case there are more aftershocks." Kicking my shoes off, I added, "You do know how to swim, I hope."

"Yes, Kev, I know how to swim."

I said, "Good," and vaulted over the dock railing feet-first into the lake. The water was surprisingly warm but it grew noticeably cooler the farther I got from shore. Halfway to the cruise boat, I began dog-paddling to get my bearings and look for Kris again.

I was worried for a moment because I couldn't see her anymore, but then I spotted her among the passengers lining the rail. I was glad to see she had a life vest on, but just then a fat pig of a man pushed her out of his way so he could climb onto the railing and jump into the water. I watched her stumble and fall to the deck. I decided I would have words with Mister Piggy later.

Renewing my swimming efforts I reached the boat half a minute later. I popped up out of the water and grabbed a wooden bumper that ran around the boat's gunwale. From there, I pulled myself aboard and pushed my way through the crowd to where I'd last seen Kris.

She was still down on the deck trying to get to her feet and more in danger of being trampled than drowning. I pushed two fellows who were practically standing on Kris out of my way and reached down to grab her.

One of the guys I moved out of the way didn't like being shoved and pushed me back, nearly knocking me down. I came up like a jack in the box and kneed him where it hurt the most. He fell to the deck groaning. His buddy didn't come to his defense and I grabbed Kris.

"Kev! God, I'm glad to see you!"

"It's good to see you, too, Sis. Now we're going to jump off this boat and I'm going to tow you back to the dock. You have a life vest on, so that will make the job easy"

She was scared, but game. "What do I do?"

Before I could answer her question, Kris cringed as another explosion rocked the boat. The crowd around us was getting excited. It was time to go.

"Kris, I'm going to lift you up to the railing. Sit on it and hold on while you swing your legs over to the water side. You can hang on there a few seconds while I get back in the water. When I yell 'Okay,' push off the railing and jump down to me. I'll be right below you."

Kris nodded and I hefted her up so she was sitting on the railing. "Swing your legs over."

She did and I yelled, "Now, hang on a second."

I vaulted over the railing and back into the water. Kris was right above me when I yelled, "Take a deep breath and push off the railing. I'll grab you when you get to the water."

Again she did exactly what she was told and hardly got her hair wet. Pulling Kris close to me, I said, "I'm going to tow you on your back by holding onto your life vest collar. All you have to do is relax and let your arms and legs float. Okay?"

Kris looked terrified, but she nodded and we took off. About halfway to the dock, there was suddenly a lot more light on the water. I looked up and saw several people with lights, including one of the deputies, but most of the light came from a TV news crew, apparently recording Kris's rescue for posterity.

A few seconds later there was another flash of fire and a corresponding explosion. Pieces of burning debris landed near us, but not close enough to do any damage. At least any damage to us. The boat was tearing itself apart.

It only took another minute or so to reach the dock where a deputy was on his knees reaching for Kris. When he had a good grip on her arms, he lifted her out of the water. I followed, but by the time I climbed onto the dock, the deputy was helping someone else and Kieley was holding onto Kris with one hand and my shoes in the other.

"Kieley, please take Kris to the car and get her dried off. I'm going to find Mark." before Kris knew what was happening, Kieley had her headed toward the Jeep.

A moment later, I heard a voice behind me yell my name. I turned and saw Mark in the water. I reached down and gave him a hand onto the dock. Pulling him up, I touched the upper part of his left arm and he flinched. Even in the dark, the angry red burns on his arm and shoulder were clearly visible through his wet white cotton shirt.

On the dock, the first thing Mark said was, "Is Kris okay?"

"She's fine, Mark. She probably has a few bruises thanks to less than gentlemanly male passengers, but I don't think any serious damage was done."

I could see the flashing red and amber lights of several fire department rescue vehicles in the parking lot and steered Mark toward them. On the way I spotted the big slob who pushed Kris down on the boat. He was waiting to be interviewed by a TV news team.

I told Mark to wait just a second and walked up behind Mister Piggy. When I tapped his shoulder, he spun around and snarled, "What the hell do you want?"

"Just this." I swung hard and sunk my right fist into his fat gut at least a foot. He gasped and staggered backwards. He was headed for the dock railing, and I hoped he would crash right through the wood, but it held.

He was bent double and groaning loudly when I said, "Listen, you miserable coward, you damn near killed my little sister back there on that boat. I have business to take care of right now, but if you're still around in a few minutes, I'd be pleased to beat the crap out of you, after which I'll make sure the sheriff throws your sorry ass in the slammer on an assault charge."

When Mark and I last saw the guy he was pale as a sheet, still holding his fat gut where I slugged him, and waddling as fast as he could go toward the parking lot. Mark said, "Damn, Kev, remind me not to piss you off!"

"Just treat Kris right and you'll never have to worry about it."

The TV news team preparing to interview the guy hustled after us. The fellow with the microphone said, "Can we interview you about what happened out there?"

"Maybe later. Right now I need to get this honest-to-god hero some medical attention."'

The two news guys looked at each other and broke into a trot behind us. When I got Mark to one of the rescue trucks, I said to the paramedic, "This man is a doctor and he was burned trying to rescue people aboard the boat. I think he can tell you what he needs."

The paramedic looked at Mark and said, "Be right with you, sir. I need to finish this dressing."

Mark looked at what the man was doing and said, "Here, let me put some pressure on that while you finish taping it."

The paramedic simply said, "Thanks, Doc."

I said, "Looks like you're in good hands here, Mark. I'm going to check on Kris and Kieley." Pointing toward the nearest row of cars in the lot, I added, "That blue Jeep over there is ours if you need me before I get back."

Kris was in the front passenger seat of the Jeep wrapped in a blanket Kieley found somewhere. Kieley was behind the wheel with the engine running to provide some heat inside. She rolled the passenger-side power window down so I could talk with Kris. Kieley also handed me my shoes through the opening.

Leaning against the Jeep to get my shoes on, I said, "Hiya, Sis. How are you doing?"

Kris looked at me anxiously. "I'm okay. Did you find Mark?"

"Yes. He has some burns on his arms, but paramedics are helping him do whatever they do for burns. Are you sure you're all right?"

"Yes. I've got a couple of bruises that are going to be colorful. Mostly, I'm embarrassed."

"Why, for heaven's sake?"

"Because I didn't have the nerve to tell Mark I don't know how to swim. He put that life vest on me and said to swim for the dock while he tried to help the people who were trapped under some parts of the boat when it ran into the ground, and I was afraid he'd think I was a ditz because I never learned to swim."

Kieley slowly shook her head. "I don't believe you, Kris. You risked your life because you were afraid of what some guy would think because you never learned to swim."

Kris's voice was barely audible when she said, "Mark is way more than just some guy."

I said, "Kris, how 'bout we keep your lack of aquatic skills just between us. Kieley, however, is going to teach you to swim as soon as we get settled into our new home. Is that right, Kieley?"

"Most assuredly. They'll be calling you 'Ariel' when I'm through with you."

Kris looked at me. "Thank you for saving my life . . . again."

Light from the Jeep's dashboard showed me a smile on Kieley's face. "Life saving is one of the things Kev seems to do best and he's been getting a lot of practice lately."

Kris said, "Kev, would you please take me to Mark? I don't want him to leave before I see him."

"Okay, kiddo, let's go see Mark, but you don't have to worry about him going anywhere without you. The first thing he said when I fished him out of the lake was, 'How is Kris?'"

She smiled. "Really?"

Opening her door, I said, "Really. "

Mark Denton was right about where I left him, but he no longer had a shirt and his left shoulder and upper arm were covered in some kind of wrapping. Mark was sitting on the truck's back bumper, but when he saw Kris, he jumped up.

"Kristina!"

Kris was staring at the wrapping on his shoulder and arm. "Are you okay, Mark? I had no idea you were . . . ."

He put his right arm around Kris and said, "I'm fine. I have some first and second degree burns, but they'll heal. How are you doing?"

"I'm okay." She glanced at me after she said it. I got the hint.

"All right, you two, I get the picture. I'm going back to the Jeep, but Kris, you are not to leave without us. We're going back to rule number one. You can explain that to Mark, and he is welcome to join us, but we stick together until further notice."

I could tell from her expression, Kris got the message. "Okay, Kev."

Mark unwrapped his right arm from around Kris and offered me his hand. "Kev, thanks for your help back there."

We shook hands and he added, "Don't worry I'll bring Kris back to you and Kieley in a few minutes."

Kieley was in the Jeep's front passenger seat by the time I got back. As I got in the other side, she asked, "How is young love progressing?"

"Actually, it worries me a little."

She immediately put on a concerned look. "Why, Kev? Is there a problem?"

"Only if you consider Kris moving out of our house and into Mark's a problem."

"Oh. Do you think that's likely to happen soon?"

"Let's just say there is nothing like surviving a life-threatening experience to speed cupid's arrow to its target. You and I learned that from very personal experience."

Kieley leaned over the console and kissed me. "Yes, I do seem to remember something like that happening to us."

The passenger side window was still down a couple of inches, and as we reprised the kiss, I heard a familiar voice say, "You guys! I can't leave you alone for a minute!"

Kieley slowly turned to the window. As I pressed the down button, she held up her left hand, and said, "See these rings, Kris? They are a license to do anything we want, including screwing our brains out on the front seat of this Jeep in a parking lot if we want."

Sounding sincerely shocked, Kris said, "Kieley! You shouldn't say things like that!"

I couldn't help laughing. "Kris, the man is a doctor. Presumably, he knows about such physiological activities as screwing one's brains out."

I could tell Kris was embarrassed as she turned to look at Mark. I think she was going to apologize for her family's crude behavior, but he said, "He's right, Kristina. I learned all about screwing one's brain's out in Procreation 101 at med school."

Kris's jaw dropped as she stared at her doctor for a moment, and then she turned back to the Jeep's window. "See what you've done? You two have corrupted Mark!" The three of us were laughing while Kris stood there shaking her head in apparent despair.

Then Mark said, "Kev, I can leave now. Do I have your permission to drive Kris back to the hotel?"

Kris spun back to face Mark. "His permission? Geez!"

Kidding him, I said, "I guess so, but we'll be right behind you, so keep both hands on the wheel."

"Actually, I was going to ask Kris to drive. I want to keep this arm and shoulder immobile."

I shook my head. "Sir, you are a brave man."

Kris said, "Oh, hell! Come on, Mark."

Back in the Regency's parking lot, Kieley and I said goodbye to Mark, and Kris said, "Are you sure you can drive home all right, Mark?"

"I'll be fine, Kristina." He punctuated that with a kiss on her forehead and she kissed his cheek.

Kieley took me by the arm and said, "C'mon, Kev, cut Kris a little slack."

While we watched from the lobby, Kris and Mark exchanged a very adult kiss. When Kris hurried into the hotel lobby, she was surprised to see us there. "I figured you guys went up the room."

I said, "Nope. Rule number one."

Kris looked at Kieley. "Then you saw us . . . ."

Kieley laughed, "Good grief, Girlfriend. I saw you and Bailey kiss hundreds of times."

Kris glanced at me, and then said, "This is different. Mark is my future husband and that was our first real kiss."

With what I'm sure was a surprised expression, I said, "Oh? Does he know that? I mean the 'future husband' part?"

Kris grinned at Kieley and me. "Not officially, but he's catching on to the idea."

TWENTY-ONE

Tuesday, August 30, 2022
470 Tuscarora Road, Crystal Bay, Nevada

When Kieley and I went to bed Monday night, we both were grateful the night's events turned out as well as they did, but we were not holding out much hope for the purchase of our new home to go smoothly. We figured the quake a few hours earlier would certainly cause delays.

Apparently, though, folks at the lake were taking California's quakes in stride now. The only delay we encountered was a last minute mechanical inspection I insisted be done before we closed the deal to make sure the house wasn't damaged during the quake. The only damage we found were a few pictures hanging at odd angles and an extremely ugly ceramic bird figurine that fell from a shelf and thankfully shattered when it landed on a hardwood floor.

When we found ourselves standing on our new master bedroom deck Thursday evening, Kieley and I decided it must have been our turn for a break. Maybe Old Man Fate even approved of our decision this time.

From the southeast corner of the deck we watched the sunset and counted our blessings. "Kev, did you ever think we would actually make it here? I mean married with our own home and everything?"

"I think it was more like I couldn't imagine us not making it. Our love is a natural thing, just like that sunset out there. I couldn't believe God would create something so beautiful and not allow it to shine."

The air was cooling quickly as the sun went down and Kieley cuddled closer. "Your buddy, Mister Fate, gave me a few anxious moments, but I had faith in us. If we really wanted to be together, we would be together."

The door from our master bedroom to the deck opened and

Kris stuck her head out. "I hate to interrupt, but it's almost six-thirty. We need to get going before visiting hours end."

The place Kris was so anxious to be before visiting hours ended was Incline Village Community Hospital. She wanted to be there because Mark Denton checked himself in to have his burns treated and they decided he ought to stay overnight.

I said, "Okay, Kris. It's not far. We'll lock up here and meet you out at the Jeep."

Kieley and I shared a kiss that said more about our love than words ever could. Then we backtracked through our new home, locking the outside doors as we went.

I started the Jeep's engine and heard Kris say, "Golly, this might be the last time I have to share the backseat with everybody's dirty laundry."

Kieley said, "Not quite, Kris. In the morning we have to make a trip to the store for supplies and groceries before we come here."

I said, "That's not going to work. Unless we unload the Jeep first, there won't be room for all the stuff on our shopping list. How 'bout we swing back by here after we see Mark and unload the Jeep into the house? Then we'll be all set to go shopping in the morning."

Kris and Kieley agreed with that idea, so we had a plan. Looking up at our new house as I backed out of the driveway, I admired our good taste. It was a beauty.

We pulled into the Incline Community Hospital parking lot and Kris was out of the Jeep almost before we stopped moving. I remembered her doing the same thing when we arrived in Buttonwillow to meet Bailey.

Looking at Kieley, I said, "When it comes to her men, Kris is not a patient woman."

"You noticed that, huh?"

We knew where Mark's room was because we stopped by to see him at lunch. When we got to his room this time, Kris was already there and sitting on the edge of his bed.

Mark greeted us enthusiastically. "Hi, Kieley, Kev! Thanks for coming to see me."

With a grin, I said "Yeah, we had to see you here because some guys will do anything to avoid a little work."

Mark returned my grin. "Not so, my friend. I become an outpatient after breakfast in the morning. I'm not up to much heavy lifting yet, but I'll be there to supervise by mid-morning."

"Good. I don't feel so outnumbered when you're around."

"Can I bring anything?"

"I can't think of anything, unless you happen to have a hand truck."

"Actually, I do. I'll pick it up when I go home to change in the morning. Will that be soon enough?"

"That works just fine."

At five minutes before eight o'clock a pleasant sounding woman on the public address system announced visiting hours were ending. Kieley and I bid Mark a good evening and left his room so Kris and he could have a couple of minutes to themselves.

By eight–thirty everything but my briefcase and camera gear was out of the Jeep and stashed in the entryway beyond the inside door to the garage. Pulling the rope to close the garage door, I reminded Kieley to add garage door opener remote batteries to our shopping list.

Wednesday, August 31, 2022
Raley's Market Parking Lot, Incline Village, Nevada

While Kris ran the two shopping carts we filled back to the store, Kieley and I organized the load in the Jeep so we wouldn't be scattering groceries all over the interior on our way home. The tab for our purchases totaled more than two hundred bucks and I knew there would be many such shopping expeditions. We were equipping an entire house more or less from scratch and four bathrooms require a lot of toilet paper.

Kieley stood back and appraised our load. "All that and I'm already thinking of things we forgot."

"I'm not surprised. Also, we need to go to the Ace Hardware store over there for a minute to pick up some basic tools. There are a few in the Jeep, but not really the stuff we need for hanging pictures or making household repairs.

I was absolutely thrilled to discover Ace carried Craftsman tools. That meant what we picked up today would serve us well for a long time to come. In addition to basic hand tools, I also picked out a good cordless drill with a set of titanium bits and a small Craftsman roll-around tool cabinet.

On our way home, Kieley tallied our receipts and informed me we had just charged about twelve-hundred bucks worth of groceries, supplies, and tools.

Kris said, "Well, it would have been a lot cheaper if it weren't for all that man-stuff you made us buy."

"Yeah, Kris, and that way I could have had the fun of watching you try to drive a picture hanging nail with the heel of a stiletto shoe."

"Well, I bet I could."

I noticed a white Four Series BMW coupe following us. When it pulled into our driveway behind us, I figured Mark had arrived. I said, "Kris, don't look now, but I think you are about receive your first visitor in your new home."

In the rearview mirror I saw her turn around and look. She yelled, "Mark!" and jumped out to greet him.

I looked at my watch. "Geez, it's already ten. This shopping business is time consuming."

Kieley gave me a sly look. "And you thought women just shop because we like spending money."

"One does not necessarily preclude the other."

Kris and Kieley spent the rest of the morning putting groceries, utensils, and cookware away and distributing the supplies we bought throughout the house. I put Mark to work in a chair beside the new tool chest. He unpacked the tools and organized them in the chest. While he did that, I moved cardboard boxes to the rooms in which they belonged using the handy-dandy hand-truck Mark brought to the party.

It was just about noon when I heard Kieley say, "Damn, I already have a full notebook page of stuff we still need to get, and a page full of stuff we need to do, like insurance, Dish Network, mail delivery, and all the utility stuff."

Kris said, "One thing we need to get for sure is some music and something to play it on. This place needs livening up!"

That reminded Kieley of something else. "Yes, and we need to get a computer set up in the office so we can order stuff from Amazon."

Mark, who was standing next to me, said, "Is this what married life is like?"

"Don't worry. A skilled cardiologist probably makes almost enough to pay the bills."

He laughed. "ALMOST enough?"

"Probably."

Kristina came in, and hearing the last part of our conversation said, "Don't you listen to him, Mark. Brother Kev is just suffering from sticker shock."

Putting my hand on top of Kris's head, I said, "Hell, Mark, I can make you a real good deal on this model. She's sexy and cute and only costs around ten grand a month to maintain . . . for the rest of your life."

Looping her arm around Mark's good arm, Kris said, "Kevin!

You scare this handsome doctor off, and I'll never speak to you again!"

"Promise?"

"OH!"

Kieley showed up to see what all the fuss was about. "Am I the only one around here doing any work?"

I said, "It's lunchtime, woman. Get out in that kitchen and rattle those pots and pans!"

"I can rattle the pots and pans if you insist, but I can't cook anything in them yet."

"Why not?"

"The guy from the gas company won't be here to turn on the gas for at least an hour."

"Oh."

"Yes, oh." She turned to Mark. "Who delivers the best pizza in this high class ghetto-hood?"

"That's easy. It's Pete's next door to the Nugget in Crystal Bay. I recommend their meatball pizza." He quickly added, "But that's not necessarily a medical recommendation."

Kris quickly said, "I'll call the order in. Come on, Mark."

Watching them disappear out into the garage, Kieley said, "I bet a buck if you opened that door right now, you'd catch them smooching."

"That reminds me. Put a garden hose with a high pressure nozzle on that new shopping list of yours. We're gonna need it for controlling the wildlife around here."

Kieley shook her head. "Gosh, you're sure being a grump!"

"Trying to promote Kris's love life does that to me."

"Yes, and you're doing a wonderful job of it, too."

We ate lunch at the table on the deck outside the great room, which we designated "Deck Number One." Pete's Pizza was every bit as good as Mark said it would be and we were back to work with our various projects by the time the utility guy showed up to turn on the gas.

Mark and I ended up in the office, where I fired up my laptop to see what kind of satellite signal we had. At our six-thousand foot elevation it was five of five bars. I checked my e-mail and discovered a note there from a fellow in whatever was left of Los Angeles who was interested in buying my house in the Hollywood Hills, thus proving it takes all kinds.

I replied I was somewhat interested in selling the property and suggested he make an offer. If the offer was acceptable, I would send him my snail mail address so we could proceed with the transaction. I also made a note to set up a mail drop with a Postal Express I saw on our travels through Incline Village and to have anything at the Las Vegas mail place forwarded.

I mentioned the offer in passing to Mark. He said, "Is the house habitable, or does this fellow just want the property?"

"To be honest, I don't know what condition the house is in. It was okay when we were there ten days ago, but there have been three major quakes since then. I figure the fellow's offer will tell me something about that."

Mark looked at me for a long moment and frowned. "Kev, May I be real honest with you?"

"I certainly hope so. They say that's the best policy."

Denton focused on the office's hardwood floor for several seconds, and then said, "Kristina told me a good deal about your adventures from the time you and Kieley helped get her out of San Francisco. You are a real hero to her and so far everything she's said, along with what I saw firsthand last night, makes me think she's right. Without a doubt, you are willing to fight for your little family."

I shook my head. "Don't paint me bigger than life, Mark. Kristina is important to Kieley, so she's important to me. It comes down to the fact that I am the guy around here, and I was brought up being taught the guy respects and protects the woman, or in this case, the women, in his life. That's it in a nut shell."

Mark nodded. "I understand the relationships. The part I don't get is how a photographer—even a darn good photographer as I understand it—can afford to pay eleven thousand dollar hospital copays, own a Rolex watch, buy an expensive custom-designed diamond engagement ring, and pay cash for a one-point-five-million dollar house at Crystal Bay."

"I see. You want to know what I'm worth and how I got that way, is that it?"

He shook his head with vehemence. "No. Frankly, I just want to know you're legitimate and not involved in something illegal."

"Mark, you described Kieley, Kris, and me as a family. That is exactly what we are, and when pressure is put on one member of the family, we all face the situation together. Excuse me a minute."

He frowned as I walked to the office door and hollered, "Kieley, Kris, would you please come to the office for a minute."

Kris ran into the room not ten seconds later. Kieley was close behind her. "Guys, we have a small issue brewing here and it's becoming a family matter. That means you need to be involved."

Denton held up his hands. "We don't need to make an issue

out of this, I . . . ."

Turning to Kieley and Kris, I said, "Mark is wondering how a lowly fashion photographer can afford to pay Kris's hospital copay, afford a Rolex watch, an expensive engagement ring, and pay cash for a one-point-five-million dollar house at Crystal Bay."

Kieley said, "Kev, please go easy here. Kris's happiness is at stake."

"That is exactly why I am not going easy and why I asked you in here. I think it is important for both of you to know what's going on."

Turning to Mark, I said, "Doctor Denton, you've asked me a question and what you are asking me might not be any of your damned business. Whether it is or not depends on why you want to know what you asked about. Looking out for Kris's welfare might be one good reason. Another reason might be you are concerned about getting involved in something shady and you will bail out on Kristina just like her former cop boyfriend did if you thought that was the case. Now, kindly tell us which it is."

Kris said, "Kev, please . . . ."

I held up my hand to hush Kris, and we all watched Mark. He looked very uncomfortable, but said nothing for several seconds. Finally, he looked at Kristina. "Kris, you have come to mean a whole lot to me. That started when you were my patient and when you left Las Vegas I missed you. Being concerned about your welfare naturally goes along with that."

Kris was sitting across a small table from Mark. She stretched her arm out and took his hand, but said nothing.

Denton continued, "I did some checking, and what little I could find out about Kevin didn't fit the man I knew. Then, when a quake destroyed the hospital along with the rest of Las Vegas, I came up here to find you and make sure you were okay because I guess . . . No, I know I want to spend my life with you."

I looked at Kris, but her eyes were glued on Mark Denton. Then I looked at Kieley and she nodded, so I said, "All right, Doctor Denton, are you saying you asked about my finances because you were worried about Kris being involved in something crooked?"

Mark looked at me and said, "I wouldn't put it exactly that way, but yes, Kris is why I'm concerned about who you really are and where your money comes from."

My wife was now watching me closely. I said, "Kieley, since what's mine is now also yours, would you please tell Mark what he wants to know without being specific about amounts? Those details really are none of his business right now. I'm asking you to do this for two reasons. One, I'm liable to put it badly because I'm pissed, and two, I don't think our guest will believe anything I tell him anyway."

Kieley nodded, and then turned toward Doctor Denton. "Mark, if Kris wasn't head over heels in love with you, I would throw you out of our home. I would do that not because you are concerned about Kris, but because your bedside manner stinks. There are a lot of ways you could have gotten answers to your questions, but you chose a very undiplomatic approach."

He said, "Kieley, I apologize . . . ."

She said, "Mark, you'll get your turn to talk later. Right now, it's my turn."

Denton nodded and Kieley said, "First, Kevin is really exactly who he says he is. Now, what I am about to tell you about him isn't just stuff he told me. I have seen the documents involved and I am now signatory to all of his bank accounts. He did that so if anything happened to him, Kris and I would have an income to live on for the rest of our lives.

"Kev asked me not to be specific about amounts, but I will say his holdings are substantial enough to provide a monthly income of roughly twenty-five-thousand dollars after taxes. Kev inherited the original sum from an uncle who admired Kevin's determination to earn a living from his craft. The Rolex watch was a birthday present from the same uncle. The money for this house is a drop in the bucket compared to the total amount." Kieley turned to me and asked, "Are those the main points you want Mark to know?"

I simply nodded. Kieley turned back to Mark. "Does what I've told you satisfy your . . . curiosity?"

He nodded and Kieley threw him a curve ball that even surprised me. "Mark, you say you've fallen in love with Kris. I don't doubt that, but I wonder if you really know what love is. For that reason, I want you to leave our home now . . . ."

Kristina turned to Kieley. "Kieley, what are you doing?"

"What I am certain is best for you. In fact, I'm doing the same thing I hope you would do for me if the circumstances were reversed." Turning back to Mark, Kieley continued where she left off. "I want you to think about what you mean when you say you love Kris. You are welcome to come back when you can answer that question to Kris's and my satisfaction."

Kris stood and looked at Mark, and then it was her turn to surprise us. "I think I love you, too, Mark, so I hope you will come back soon so we can talk about what that means. In the meantime, I would appreciate you doing as Kieley asks."

Mark and I both stood and I offered him my hand. He shook it and turned to the office door. He stopped there and said, "Kris, I can only hope that someday I will be loved by someone as much as Kieley and Kevin love you."

When Denton left, Kris put her head down on the table and cried. Kieley held her and I walked to one of the front bedroom windows and watched Mark Denton drive away in his BMW. I wondered if we would ever see him again. Unless I'd completely lost my ability to judge a person's character, I thought it likely we would.

I locked the front and deck doors and met Kieley going upstairs to our bedroom. We held hands up to the master suite. Kieley said, "Kris has gone to bed. We've had a long, eventful day, so I'd like to do the same."

"Am I invited?"

"Of course! I'm sorry. The way I said that sounded strange. The truth is I want to be as close to you as possible during our first night in our new home."

I smiled. "I was hoping you felt that way, because I sure do."

Twenty minutes later we were cuddling under the fresh linen Kieley put on our king bed earlier in the day. She propped herself up on her arms, a position I have come to think of as her bedtime talking posture.

"Kev, did we do the right thing by Kris tonight?"

"I'm certain we did, although I'm not sure she would agree with that."

"You might be surprised. She's upset, yes, but when push came to shove, she made it clear to Mark that if he wants her, he has to respect her family."

"I know. That really surprised me. You know what? I'd like us to go downstairs and look in on her to say goodnight."

"All right, Kev. I think Kris would appreciate that, but please put some pants on before we go."

I gave her a mock glare. "You spoil all my fun, woman."

She kissed me and said, "Maybe I can think up some different fun when we come back."

Kieley turned on a hall light outside Kris's bedroom and we saw Kris's door was open, so I knocked softly on the doorframe.

A voice from the bed said, "Kev, is that you?"

"It's both of us, Kris. I didn't get to say goodnight before."

She sat up in bed and I sat on the bed next to her. Kieley stood behind me with her hands on my shoulders.

I said, "Kris, I want to say something you already know, but I think it bears repeating, especially when things seem kind of tough."

"What, Kevin?"

"Kieley and I really love you and your happiness ranks right up there with Kieley's where I am concerned."

"Thank you, Kevin. I think I got a reminder of that tonight. You guys weren't trying to ruin my future. It was just the opposite of that. You were making sure I would be happy when all is said and done. That makes me love the two of you even more, and that is what love is all about."

Kris kissed my cheek and Kieley leaned down to kiss her forehead. I said, "Goodnight, Kristina. I wish you the sweetest dreams you ever dreamed tonight."

"Thank you, Kieley and Kev. You guys are the best family a girl could ever want."

TWENTY-TWO

Thursday, September 15, 2022
Birthday Shopping – Reno, Nevada

Being the day before Kieley's twenty-fifth birthday, Kris and I went on a shopping spree in Reno. I think we had as much fun picking out Kieley's presents as she was going to have opening them.

A limo picked us up at home, ostensibly so Kieley would have my Jeep for some shopping she needed to do. The fact that she had to use my Jeep, was another reason for the limo. I already knew what Kieley's main present would be. We once discussed getting her a vehicle of her own, but there were so many other things to do, all our discussion accomplished was the decision she wanted a Jeep like mine.

For that reason, the first stop Kris and I made in Reno was Lithia Chrysler-Jeep. There, we dismissed the limo and set about picking out Kieley's new Jeep. The 2023 models were in and we agreed Kieley deserved the latest Jeep. As for the color, Kris was certain Kieley would love Jeep's "Firecracker Red."

That choice made, I simply told the salesman to find us a red one with every option known to man on it. Of course, he happened to have just such a Jeep, and after some negotiation, we agreed on a price. He even threw a giant white bow into the deal. The bow was designed to be stuck on the Jeep's roof, thus instantly turning it into a birthday present.

I offered to let Kris drive to our next stop, but she didn't want to take a chance on putting the first dent in Kieley's new Jeep, so I drove us to the Reno Macy's department store in the Meadowood Mall. There, Kris picked out a three-piece gift set of Calvin Klein's Obsession, Kieley's favorite scent, which would go to Kieley with Kris's name on it.

After that purchase, Kris helped me pick out a couple of very enticing camisoles of the sort Kieley liked to wear. We also picked out a robe and chemise nightgown in which I could guarantee she wasn't going to do much sleeping. With our Macy's purchases wrapped and stowed aboard Kieley's Jeep, we made tracks for the Reno Best Buy store over on Virginia Street.

In Best Buy's computer department we chose a state of the art all-in-one Lenovo computer and accessories for Kieley to use in our new home office. Next, we picked out a Sony five-speaker sound system with Bluetooth to drive additional wireless speakers. We also bought, three outdoor speaker sets for use on the decks.

Once we got all that into the red Jeep, we headed to our last stop, Sounds of Reno further up Virginia Street, to get some music for Kieley to play on her new sound system. Kris ended up with a few dozen CDs by Kieley's favorite artists—Katy Perry, Chris Issak, Taylor Swift, and others of the same ilk. The background ambiance at Kieley's and Kevin's home was in for a major upgrade.

On the way home, Kris suddenly said, "You know you're spoiling Kieley, don't you?"

"I do. You think that's a bad idea?"

"Absolutely not! If anyone deserves spoiling, it's Kieley."

"That's the way I look at it. On another subject, am I correct in assuming you have not heard anything from Doctor Denton?"

"Not a word."

"You think Kieley was too hard on him?"

She shook her head. "No. I kinda felt that way at first, but the more I thought about it, the more I realized you and Kieley did exactly the right thing."

Glancing over at Kris, I said, "I felt a little sorry for him. Kieley was as angry as I've ever seen her, and she certainly didn't cut Mark any slack."

"I hate to say it, but he didn't deserve any slack. Even if he really had my best interests at heart, he went about it all wrong."

"But you miss him, don't you?"

Slowly nodding her head, Kris said, "Yes. I never felt like that about anyone else, not even Bailey, but that doesn't change anything. If Mark loves me, he knows what he has to do. If he can't or won't do it, we both lose."

Thinking about what Kris told me, I realized she had done some growing up, and I could hear Kieley's influence in Kris's words. Of course, I'm somewhat biased on the subject, but I didn't think Kris could pick a better role model.

Back in our garage, we left all of our purchases in the Jeep, locked it, and I stuck the giant white bow on its roof. Then we walked into the house and found Kieley using my laptop in the office. Kris jumped up and sat on the table next to the laptop, and I leaned over and kissed the very sensitive spot on the back of Kieley's neck.

She shivered and said, "You two have been gone all damn day! I'm gonna check Kev's collar for traces of your lipstick, Missy Krissy."

Looking three kinds of innocent, Kris said, "What good will that do if I took his shirt off before smothering him with kisses?"

Kieley glared at Kris. "Girlfriend, you're cruisin' for a bruisin'."

There was an edge to Kieley's voice that told me she was only half kidding. I said, "Kieley, would you come with me, please? I want to prove to you that Kris and I thought of nothing and nobody but you today."

She stood and leaned into my arms. "I'm sorry, Kev. I'm a little on edge today."

I hugged her close. "Can you tell me why?"

Kieley looked at Kris and then up at me. "I think so. It dawned on me today that tomorrow I will be a quarter of a century old."

I glanced at Kris, stifled a chuckle, and gently lifted Kieley's chin with my hand so she was looking up at me. "Kieley, will you still love me tomorrow?"

"Of course I will!"

Kris came over and put her arms around both of us. I said, "And do you think Kris and I will still love you tomorrow?"

Kieley nodded. "Yes, I know you will."

"Are you going to grow warts and turn ugly tomorrow?"

With wide eyes, she said, "I sure hope not!"

"Then I think I can safely guarantee that tomorrow you will be just exactly as you are right now, except you will have a great big smile on your face because you are totally blown away by the birthday party we have planned for you."

Kieley broke into a grin. "It is impossible for me to stay upset about anything with you around. Thank you, Kev. And you, too, Kris. I love you both."

Kris said, "Good, because we love you, too. Now come with us into the garage."

When we got to the entryway door that opens into the garage, Kris produced a scarf which she tied around Kieley's head as a blindfold. I said, "Good idea, Kris. Are we all set?"

Kris said, "Yes, Big Brother, we are ready. Open the door."

I opened the door and guided Kieley through it. Kris followed us, flipping on the lights, and I said, "Okay, Kieley, here are your birthday presents."

Kieley said, "Can I take the blindfold off now?"

"Oh, you want to SEE your presents, too? What do you think, Kris?"

Kris said, "Well, I wouldn't, but you sleep with her, so maybe in the interests of marital bliss, we should take the blindfold off."

Kieley said, "You guys!"

I said, "Okay, okay. Kris, take the blindfold off."

Of course, Kieley could hardly miss the bright red Jeep four feet in front of her. "Oh my gosh! Kev, I love it!"

She walked all the way around Jeep, admiring it from every angle. Then she tried the passenger-side door and found it locked. "Where's the key? I want to see what it looks like inside."

I held the fancy Jeep electronic key fob up. Kieley made a grab for it and I pulled it out of her reach.

"Kev, come on! I want to see the inside."

"You can't do that until tomorrow."

She made a pouty face. "You guys are mean. Why can't I see inside it until tomorrow?"

"Explain it to her, Kris."

"You can't see inside because your brand new Jeep is more than a brand new Jeep. It's also a giant birthday surprise package full of amazing presents, and you don't get your presents until tomorrow."

Kieley sighed. "I guess that's fair. I also guess you two did way too much shopping for me today. All this on top of a beautiful engagement ring I still can't believe is really mine . . . and this amazing house that's a dream come true. How come I'm so lucky?"

Kris gave her an excellent answer. "Because you are a wonderful loving person. I know you've earned Kev's total devotion and I've loved you since the day we met. That's why."

There were tears in Kieley eyes as she hugged Kris. "Thank you, Krissy. You and Kev are my reasons for living."

That was the precise moment Kris's phone chose to play I JUST CALLED TO SAY I LOVE YOU. She pulled the phone out of her jeans pocket and looked at the screen. Then she looked at Kieley and me with an odd expression on her face.

From that expression I had a pretty good idea who was calling. I said, "Mark?"

Kris nodded. "What should I do?"

Kieley offered her a suggestion. "I would answer the call before your voice mail picks it up."

TWENTY-THREE

Thursday, September 15, 2022
470 Tuscarora Road, Crystal Bay, Nevada, Nevada

Kris touched the screen and raised the phone to her ear. In a tentative voice, she said, "This is Kristina."

We watched her listen for a long moment, and then Kieley led me toward the entryway door to give Kris some privacy, but Kris held up her hand up to stop us. Into the phone Kris said, "I'm not sure, Mark. Hang on a minute."

Kris pressed what I assumed was the mute button and said to us, "Mark wants to come over and talk to all of us. What should I tell him?"

Matter of fact tone, Kieley asked, "Do you still love him?"

Without hesitation, Kris nodded and Kieley said, "Then maybe you should tell him to come over."

"I'm afraid."

I said, "Then tell him not to come over. We're behind you a hundred percent whichever you choose, but the choice is entirely up to you."

Kris seemed to study the cell phone screen for a moment, and then she touched it and put the phone back to her ear. "Yes, Mark, you can come over."

After listening again, Kris said, "Okay. See you then. Goodbye."

She looked at us and said, "He'll be here in half an hour. I guess I should freshen up a little."

Kieley put her arm around Kris and they walked into the house. I turned off the garage lights and followed them. Then I switched on some lights in the living room and more out on Deck Number One. It was mild enough to sit outside and enjoy the twinkling lights surrounding the lake below.

Next I took a few soft drinks along with bottles of tonic and lime juice from the fridge and filled a crystal ice bucket Kieley bought along with a black and chrome deco-style cocktail trolley. I put the ice and soft drinks on the trolley, which already held bottles of bourbon, vodka, gin, and scotch, along with other cocktail essentials, and pushed the whole works out onto the deck.

I met Kris and Kieley on my way back into the living room. Kristina looked nervous. That was no surprise, she had every right to be nervous. I said, "Kris, what happens when Mark gets here is up to you. Just tell Kieley and me what, if anything, you want us to do."

Kris looked at Kieley. "Would you talk to him please? I mean you sort of laid down the rules the last time he was here, so I think . . . I don't know . . . I just . . . ."

Kieley smiled at Kristina. "Yes, Kris, I'll start things off.

The doorbell bonged at us and I said, "Go make yourselves comfortable on the deck. I'll get the door."

I turned around before opening the door and looked across a large expanse of living room to see Kieley and Kris seating themselves at the deck table. Then I opened the door.

Mark was wearing a white cardigan over a pale blue shirt and tan slacks. "Hello, Kevin."

"Hello, Mark. Come on in. The rest of the party is out on the deck. Just go straight on through the living room."

Out on the deck greetings were exchanged and I asked Mark what he wanted to drink. He said a vodka-tonic, so I invited him to sit while I made his drink. Kieley thought she would like the same. Kris asked for a diet coke. That sounded good to me, too, so I split a can between us.

I completed my job of bartending by delivering the drinks, and then it was Kieley's turn. Speaking softly, she said, "Mark, I gave you a pretty rough time when you were here last, but I won't apologize. What I said needed to be said. Now it's your turn to say what's on your mind while we listen. The floor is yours."

Mark looked around the table making eye contact with each of us. Then he said, "I guess you know I feel on the spot here, but that's what I deserve. So, the first thing I want to do is apologize to Kevin.

"Kev, Kieley was absolutely right when she called me out on my lack of diplomacy in asking about your finances. I apologize for that. I'm not very experienced at personal relationships, and I sure showed my lack of experience that night. I hope you'll forgive me."

I nodded. "Consider yourself forgiven, Mark. We had you outnumbered and under the same circumstances I'm not sure I could have done any better."

"Thank you, Kev. Kieley, I owe you the same apology. You are a lovely person and I put you in a position of having to say things I suspect you would rather not have had to say. I'm sorry for doing that to you."

"Apology tentatively accepted depending on what comes next."

Mark nodded solemnly. Clearly, Kieley was still cutting him no slack. Actually, I admired her for that. It reminded me I married a hell of a woman.

Finally, Mark looked at Kristina. Her composure was a thing of beauty. Her expression gave absolutely nothing away.

"Kris, rather than apologize to you for making a mess of things, I'm just going to try to make things right. Kieley told me to come back when I could explain what I meant when I said 'I love you.' What confused me is I've always thought of love as an intangible feeling . . . a basic emotion.

"It wasn't until I saw love demonstrated by you and Kieley and Kevin that I realized love is as much shown in how you behave toward each other as it is a feeling. That night when the cruise boat ran aground, Kevin didn't just say he loved you, he demonstrated his love by diving in the water and rescuing you from the precarious position I put you in because I didn't know you couldn't swim."

Kris's expression changed to something between surprise and embarrassment. Mark gave her a soft smile and said, "What I learned from Kevin is when you love someone, they come first all of the time. Now, that could be difficult for a doctor who must also care for patients, but I still think I could manage putting you first in my life.

"That's what I want to do. I want to love you by putting you first in my life and making you happy as I can. I want to make a world for you in which you never have to be afraid of anything ever again—a world in which no matter where I am or what I'm doing, you come first."

Now Kris had the beginning of a smile on her face and a small tear was just departing from her right eye. Mark concluded what was on his mind by saying, "With that as a basis for our relationship, would you consider becoming my wife and life partner?"

Now there were more tears on Kris's face, but she still held it together. Looking Mark square in the eye, she said, "First, thank you for coming here tonight, Mark. I know it wasn't easy for you, but by coming to talk to us, you've proven your love to me." Glancing toward Kieley and me, she added, "I think Kieley and Kevin will agree with that."

Kieley gave Kris a small nod of her head, and I sent her a smile. What made me smile was Kristina was standing tall on her own two feet without leaning on Kieley. Sister Kris was taking charge of her own life again.

Kris continued her reply to Mark's question. "As for your proposal of marriage, you just made me the happiest woman on earth and my answer is yes—a thousand times yes!"

Mark walked around the table to her side and knelt on one knee. He opened a ring box so she could see the glittering diamond inside and said, "This was my mother's engagement ring. It brought her more than fifty years of happiness at my father's side. I think it might be good for at least another fifty years, maybe more."

He slipped the white gold ring onto her finger and I took Kieley's hand in mine. Raising my glass, I said, "To Kristina and Mark. May they be as happy in their union as Kieley and I are in ours."

THE END

MEET H. P. OLIVER

H. P. Oliver began his writing career earning a degree in journalism from San Jose State University and spent the next twenty-some years writing award-winning entertainment and educational media. Now he applies his creativity and imagination to writing period mysteries and thrillers.

About mystery writing, Oliver says, "To be truly engrossing, a mystery needs a little meat on its bones—something more than just figuring out who did the evil deed. Taking a story back or forward in time or even basing it on historical events is a great way to endow a good yarn with even more color and depth. Historical periods and locations give the writer an opportunity to take most readers where they've never been before."

H. P. Oliver lives in northern California and spends much of his time working on projects throughout the western states. In addition to his love of history, Oliver's interests range from vintage film to restoring classic cars.

For information about H. P. Oliver's books, including synopses, previews, video trailers, and purchase links, visit his fan site at www.HPOliver.com, where you will also find a large collection of free original illustrated short stories and other fascinating features. Plan to stay a while and explore.

BOOKS BY H. P. OLIVER

◆ CLASSIC MYSTERIES IN HISTORY ◆

THE TRUTH BE TOLD
(E-Book)

AND THE ANGELS SING
(E-Book)

SILENTS!
(E-Book & Paperback)

WINGING IT
(E-Book & Paperback)

GOODNIGHT, SAN FRANCISCO
(E-Book & Paperback)

SO LONG, L A
(E-Book & Paperback)

ESTELLE
(E-Book & Paperback)

◆ JOHNNY SPICER ◆

JOHNNY SPICER: THE FIRST CAPERS
(E-Book)

PACIFICA
(E-Book & Paperback)

REVOLVER
(E-Book & Paperback)

TEMBO
(E-Book & Paperback)

S. N. A. F. U.
(E-Book & Paperback)

PAYBACK
(E-Book & Paperback)

JOHNNY SPICER'S LOS ANGELES NOIR
(E-Book & Paperback)

H. P. Oliver's books are available at Amazon.com